FEASTING
WITH
PANTHERS

FEASTING
WITH
PANTHERS

LYLE BLAKE SMYTHERS

PINK
NARCISSUS
PRESS

This book is a work of fiction. All the characters and events portrayed in this book are fictitious, and any resemblance to real people or events is purely coincidental.

FEASTING WITH PANTHERS

© 2012 Lyle Blake Smythers

Cover illustration & design by Duncan Eagleson

Published by Pink Narcissus Press
P.O. Box 303
Auburn, MA 01501
www.pinknarc.com

Library of Congress Control Number: 2012900348

ISBN: 978-0-9829913-7-4

First trade paperback edition: May 2012

This is for my mother, Laura Hunter,
who published short stories but never wrote her novel.
I think that she would like mine.

There are three smiles more terrible than frowns:

The smile of snow melting,

The smile of a treacherous woman,

And the smile of a panther about to feast.

—variation on a fragment from a set of ten triads, ninth century Ireland

Contents

PART I

DERVISH IN DISGUISE

Chapter 1
A Body in the Snow

We found the first one-eyed man at dawn.

The snow in the mountain pass was pale green, like seawater in strong sunlight, and our torches made the trail of blood look black against the path. The sentry cat screamed when he saw the body.

Our boots crunching on the snow, we hurried down after the cat. His markings never showed in dim light, so his large frame appeared to be a solid dark shape as it flowed down the slope, moving with the swift smooth strength for which we bred these animals. He gave short shrill cries as he went.

The man's body was a dark irregular mass, sprawled on the snow like a dead turkey vulture. As my party reached it, however, we could see faint signs of life. The cat, now crouched at the man's head, recoiled slightly when his breath suddenly made a cloud in the cold morning air. One black-sleeved arm, protruding from his cloak in the unnatural twisted angle of a broken limb, moved slightly as we came down and spread around him.

We could see more clearly with each racing moment. The clean dawn light was filling the pass, making our torches wane like crushed fireflies, and now I could make out blotches of blood on the dark cloak. Crimson roses against an ebony panel, I thought, ever the warrior poet.

The man lay face down, his head turned away from me. I gestured to Terhune.

"Turn him over. Gently."

He scowled. "This might be a trap. These mountains are full of bandits."

"Are you mad? Look at the blood. Besides, that arm's broken or I'm a monkey." He still hesitated, so I stooped to move the man myself.

Long, shaggy, bright red hair stood out against the snow. As I laid hands on the body, I noted that there was something odd about that hair, as showy as the red head of a vulture, but my keenest curiosity at the time was about the man's face. Rolling him over, I shifted my grip, and the entire head of hair came off in my hand.

The sentry cat, who had never left his position next to the body, flattened himself against the ground and hissed like a dragon. Even under the jolt of my own surprise, I recognized the danger of his lashing out and possibly damaging our find, so I took a few seconds to stare directly into his eyes and speak firmly: "Styx! No!" Those green-gold eyes blazed out of the chocolate mask of his face, which was in visible contrast to the lighter cocoa of his body now that the sun had risen. I was nose to nose with a genetic creation larger and much more lethal than his domestic ancestors, but Styx and I understood each other very well. He blinked twice and then backed away.

After glancing at the wig in my hand and tossing it aside, I finally looked back down at the person before me. He was completely bald, yet unnaturally so; I could tell that his lack of hair was the result of a razor, not advanced age.

Despite the fact that his head was fully shaved, including the eyebrows, he was one of the most spectacularly good-looking boys I had ever seen. I judged him to be around seventeen, a very pretty boy on the verge of turning into a stunningly handsome young man.

High cheekbones and a fair complexion gave him an aristocratic look, saved from being severe by a generous mouth with smile lines at the corners. I could see that his head and his strong jawline were marked with a reddish -gold stubble, a clue that his natural coloration was much subtler than the garish red of the wig. A few elfin freckles were lightly sprinkled over the bridge of his finely shaped nose.

His left eye, now fluttering weakly as he began to regain consciousness, revealed itself to be a scintillating green, somewhat darker than the snow beneath his head, and flecked with bits of amber. His right eye was hidden by a black patch.

He looks like a prince, I thought. Not one of the so-called princes you find nowadays, greedy brats bellying up to the groaning boards of royal dining rooms in a dozen kingdoms from here to the equator, but a real prince from one of the old fairy tales. I'd found a prince.

My men were full of speculation.

"He must be a pirate."

"A pirate? Don't be stupid. Do you know how far we are from the sea?"

"Yes, but he's got an eyepatch. In books they always—"

"He's a dervish." Terhune turned his massive head and spat, although I could not tell whether it was a gesture of disgust or merely a move to expel some of the tobacco juice he always had in his mouth.

I knew the word. "A dervish. Yes, I've never seen one, but I've heard they shave their heads."

"And their eyebrows too. They have to do it when they take their religious vows and go out into the world as wandering mendicants."

"Wandering what?" my underling with the theory about pirates wanted to know.

"Beggars." Terhune spat again. "They dedicate them-

selves to traveling the open countryside, with no more possessions than they can carry on their backs, their only joy in
life being the spreading of the True Word." His voice was
carefully expressionless, totally devoid of irony.

"Do they always start so young?" I asked. "He's
nothing more than a boy."

"But what a boy," threw in another of my warriors,
one whose furs hung open to show old scars on his throat
and upper torso. "If he's this handsome with his head shaved,
imagine him with a full head of natural hair. He could have
his pick of any woman in the kingdom."

And more than a few men, I thought. Suddenly I felt
very protective of our discovery. I watched him as he gave a
little sigh and sank back into unconsciousness, his beautiful
face vulnerable and open to the brightening sky. Who was I
trying to protect? The younger brother I never had?

I made a decision. "Terhune. Take some men and
make a litter. You can use those old thorn trees over there.
We'll carry him down to the village and have the doctor
look at him."

He grumbled something about not being in the
business of picking up every bleeding orphan he tripped
over, but he went. I crossed to where Styx was sitting with
his long dark tail wrapped around himself, his head slightly
cocked while he kept an eye on the body.

"You know something, Sticker? I think you and I
have got ourselves a house guest." I scratched him behind
the ears. "At least it's good timing since we're between jobs.
We won't have anything to do now that we've finished that
assassination."

He gave me a cryptic green-gold look.

Chapter 2
Bandits and a Badger

By the time we reached the foothills, the sun was high enough to lend warm highlights to the buildings of the village below us, making them look like huge sculptures of rose quartz. The roofs were bristling with tall stone chimneys, from which the smoke of countless cooking fires rose to stain the sky.

Off to our right, a stand of cedars formed a curving wall of vegetation that marked the beginning of the lowlands. Clumps of snow caught in their branches turned the trees into mutated versions of the snowball bushes that bloomed every spring outside the inn where I lived.

Thinking of the inn reminded me of my guest. I threw a glance over my shoulder at the crude litter carried by Terhune and another burly warrior. My prince was still in dreamland, his long black-cloaked body sprawled across the thorn tree latticework like an inkstain over a mathematical diagram. His mouth hung slightly open to reveal perfect, very white teeth.

My eyes swung back to the trees near us. The dark bars of the trunks stood out against the snow, meticulous brush strokes on pale green rice paper. It seemed so much like a scroll drawing that I almost expected a stag to emerge from the cedars, stamping his front hooves against the frost-hardened tree roots while his hot breath billowed from his nostrils. Then, as I watched that forest picture seemingly frozen in time, it moved.

The change was subtle, as if a trunk near the edge of the copse had shifted slightly to one side. I realized immediately what I had seen. Someone hiding behind one of the trees had moved to the next tree. Someone or some thing.

Now each cedar along the edge of the suddenly sinister wood was acquiring a ghostly double of itself, one that separated from the parent trunk with slow and silent menace. And each ghost tree appeared to have a widow-maker, one of those loose dead branches which can fall out of the sky to deal death without warning. Within seconds I recognized the widowmakers for what they were, swords held parallel to the ground.

"Gentlemen," I said softly, "get ready to draw." I stopped and turned to make sure that Terhune and his companion were putting down the litter.

As I turned back, a dozen bandits sprang from the copse. They were clad in dark olive leather armor, and the sunlight gleamed on their blades as they ran up the hill towards us. My men, disguised as merchants, had no armor, for our mission had been one involving treason, stratagems, and spoils.

"Surround the boy!" I cried. We turned our backs on the litter and encircled it, standing shoulder to shoulder and drawing our weapons to present an unbroken ring of steel to the enemy.

They surged onward up the slope, swarthy men who had the look of outsiders, perhaps from south of the kingdom. Their long black hair streamed behind them in the swiftness of their charge.

"They've no crossbows," Terhune muttered. This was cold comfort, since we had none ourselves.

Like most of my men, I held my sword in my fighting hand while keeping my long dagger ready for parrying and thrusting in the other. Behind me and to my left, the giant with the scarred throat and chest was using both hands to wield his favorite weapon, a huge double-headed ax.

The bandits came at us in a tightly packed wall, giving fierce cries in a language I did not recognize. I was not surprised to see that many of them carried secondary weapons at their sides, everything from shortswords to a sickle and a meat cleaver. One even had what looked like a sword cane, probably lifted from a city prickmedainty; to his right he swung a long slender blade, while holding its polished sticklike casing in the fashion of a cudgel to guard his left side.

Their band smashed into us with a savage howling and the clang of steel against steel. I was immediately engaged by a mighty-thewed opponent who tried to run me through with a very long pike; his lunge, however, carried him off-balance when the point failed to connect, and I brought my sword down in a vicious whack that split his skull.

His place was promptly taken by another, so I wrenched my blade free from the pikeman's corpse and whirled to strike again with no time to check on the fighting elsewhere in the circle. My ears rang with oaths, exclamations of pain, and those foreign battle cries.

It seemed that my men were saving their breath when they could, and I smiled grimly as I saw that one by one the bandits were falling, some wounded but many dead. As I continued to hack away, the dark metallic smell of fresh blood rose around us, and men's entrails spilled to make steaming ropes of wetness on the snow. I made another kill.

"Catalan!" The shout came from one of my men. "On your right!" I whipped my head around and confronted the tallest bandit, a skeletal lantern-jawed man whose eyes flickered like phosphorescent mushrooms in his dark face.

"Give us the dervish!" he snarled.

His voice was oddly muffled and full of echoes, as if we were both underwater. His left hand, encased in a heavy gauntlet of the same dark olive leather as his armor, held a particularly nasty dagger. Its crooked serpentine blade was designed to rip out as much living flesh as possible when jerked free of a deep stab wound, but what struck my mind even in this moment of danger was the way its twisted metal suggested a distorted echo of reality, just as his voice did.

"Never!" I cried, throwing my weight behind a strong slashing blow that flung me sideways as it carried my gore-clotted sword around me in a glittering semicircle. With triumph I felt its edge slice through the bone and sinew of his left wrist, and I saw his severed hand fly into the air, the fingers still clutching the handle of his cruel weapon.

He shrieked like a rusty portcullis. The shrill sharp-edged cry pierced the battle noises around us the way his nightmare blade would have pierced my body. As his mouth continued to gape I saw a hideous gray worm of a tongue, like the organ I had once seen inside the mouth of a flightless nocturnal parrot on display at a fair.

And just as that unfortunate bird had sawed the air with its useless wings when prodded by its owner's stick, the bandit waved his stump while it pumped out black blood.

The strangled voice leaked from the dark withered throat. "Prepare to die." His right hand flew up to menace me with a short copper-colored trident, the prongs of which were smeared with a dull blue paste. Poison.

Then a chocolate blur sped past my shoulder as Styx launched himself at my opponent. The huge pantherlike body struck the bandit with enough force to make him drop the trident, and he went over onto his back with Styx on top of him. The bloody stump was still waving in the air as the sentry cat sank his fangs into the man's throat.

With more strength than I would have expected from his bony body, which was rapidly losing blood, the bandit used his remaining hand to wrench Styx from him and fling him to one side. Styx landed shoulder-deep in a snowbank; he crashed out of it and crouched close to the ground, growling around the mouthful of flesh he had torn from the bandit's throat.

Conscious that the battle around us had spun down to a halt, I moved forward to finish off my enemy. He had rolled over onto his knees, and now began a transformation the likes of which I had not seen outside of nightmares.

His long face ran and melted like a wax image thrown into a furnace, becoming suddenly furry and even darker than before. His body was collapsing in on itself, elongating into a tubelike creature, while the dark olive leather armor turned into black fur and his limbs shrank and twisted themselves into four strong legs ending in clawed feet.

Within the space of half a dozen breaths, the man was gone. I was staring at a sleek and vicious mammal, obviously carnivorous and dangerous; its ears flattened on the top of its triangular head, and when it opened its mouth to hiss at me I saw the rows of ivory fangs. From my knowledge of old illustrated books I recognized the fabled black sable, which no living man had seen because it was believed to be extinct.

Its eyes gleamed with a murderous redness as it turned away. By the time Styx sprang into action, the creature was already darting towards the woods, streaking over the snow in an undulating fashion while its breath left puffs of vapor floating in the frosty air behind it. Styx was still only halfway to the copse when the beast lost itself in the cedars.

A horrible hissing noise, not unlike that which had come from the mouth of the sable, made me turn around. All the men still standing were members of my band. The enemy bodies that lay on all sides of us, both dead and dying, were dissolving into stinking black foam that fumed like acid as it ate into the snow. A sharp, corrosive smell stung my nostrils. Soon there were only three bodies that were recognizably human, those of my men who had fallen. Only one of them was alive, and his right shoulder was laid open to the bone.

Without really being aware of what I was doing, I stooped and picked up a dark brown fur hat that had fallen from the tall bandit's head before his transformation. Like me, my men seemed to be in a state of shock. We gazed at each other with a wild surmise.

A muffled cry came from behind me. "No, no! Don't!" My dervish was writhing on his bed of branches, his face contorted in agitation, his uncovered eye jumping as he struggled just beneath the surface of consciousness.

I knelt beside his litter and laid a shaking hand on his head, dislodging the gaudy wig which I had replaced when we left the mountain pass. Words continued to spill from his trembling lips.

"Please! I didn't mean for you to get hurt! No!"

My men were buzzing with speculation again, like a cloud of disturbed wasps. One of them muttered, "Demons."

But I knew that this was not the answer. "You all saw them cut and bleeding from our swords. There's no way to hurt demons like that unless you use magic against them."

I looked at the still smoking puddles around us. "But we know one thing. Whoever these men were, they had magic on their side."

Half an hour later, with the aromas of many breakfasts blowing in our faces, we ran into a clump of peasants at the edge of the village. They were clustered about a large barrel centered in an area of snow which had been trampled flat, and even before I stepped forward I knew what I would see inside.

Crouched at the bottom of the barrel, its sturdy six-pound body flattened out to its full length of a foot and a half, a male stink badger leered up at me. I knew it by the yellow crown that branded the top of its head and extended down its dark brown back. We had come upon a badger baiting.

I found this a fortunate diversion, as the grinning ostlers and tradesmen were far too spellbound by their forthcoming sport to take notice of the mysterious burden my men were bringing into the village. The rest of my band halted at some distance behind me, on the periphery of the crowd, as a pair of muscular lads brought forth an unfortunate wire-haired terrier. Struggling madly in their hands, it seemed to know what I knew, that once dropped into the barrel it would have to fight the badger until one of them was dead. Styx sat down beside me and surveyed the scene with bored disdain.

Terhune rumbled in my ear, "I hope for the dog's sake that the scent glands have been removed." I nodded briefly; I had seen stink badgers spray their enemies with the smelly liquid which their scent glands produced. The horribly pungent fluid, far worse than that of their cousin the skunk, had been known to blind dogs for life.

The terrier whined and jerked, its bulging eyes rolling and showing plenty of white, and I felt a twinge of sympathy for it. If the badger wasn't weak from hunger, it would probably kill the dog, with or without its scent glands. This cruel, bloody sport had given the word "badger" its secondary meaning. I prepared to move on.

"The torment of helpless animals does not appeal to you, sir?"

I raised my eyes to the figure standing on the other side of the barrel from me. Unlike the familiar village oafs now milling about in their impatience, he appeared to be a stranger. A black hooded cloak muffled him entirely, and the raised hood was filled with darkness visible, a total blackness that was unnatural even though he stood with his back to the sun.

He continued to speak: "In the regions north of here, I believe, people are somewhat more civilized. They form clubs to set up badger hunts."

His voice reminded me of clotting blood, soft and

moist and oozing, with slight traces of a one-time warmth now departed. He kept his hands tucked into the voluminous sleeves of his all-concealing garment. I saw no weapons.

"Only somewhat more civilized," I responded. "They use terriers like this one here, since they love to dig, to follow the badger into its hole. Hence the name terrier, from a very old word terra, meaning earth. Then they use shovels to dig down and force the badger to the surface, where the terriers are set loose on it. A charming sport."

I watched him closely. Although we did not know one another, he had started the conversation. His next words, and the action that accompanied them, struck me like a chilling shower of hailstones.

"Sometimes it is necessary to keep following your prey assiduously until you capture it, no matter how drastic the methods used." As he said this, he turned his hood in the direction of the litter where the dervish still lay unconscious, and I imagined unseen eyes feasting on my find.

Trying to keep my face expressionless, I signaled to Terhune and turned abruptly to stride down the main street of the village, knowing that my band would follow. My inn was not very far from the edge of the village, and we could reach it in a matter of minutes.

He can't be after the boy, I thought. He was already here when we entered the village. Then I realized that the bandit ambush had obviously been set up ahead of time, planted in the path the dervish would have taken as he came down the mountain pass. The wise thing to do would be to get him safely inside the inn, where he could be defended easily by a couple of well-placed men. I quickened my pace.

The Floating Head was doing a brisk business on this bright winter morning. A coach rattled into the courtyard and pulled up before the long half-timbered building, where a pair of sturdy bays had obviously just arrived and stood stamping on the cobblestones while footmen unloaded the saddlebags.

Within moments a stream of gaily-clad passengers was pouring from the coach to fill the courtyard, like a cloud of exotic jungle birds from the far south. After drinking and riding all night in a carnival atmosphere that made the entire trip a rich man's parody of a direly urgent journey, they were looking for more party refreshments rather than an honest breakfast.

Off to the side, beyond the robust ostlers waiting to lead the horses away to the stables, appeared a disheveled kitchen scullion. She must have slipped out from under the watchful eye of the cook and crept out here to share in the excitement of the coach arrival. I beckoned to her.

She gave me a sudden, distrustful look but sidled forward, recognizing me as a permanent lodger who usually carried cash. I dug a nickel coin out of the moneybag that hung at my belt as part of my merchant's disguise.

"Go fetch the doctor and bring him up to my rooms. Tell him the patient has a seriously dislocated arm that may be broken." She reached for the coin, greed spinning in her dull eyes, but I had more instructions. "After you get the doctor, send up a large breakfast. Hot meat pies. Muffins. Eggs. Enough for two. And lots of coffee." She snatched the coin and vanished into the crowd.

Terhune appeared at my elbow. A curt order sent him and the other litter bearer moving across the courtyard with their burden. I watched them maneuver past the heavy oaken doors, and my mind's eye followed their progress over the hay covering the sunken floor of the great front hall, up the narrow stairs, and down the long dimly illuminated passage to my rooms. With that vital bit of business completed, I was at last free to think about the stranger who had accosted me at the badger baiting.

Turning to dismiss the rest of my men, I made a discovery that was half expected, half feared. As if summoned by my thoughts, the hooded figure had materialized at the edge of the courtyard. He stood very still, his hands still tucked out of sight into the sleeves of his cloak, exactly as I remembered him. Except for one detail.

My startled exclamation made Styx whirl around, ready to fight, and I reached for my weapons. A bolt of fear ran through me. Then I was heading for the doors of the inn, my brain burning with the strange image I had seen.

Within the darkness of the man's hood had blazed a constellation of glowing red spots, arranged in concentric circles, and far too numerous to be his eyes. Or so I had thought at the time.

CHAPTER 3
WAR GAME

Out of his cloak and his drab shapeless habit, dressed in a caftan of tan from my personal garderobe, the boy proved to be tall and lean, with the broad shoulders and narrow waist of one who has worked regularly and strenuously in the outdoors.

He stood before the roaring fire, which threw out pools of ruddy light to rise and fall on the walls like a tide of blood. After having slept all through the ominously quiet day and then a spot of supper at sundown, he seemed considerably refreshed.

A sling now supported his right arm, which together with his eyepatch had prompted the elderly little doctor to make a witticism about some people deteriorating faster on one side of the body than the other; however, the boy still looked quite muscular and healthy.

"I always thought religious men spent all their time huddled over old documents," I said with a smile. "But you don't exactly look like someone confined to an intellectual life."

He smiled back. "I've only been a dervish for a short while. Before that I was a woodcutter."

There was money in his voice. The accent was

refined, the pitch a pleasant light baritone, the intonation that of a man who does not expect to be contradicted. Yet the hands that toyed with his cup of brandywine were strong and calloused, the hands of a manual laborer. My eyes drifted back to that perfect face which kept making me think of the aristocracy or even royalty itself. There were many contradictions here.

I threw myself down in an overstuffed armchair. "There are several things I want to ask you, as I'm sure you can imagine. One thing I'm curious about is why you became a dervish at your age."

He jerked as if I had struck him, and some of the brandywine sloshed over the edge of his cup. "I—It was in penance for..." His lips moved soundlessly as he tried to find words that would not come. He blushed suddenly, the one clear honest eye that was visible beginning to glint with moisture, and something turned over inside me at the sight of that handsome boyish face becoming suffused with a guilty surge of blood. Like the larger blood-dimmed tide with which the room was awash from the fire. I wanted to protect him from his personal demons, but I didn't know what they were.

Instinctively I looked away from his face, which was working with naked emotion, and stared instead at the drinking vessel I had given him. It was a handleless cup of cream-colored ceramic, around the rim of which snaked a red and black dragon. The beast depicted was delicate and ornamental, more like an exotic fighting fish than any dragon I had ever seen before, the typical product of an artist of the Far East whose only familiarity with the animals came from books of legends.

The boy followed my gaze and smiled again, probably in relief. "Not much like the real thing, is it?"

I felt mild surprise, although by this point nothing should have taken me unawares. "You've seen a real dragon?"

"Yes." As quickly as he had gone from anguish to

sardonic amusement, he grew grim and introspective. It was like a trick I had seen a traveling player perform, in which he pantomimed donning a series of contrasting masks by moving his hands up and down while changing his expressions with startling rapidity.

I decided to take control of the situation. "It's time we introduced ourselves. I am Catalan. A very old name. But it suits me because I am interested in very old things. Legends. Myths. I can't seem to stop them from turning up in my poems."

"I know."

My expression seemed to amuse him, for his grin this time was an explosion of light. It was the first time since he regained consciousness that I had seen him look his age.

"You know my work?"

He laughed softly. "I wasn't always a woodcutter. I grew up in a royal household, where I was trained to be a scribe."

Aha.

"My name is Talin." The way he pronounced it made it sound like the talon of a bird of prey. I remembered that I had first thought of a turkey vulture upon seeing his body, ungainly in its large black cloak, sprawled across the snowy path. Now, however, regarding the clean lines of his limbs and the proud angle at which he held his well-shaped head, I was reminded more of an eagle, the inevitable symbol of royalty for centuries too numerous to count.

"Actually," he went on, "it's a remarkable coincidence that you were the one to find me, because I was coming here to see you."

This strange boy continued to surprise me. He was like a toy I had seen in an eastern bazaar, a wooden doll which opened to reveal smaller and smaller replicas of itself, each one popping open to disclose another piece slightly smaller yet still wondrous.

As I opened my mouth, he raised one broad hand to silence me.

"I'll explain all that I can. Just give me time." For a moment he looked down into his brandywine, swirling it into a miniature whirlpool. Then he threw the drink down his throat with a sudden, almost defiant gesture.

"I am acting as an agent for one of the players in a contest." He turned his head and locked his dark green eye with mine. The fine flecks of amber in his iris seemed to be revolving steadily, in time with my quickened pulse. His vibrant young voice continued to sing.

"I serve a particular fine Lady, whose name is not vital at the moment." That capital L soared above the rest of the words, an alabaster tower decorating the otherwise mundane cityscape of his sentence.

As he paused briefly, I sprang in with one of the many questions seething in my brain. "And what is the object of this contest?"

"My Lady's opponent in the contest is a mighty Lord, one who has in his possession the individual components for an ancient simulated war game. These are a large playing board, constructed of alternating inlaid squares of mvuli wood and stained sandalwood, and delicately carved figurines of onyx and ivory. The original object of the war game was to manipulate the playing pieces in such a fashion that the king of the opposing army was trapped and eventually destroyed."

"Yes. A situation referred to in the old texts as Checkmate. A term which could be literally translated as 'the king is dead.' The war game you are describing is a a very old, very popular one called chess. Tell me more about the contest."

"My Lady's opponent divided the war game into its three basic components–the ivory playing pieces, the onyx playing pieces, and the board itself. He established a cunning hiding place for each of these three components and then challenged my Lady to find them all and reunite them into the original game."

I was intrigued. "And you have to do all that for her?

Find both armies of figurines, as well as the playing board?"

His eyelid rose in momentary surprise, creating a vivid green flash like that optical phenomenon sometimes seen in the distance just at the moment the sun sinks below the horizon.

"Absolutely not. All I'm in charge of is the white playing pieces. The ones carved out of ivory. All the clues I've gotten so far were supposed to be limited to them."

The heat of the blood-red fire, still roaring against the right side of my face, suddenly seemed intensified. I leaned forward in my seat.

"Why don't you tell me exactly how serious this contest is? After all, when I found you, it was obvious you had recently been violently attacked. Shortly after I took you into my custody, a group of bandits ambushed my party, and one of their number stated explicitly that you were what they were after. We managed to get you safely here to the village, where a very strange hooded figure suggested he had a special interest in you. In short, it appears that your movements have been closely followed ever since you made it through the mountain pass."

He sighed deeply. "It seems that the powerful Lord opposing my Lady in this contest is taking the game very seriously. I believe that he has dispatched his minions to prevent me from achieving my goal, just as I must assume that he is moving to thwart any other agents of my Lady. Of course, I have been kept in ignorance of any agents who may have been assigned to seek the onyx figurines or the inlaid playing board."

I poured myself another healthy slug of brandywine and offered him the ceramic jug, which he refused. "I gather you're not quite ready to discuss what led you to shave off all your hair and become a dervish. I get the impression there's more involved than simply seizing an excuse to remove your hair, which seems a bit distinctive in color." I ran a hand along my jawline, to indicate that I had noticed his red-gold stubble.

The beautiful emerald eye clouded over, and he cleared his throat uncomfortably. "It's not important why I became a dervish. Except that I didn't do it in order to disguise myself. The people who are watching me are well aware that I took my vows, and everything that goes with them, because I did it quite publicly."

I could not resist falling into the role of the wiser older brother. "Speaking of disguises, didn't you think it foolish to choose a wig so similar in color to your own hair?"

He smiled wryly. "Perhaps. It pleased me to be wearing a portion of my former self. It is said that when a fugitive changes his name and goes into hiding, his most common mistake is to select a new name beginning with the same letter as his old name. But as to the question of hair, the shades of red are quite different. My real hair is closer to gold. And of course the people following me are not looking for a red-haired boy, or a boy with any hair at all. They are looking for a dervish, who has observed the custom of his kind by shaving his head and eyebrows."

I remembered the lantern-jawed bandit snarling, "Give us the dervish." Yes, they had known what they were seeking. And they had penetrated the boy's disguise. I was thinking of the hideous transformation that had concluded the battle in the snow when the door to the hallway crashed open.

Chapter 4
The Moving Finger Writes

Styx padded in, having banged the door open with his flat head, and crossed to throw himself down on the hearth. Even lying down, he was so large that his paws stretched well beyond the andirons on either side of the fireplace. He began to make his pleasure purr, rumbling like an old windmill. The fire turned his eyes into smooth jewels.

I felt that I had to get to the crux of the matter. "All right. Why were you coming to see me?"

Talin sank into my most comfortable piece of furniture, a soft peach-colored armchair whose arms had been worn down to blunt stubs. With a peculiar, almost mischievous look on his face he began to recite:

"Joy stalks the darkling mountainside
On padpaws soft as pipesmoke.
Her laughter fills the porcelain hills
And makes the demons choke.
A panther she, with golden eyes
And fur of finespun amber;
To still the dark and wake the lark,
Through cloud she likes to clamber.
The demons scurry from her sight

As beetles do from torches.
Her lamps of fate illuminate
Her path, which never scorches."

My former astonishment was nothing compared with what I felt now. I set the brandywine jug down very gently on the floor, as if it were spun out of spider silk and might disintegrate. Then I stood up slowly.

"What–Where did you hear that?" I stammered.

His eye was twinkling with barely suppressed amusement. "It's one of your poems, isn't it?"

"Yes, it's one of my poems, but it's one I just wrote this past fall. It hasn't been published yet. I haven't even distributed copies to my colleagues. As far as I know, no one has ever laid eyes on it but me."

His mobile mouth turned up at one corner. "That's one of the strange things about the clues I've been getting in this contest. They carry information that could not possibly be public knowledge at the time I receive them, and they always come to me in dreams."

I sank back into my chair. "You dreamed the text of my poem? How is that possible? And what could it possibly have to do with your quest?"

"Look. One of the things you have to accept right away about this affair, this grand contest, is that there's lots of magic involved in it."

"I know. Remember what I told you about the disappearance of the enemy bodies at the end of the ambush in the foothills."

He nodded vigorously, and his shaved head glinted in the firelight. "Exactly. Both the Lord and the Lady are using magic against each other. Apparently he has sent a number of his own agents into the field to stop my Lady's men from succeeding, and he is backing them up with his rather powerful spells.

"Fortunately, my Lady is doing everything she can to protect me and whatever other agents she has. In addition, she has sent me vital clues by long-range mindlink. Through my dreams."

I was becoming exasperated. "I don't understand where these clues come from, or what they have to do with my poem."

"Under the terms of the agreement entered into by the Lord and Lady, he is obligated to give her legitimate and valuable clues at certain intervals. She in turn has been passing those clues on to her agents, depending on what component of the war game the individual clue concerns."

I was fighting hard to maintain my composure, but I could feel my chest rising and falling more rapidly than normal, and heat was radiating from my face. "My poem has nothing to do with your ridiculous game," I protested, rather loudly.

His smile was that of an angel refusing a soul entry into heaven. "I'm afraid it does. Ever since the contest began, I have been following a pathetically faint trail, with very little help from my Lady. If I get the chance to tell you about it, you may judge for yourself. But once she got a major clue from her Lord, one pinpointing the hiding place of the ivory pieces, she was able to put it into one of your poems and then send me the text of that poem in a dream."

The room was suddenly too hot, and my sentry cat's purring throbbed in the silence. "No one puts anything into my poems," I said quietly. "I may be influenced at times by the old classics, but my work is my own."

Talin moved forward to the edge of his chair and made a placating gesture. "I'm sure my Lady didn't tamper with the wording or the actual literary quality of the work," he crooned. "She only subtly influenced your choice of subject matter, so that the topic of your poem would point to the final resting place of the ivory playing pieces which I seek."

"This still doesn't make any sense." I clutched my hair in both hands, as if I would tear it out. "Once she got the major clue to the whereabouts of your prize, why would your Lady go to the trouble of putting it into one of my poems and then send you the poem? Why not just send you the clue itself?"

He grew painfully earnest. "Because I am being tested as well. Myself and my Lady's other agents. Her success or failure will depend not only upon her own powers but also upon her ability to select intelligent and resourceful searchers. If she made the quest too easy, it would be a bad reflection upon her. Conversely, a highly challenging trail of clues that nevertheless leads to a successful outcome will make her shine that much more brightly."

I was still not prepared to accept the possibility that my own mind had been interfered with. "So my poem came to you in a dream. Why is it inevitable that she had a hand in its inspiration? Maybe I just happened to write a poem mentioning this clue, whatever it is, and she chose that way of passing it on to you."

A strange expression seemed to flicker across his face and then was gone; perhaps it was pity, or perhaps merely the constant movement of the firelight. "I think what you're suggesting would be a coincidence of immense magnitude. I believe that you are involved in this quest, whether you wish it or not."

I took a deep breath and clasped my hands together to stop their shaking. Sorcery always made me nervous.

"All right. Was there anything in your dream to point out where the clue lies in the poem? Or to lead you to me? How did you know where to find me?"

"In the dream I was on a beach at night, under a brilliant full moon. I was down near the water line, where the surf was boiling and foaming at my feet, and the damp hard-packed sand was smooth silver in the moonlight. Ghost crabs were skittering here and there.

"Then, as if a moving finger was writing there in the silver sand, words began to appear on the beach. The letters might have been carved from ebony, they stood out so blackly. After the writing stopped, I had time to read the message three times before the rising tide obliterated it. It was the text of your poem, and it was signed with your name."

"No instructions to you? No directions on how to find me?"

"As I said before, your work and your reputation were known to me when I was training to be a scribe for a royal household. I already knew that you lived here in Andor."

"And what is the clue in the poem?"

"Each agent was to receive three clues about specific places or points of the compass, each one leading him closer to the object of his quest. Since this is the second clue, I am hoping that it will lead me to the general location of my pieces, with one more clue to come when it is time to find the actual cache. I wanted to ask you especially about where you were when you wrote the poem and what you were thinking about when you referred to the darkling mountainside and the porcelain hills."

I rose again and went to the small window opposite the fireplace; its thick glass was wavy and filled with bubbles, and in it I saw nothing but a twisted version of my own confused face.

"There is no area officially known as the Porcelain Hills," I said without turning around. "I was inspired to write the poem one day when I was out with Styx, up in the foothills north of here."

"Styx?"

I faced him and nodded at the big beast blinking in front of the fire. "My sentry cat. We were on a simple day trip up in the hills just for a bit of exercise, and watching him stalk along the slopes aroused me to the sheer astonishment of his physical beauty, and how it might embody the quality of joy.

"Joy has been traditionally personified in literature as a feminine entity–there is an ancient piece describing Joy as the beautiful divine spark, daughter of heaven, into whose holy resting place we step drunk with fire–so I changed the gender of the cat to a she panther. Otherwise the references are merely visual. The darkling mountainside is the major slope that rises above the foothills, and I used the other phrase because those hills have the qualities I associate with porcelain–hardness, whiteness, sonority. If you shout up in those foothills, there is a wonderful ringing in the air, like the sound produced when you flick a fingernail against a fine porcelain vase."

The dervish rose as well and came to stand within inches of my face. Although I am rather tall, I was uncomfortably aware that his bewitching eye and the corresponding black patch were exactly level with my own eyes.

"Take me there," he said.

Before I could answer, there came a peremptory rap on the door, and my landlord bustled in. Orn was a short bandylegged man, with watery light blue eyes, thinning blond hair, and a beard large enough for several birds to nest in.

"Catalan!" He waved his arms in a frenzy of excitement, and the close air of the room became redolent with snuff and garlic.

I smiled largely, knowing Orn's temperament and his predilection for false alarms.

"There are men watching the inn."

My amusement was killed in an instant. "Where?"

"At least five in the front and an unknown number out back, in the baker's yard." He gasped and wheezed like an asthma victim. "Cook tells me they've been there for at least an hour, but she didn't want to raise a brouhaha. Heavens, no, the entire population of the Floating Head may be in for doom from the moon, but she was never one to raise a fuss. Ha!"

His agitated tone had caused Styx to roll over with silky smoothness, to crouch unwinking on the hearth. As he was silhouetted against the dying fire, the dark chocolate markings on his face, ears, and paws blurred into the cocoa-colored fur of his body, creating a sculpture of solid jet. The statue's only movement was the stately pavane conducted by his tail, which swayed like a black cobra in the ruddy illumination.

I raised both hands to Orn and attempted to be the voice of reason. "So what makes you think they have anything to do with me?"

"What?" He sputtered and popped, just as a resinous chunk of pine would have if thrown into our smoky fire.

"What I mean, Orn, is this: Who are these men, and what do they want?"

His jaws snapped open and closed, and I got a wave of more garlic. "How do I know who they are? But they must want you or somebody who came with you, since the only other arrivals we've had at the inn in the last twelve hours have been that lovely charm of finches you saw when you came in this morning." He paused, tugging at the curls in his beard. "Why is it so dark in here?" he demanded querulously.

"We were talking." I moved to put another log on the fire, but Orn stopped me with an impatient noise that sounded like a cat sneezing.

"Don't! The watchers will see the light flare up in the window and know that something's up." He looked at Talin as if suddenly aware of him for the first time.

I proffered a foolish thought. "Maybe the watchers are after one of the party that arrived this morning."

"Fiddlesticks! They're harmless rich idiots from the city. The finest collection of prickmedainties and fancy boys this side of the capital. I imagine this young buck is the cause of our troubles."

"All right. In that case we need to leave right away. Are there horses ready?"

"Are you mad? Your life wouldn't be worth a bulrush. The only way out is through the tunnel to the Widow's house. You can send the boy out that way since it seems that's who they want. It's none of your business."

I remembered the dervish's clear vibrant voice telling me, *I believe that you are involved in the quest, whether you wish it or not.* I cleared my throat.

"Yes, it is my business. We both go through the tunnel. Send me Terhune."

He gave vent to a minor explosion inside his beard. "All right. But don't try to leave the village on horseback. My advice is, if you want to get away clean, keep your party as small as possible, go north through the hills, and hole up in the old waystation cabin on the mountain. I'll get to you tomorrow with supplies."

"Fine. Talin, get your cloak. Sticker, we're moving." I grabbed my cloak and my leather pouch, which was always filled with the daily necessities, and headed for the door. Styx flowed to his feet and oozed after me, his tail lashing from side to side.

Talin moved with us, snatching his dark cloak and wig from the hook where they were hanging on my claw-footed coatrack.

Within seconds we were in the hallway and headed for the stairwell. I could hear a girl singing.

CHAPTER 5
WE FLEE THE FLOATING HEAD

Orn's daughter was on the stairs, inspecting the treads to make sure the maids had done their job and removed the red clay from the filthy foothills. Snow was left to melt.

As we came down she raised her finely etched face, with its helmet of tight chesnut curls, and watched us through those metallic blue eyes of hers, without ever stopping her otherworldly singing. Her voice rose and fell in lovely fluting tones, as if some wet bird-haunted lawn had lent her the music of its trees at dawn.

She was about Talin's age and almost as beautiful as he was. She finally stopped singing when she saw him. The guttering candle stubs in the wall brackets were throwing visible spiderwebs all over our faces, but there was enough light for her to get a good look at the boy.

Orn produced his sneezing cat noise again. "All right, Diarfa, that will do." His twitching hands made vague shooing motions in her direction, suggesting she was some easily excited fowl. "Move along now. These gentlemen are in a hurry."

"Are they now?" Her speaking voice was deeper and throatier than when she sang, reminiscent of a sultry barmaid too fond of her whiskey. She straightened to her full height, and I noticed that she wore her usual choice of male doublet and tights. Tall, trim, and tightly muscled, with no breasts nor hips to speak of, she had the body of a young boy, which made her very popular with certain male clientele of the Floating Head. If you squinted your eyes just right, you could pretend that she was indeed a male youth.

"Catalan I know, but this other I do not. Where have you been hiding him? Are they in too much of a hurry for an introduction?"

Orn grew even more exasperated. "Yes, they are. Now move." He paused to think. "You can talk to them downstairs. They're going through the tunnel. I want you to get some provisions for them from the kitchen, just bread and cheese will do. I have to find Terhune."

"He's probably in the front room having a drink," I said, then turned to Diarfa. "Can you meet us at the far end of the tunnel, just beneath the Widow's house? We need to get away from the windows." I tried to sound courteous but urgent.

"All right, Catalan," she agreed with careful dignity. "Father, please try to remember I am not one of your scullery maids."

As she moved down ahead of us, Orn snapped, "Scullery maids have big mouths. I trust you to keep yours in control." She shot him a dark look and continued to descend.

At the bottom of the stairs Orn said, "I'll put the signal in the back window so they'll know to open the other end of the tunnel." Then we scattered like a watch of nightingales disturbed by a kestrel. Pausing there in the great hall with Talin, while Diarfa strode evenly back toward the kitchen, I eyed her father scurrying into the front room and felt the danger of our situation quickening in my blood.

Terhune had not kept us waiting. Reeking of his chewing tobacco, he herded Talin and me along the narrow tunnel, while the dancing torch threw goblin shadows on the walls and the heavy close air grew fragrant with burning pine.

The small square room at the end was lined on all six sides with smooth cedar panels that gleamed in the torchlight. The three of us crowded in, stooping slightly because we were all tall. It was like being stuffed inside a cigar box.

Behind us Styx padded up and crouched in the dark mouth of the tunnel, which was irregularly shaped and edged with ragged cobwebs. His eyes caught the light and threw it back as disks of cold fire. After we had stood in silence for a couple of minutes, Terhune idly shifting his pack from one hand to another and periodically spitting on the cedar floor, I saw a flower of flame sprout at the tunnel end from which we had come.

Our anxious breath made clouds in the frigid air. The vapor hung in a transparent curtain, through which the distant blossom of light grew closer and coalesced into six separate candle flames.

Suddenly Diarfa sprang into view, holding aloft a blazing six-pronged candelabra. Styx glided out of her way and she stopped just inside the small room.

Talin allowed himself a brilliant smile. "That's a pretty showy way to travel. Did we take the last of your father's torches?"

The girl recoiled as if physically stung. "As long as we're talking about appearances, that's a pretty showy patch you're sporting. What happened to your eye?"

No one else said anything; Terhune was not one to correct another's manners, and I wanted to hear what Talin's answer would be.

He retreated in silence to the far end of the room, where a deep alcove let him slip just outside the range of the torch and the candelabra. I could barely make him out, standing in the gloomy niche near the foot of a crude ladder. Light the color of old gold spilled down from the house above, outlining his elegant knife-edged profile.

"A mistake," he murmured. "A stupid mistake." I could not tell if he was referring to the loss of his eye or his remark to Diarfa.

"I thank you most kindly," I said to her, taking the canvas bag of provisions she had brought us. There was an awkward pause.

Diarfa's eyes, so dark blue that they looked black in the flickering light, had never left Talin for a second.

"I'll see you later," she whispered. And was gone, taking with her the spectacularly gaudy candelabra. I watched the six separate candle flames recede into the tunnel and melt back into a single bloom of light and eventually disappear.

"Let's move on." Brisk, sensible leadership. As Terhune and I entered the deep alcove where Talin stood at the bottom of the ladder, I added, "I think we should have a word with the Widow before we leave her house."

Terhune chuckled drily. "That's a good idea, seeing as how we have to go bang through her parlor, and she hasn't left it in fifty years."

I led the way up the ladder, climbing one-handed with the bag of provisions dangling from my right fist. Terhune followed with the torch, leaving Talin to bring up the rear. I gave him enough credit to assume that he would be able to negotiate the ladder with one arm in a sling, and he did not disappoint me.

We emerged into a well-lit back room full of boxes and old furniture. I noted with approval the thick wad of rolled-up wine-red carpet and the detached floor panel next to the wall, verifying that the Widow's people had seen Orn's signal. We moved through an archway into an old-fashioned parlor.

The Widow Quod squatted malevolently on the floor, eating raw tomatoes. She was a fat old woman who had gone bald long before Terhune and I were born.

Many called her the Widow Toad behind her back;

not only did it rhyme with her real name, but she also resembled an amphibian with her lumpy skin and bulging eyes. She reminded me of someone who had been all but choked to death and had just that moment been revived.

She was notorious for her prejudice against chairs, napkins, and people under the age of a hundred. When she saw us coming she wiped her mouth on her maid's robe and waved the girl away.

She was wearing so much face powder that, every time she turned her head, folds of flesh jiggled and filled the air with white dust, creating a halo. The tomato stains around her mouth made her look like a vampire disturbed in the midst of its feast. A vampire toad.

With Terhune and Talin flanking me, I advanced to stand in front of her. "Madam," I said, "I thank you for giving us access to the end of the tunnel. We are grateful for the right of passage."

She rolled her protuberant eyes up at me and then rotated them to take in my dervish. Having put on his ungainly cloak and replaced the garish red wig, he did not cut a very impressive figure, but of course nothing could dim the glory of those aristocratic features.

The Widow let loose a laugh that sounded like tearing leather.

Her voice came creaking out of the long curved crevice of her mouth. "That's the ugliest wig this side of the seashore. You just can't find decent hairpieces these days, can you? That's why I gave them up."

Talin moved to touch his wig but stopped in midgesture. I reflected that Terhune and I were the only persons in the room with normal heads of hair, now that the maid had left.

The Widow continued to stare at Talin as she clutched at her long skirt with hands that were twisted like old thorn trees.

"My, you're a pretty boy," she croaked. She reluctantly shifted her gaze to Styx, who had finished climbing the inclined ladder and was stealing into the parlor behind us. "And I see you've brought along your... animal."

The way she said that last word offended me, but I held my tongue. I wanted to bark at her, but instead I turned and looked pointedly at the door to the front hallway. It was the only way out, as the parlor had no windows.

She was not through, however. Craft clung to her fat face, cloaked her skull.

"Just who are you trying to avoid?" A hideous grin appeared, stretching her mouth even wider than I had thought possible.

"Oh, that's for us to worry about, not you," I said lightly. "We've intruded on you enough already, so we'll be on our way."

She held up one of her twisted hands, with fingers shaped like spatulas. "Let's not be too hasty. I'm thinking." There was an ominous pause, while the room's artificial flowery smell filled my nostrils.

"Ah. All the years I've seen you at the Floating Head you've never had to come through the tunnel. Hmm." Her ancient voice continued to crackle. "It must be the boy."

I could feel the blood rising in my face. "You're just like Orn," I snapped. "You're too smart for your own good." I made a move to leave the room.

The Widow suddenly thrust both her hands out to her sides, in a bizarre parody of supplication. "Now, wait. It would be the devil's own nonsense to let him go out there, if he's who they want." Her mouth gaped into a crater, the edges dripping with fragments of tomato, as she filled her lungs with the incense-laden air. I knew that she was about to summon her guards.

"Oh, no. It would be the devil's own nonsense to involve a private citizen of your stature in such a petty squabble." I gestured to Terhune. He surged forward and placed the tip of his sword against her throat, and I saw the red-rimmed hole of her mouth collapse in upon itself.

"Sticker! We're moving!" We three humans, trailed by the sentry cat, advanced past Quod, who sat there paralyzed like a troll exposed to the rays of the rising sun.

My party was at the outside door when the Widow's strangled scream reached us. "You'll regret this! You'll never reach your goal alive!"

We stepped out into the iron-dark air.

CHAPTER 6
HUNCHBACK MOUNTAIN

Starlit snow lay everywhere around us. Up here at the edge of the northern foothills, far outside the range of any lights from the village, it gleamed softly like seafoam. A rumor of a gibbous moon floated behind constantly moving banks of clouds; an hour earlier, when we struck out from the village, it had risen to give us shadows on the lambent snow, and Terhune had extinguished the torch, but now the moon was in hiding. There was still enough light that we had not yet relit the torch.

Talin spoke quietly. "Is there anyone in particular we have to watch out for here in the hills?"

"Not really," I answered. "If we were heading back up into the eastern pass, where we found you, we'd have to think about the various mountain tribes that are always watching the trail. And of course that country is full of bandits. But here in the north it's pretty quiet."

"Right," Terhune grunted. "People still remember the earthquake, even though it was ten years ago. The ground swallowed up two whole villages and half a sheep ranch. The only thing left up here is the waystation cabin, and that's a good third of the way up Hunchback."

Talin came up beside me. We were nearing the top

of a gentle rise where there were no trees to throw shadows, and the starlight reflecting off the hard-packed snow was bright enough to show me his face. He looked worried.

"That strange old woman was really angry that we didn't stay to talk to her. Would she turn us in, give us away to the men who were watching the inn?"

"I seriously doubt it. She's lived in Andor for a long time, she has no intention of leaving, and she wouldn't want to do anything to ruin her reputation there. She wouldn't have anything to gain from betraying us, except money, and she's already got more of that than she can possibly spend. She was just annoyed at not getting her own way. And I think she was somewhat arrested by your... shall we say, your physical attributes."

He turned away quickly, and I thought that maybe I had embarrassed him. Was it possible that he did not know how attractive he was? A prince who was unaware that he looked princely? His reaction was almost a guilty one, though, reminding me of how he had behaved when I asked him why he became a dervish, and again when Diarfa asked him about his missing eye.

It also occurred to me that, whereas the Widow would probably never turn us over to the mysterious agents watching the inn, she might be perverse enough to send some of her own people after us. This action could have several undesirable consequences, such as blazing a trail straight to us for the enemy agents. I quickened my pace.

As we crunched down the other side of the hill, the swollen moon burst forth from the clouds and flooded the landscape with a brilliant milky radiance. Lacking another week before it became full, the bright chunky satellite appeared to be lurching across the sky with a hump on its back, almost a miniature replica of the misshapen peak suddenly looming above us.

Hunchback Mountain slouched against the now opalescent dome of the heavens. Its famous outcropping of granite and dead trees was covered with sullen snow much whiter than the pale green drifts of the rest of the kingdom.

The last landmark before the base of the mountain was a long footbridge, which swayed from side to side while we clung to the rotting ropes that were the only handrails. One hundred feet below us lay a frozen river.

At the other end of the bridge Talin stopped and faced me, his shaggy wig silhouetted against the moon. The three of us came to a halt, while Styx prowled on up toward the first major slope of the mountain.

"You said you were going to show me where you were inspired to write the poem."

I almost laughed; I had been waiting for that question with an absurd amount of pleasure. "Actually, I never did agree to that. I only said I would come up here with you to get away from your pursuers." Taking pity on his dismayed expression, I hurried on, "But of course I'll show you."

He leaped in. "Where was it?"

"Right here."

His visible eye widened, reminding me of how very young he was. With an inarticulate cry of triumph, he whirled to survey the snowy landscape around us, while Terhune and I stayed rooted in our tracks. My eyes slowly moved to take in what Talin's hungry gaze was devouring.

The moonlit drifts on either side of the gorge reeled in drunken ecstasy, like the icing of a vast ceremonial cake damaged in transit. The low treeless ridge we had just crossed beetled above us, while in the distance we could make out higher crests we had left behind, each crowned by snow-crippled thorn trees writhing in the winter air.

"They could be anywhere," Talin murmured.

"What could?"

"You know, the ivory pieces. They could be buried under eighteen feet of snow. They could be at the bottom of a snow-filled crevasse that we can't even see. Or—or—" His face tightened in anguish. "Or they could be somewhere in that frozen river down there, stuck under several feet of black ice."

I cleared my throat. "Don't forget you have one more dream clue coming. There's always the possibility that–"

Terhune chopped off the end of my sentence with the phlegmatic calm of a farmer beheading a chicken. "We're being followed."

I flung my gaze back across the gorge. On the slope above us, Styx gave a rattling cry.

Everything was frozen into an oil painting, a twisted two-tone seascape. Black tree shadows stood out against the distant pale green ridges.

Into this scene of snow and silence drifted a small dark shape, like the fuzzy spot that floats across a man's field of vision when a fragment of dead skin has become detached from the surface of his retina and wanders about the sea inside his eyeball.

"Only one," I mused. "Not what I would call a major threat."

Terhune was more pessimistic. "That depends on what weapons he's carrying. We still have no crossbows and no armor."

"We didn't exactly have all the time in the world when we left the Head."

"It would have been the work of a moment to arm ourselves correctly–"

"Terhune, we're fine."

"What are you going to do, hit him in the head with your sack of cheese sandwiches?"

"Enough!" I rapped out. "We go to the waystation. It's the only shelter for miles."

"And easily defended, as long as no one sets fire to it," he admitted reluctantly.

"Sticker, we're moving!"

The cabin was a long, low one-story structure of painted logs that clung to the upper edge of a small clearing.

The high windows were little panes of dusty glass, and on the ancient door the paint was cracked with age.

The snow had gradually paled as we climbed, eventually turning from its normal light green to the color of bleached bones under the relentless radiance of the moon. Now I eyed the whitewashed cabin where it crouched in the clearing, like one of the northern bears flattening itself into the mountain snow to take advantage of its protective coloration.

All pigment seemed to have been sucked out of the scene, and our dark cloaks stood out like dry scabs. The moon was now a misshapen skull from an old corpse. Everything was reminding me of disease and death.

I remembered the cabin had a fireplace. "Let's get inside and start a fire."

Terhune spat. "Smoke will bring watchers on us like ducks on a June bug."

"There's only one, and he already knows where we are. We might as well be comfortable." I crunched across the clearing.

"It's bad policy," he muttered as he followed.

With Styx flowing along at my left side, I approached the small front porch. Three decaying concrete steps led up to the porch itself, which had a roof and was enclosed on both sides by heavy curtains of dead trumpet vines. The front door was flanked by two diminutive religious statues I did not recognize.

The door eased open at my touch and we moved inside, stamping the snow from our boots. The interior of the cabin was one large undivided room, dark and murky because the small windows high on the walls only allowed a bit of moonlight to leak in. Terhune lit his torch as I crossed to the fireplace.

The log lying ready seemed to leap to meet the spark from my tinderbox, and soon smoky tendrils of light were unfolding to illuminate the interior of the cabin. Substantial pieces of furniture loomed here and there. A big oval table of dark wood dominated the room, balanced on curving legs that ended in clawed feet wrapped around large spheres.

Terhune shot a dubious glance at the high windows. "I was worried about smoke, but the light from this fire is going to be even worse. It'll turn the whole cabin into a constellation."

I brandished the rusty poker I had found beside the fireplace. "Nonsense. That moon out there has the entire mountainside lit up like a midsummer afternoon. No one should notice if there's a light showing here. Besides, whoever that is following us, I think it's obvious that he already knows where we are. I told you."

Terhune turned and spat into the corner of the dimly lit room. "I don't like it."

Styx sprang up onto the near end of the table and crouched there like a vast heraldic beast. In the strengthening illumination from the fire I could see the lighter-colored fur on the inside of his ears. His eyes swam toward mine in the thick reddening air.

Talin was pacing back and forth between the front door and the table. "She'll help me," he finally blurted. "She must help me."

"Who?" I demanded.

"My Lady." By this point he was almost bouncing from wall to wall, and all the muscles in his cheeks were jumping as he clenched his jaw in his anxiety.

"Talin. Don't you think it's time you told me her name?"

He hesitated, and then it came in a rush: "Marabar. She is the Lady Marabar."

The name acted as a key, not the word made flesh as in one of the old religions but the word made metal, unlocking the floodgates of memory.

A scene from the past swam slowly up before my mind's eye, unfolding like a nocturnal forest glade under the spell of moonrise.

*A huge room cross-lit by blazing candelabras. The
light moves and seethes in the center of the chamber, like
something alive. The people crowding the room are short
and stocky, with skin the color of strongly brewed tea.*

*I am stuck in a corner of the room, at an oblong
guest table crammed with black panther people visiting
from a distant kingdom.*

*Woodwind instruments coo a warning, like the soft
cry of a mourning dove. Double doors at the far end of the
room slide open their ponderous ebony jaws, and in she
sails.*

*She stands there as tall and straight as one of the
candle flames, and I recognize the truth in the rumor that
she makes it a matter of personal pride never to use her
magic to restore her lost youth. I see a woman in her fifties,
with soft smooth skin the color and texture of a rose one
morning past its prime. The dusky pink-red of her angular
handsome face is set off by sharkskin-gray hair coiled into a
majestic bun, and her cheekbones are sharp enough to slice
an apple. Her eyes are hidden by iridescent protective lenses
of the type that cover the entire eye socket and cling there
without any visible means of support.*

*Her simple white gown is eclipsed by her crown of
pure crystal and silver. I am impressed.*

*My failure to put a name to the home country of
my table mates is capped by my total ignorance of the cus-
toms of this kingdom we are presently visiting, because I am
stupefied by the ceremonial gesture we now witness.*

*With funereal gravity all the celebrants in the
chamber rise to their feet, rotate so they stand with their
backs to the Lady, and bow away from her in a slowly
spreading wave. From my vantage point, it is like being on
the edge of a diseased, unnaturally dark wheat field bending
before a wind unseen yet irresistible.*

*Because I am only a callow youth still in my teens,
their maneuver of spinning away from her and bending
themselves double strikes me as incredibly ridiculous. I burst*

out laughing.

One by one the individuals in the crowd turn horrified faces to me, the waving wheat field transformed as the wind changes direction.

Suddenly the vision from my past slid from my mind. It had been as vivid as a fever dream. And it had only taken seconds, because the mind's eye never blinks.

Styx had started to purr rapidly as the warmth and light of the fire eddied around us, and the splashes of snow on our cloaks were melting away. The tranquil scene seemed to have calmed Talin a bit. "Tell us about where you're from," I suggested quietly.

Pain still twisted his face, and he stood there biting the inside of his cheek. His right cheek, on the same side as his monstrous and inescapable eyepatch.

"What's the matter with you?" My question was gentle yet firm. His response was to turn back to the closed door and lean against it, as if its scarred panels were transparent and would let him look back down the moonflooded mountain slope to the footbridge where I had been inspired to write my poem.

The fire made noises like the rustling of an impatient crowd. Time crawled along.

At my side, Terhune stirred himself. "Give the boy some space," he rumbled. "After a few more quiet nights of sleep he'll be as right as rain."

He eyed the shrinking flames in the fireplace. "We need some more wood," he announced in his normal booming bass. "And I could use a Jimmy Riddle." He surged toward the door, where he laid a surprisingly gentle hand on Talin's shoulder.

The young dervish, now partly in shadow, looked at him as if he were looking at a square egg. "What?"

"I'm going for more wood. There's extra logs on a covered porch out back—or there used to be. Sometimes the snow has drifted in on them, but usually they're all right for keeping a fire going."

Talin blinked in confusion, like a sleepwalker who had just awakened. "No, I mean–What was that you said about a riddle?"

"You know, a Jimmy Riddle." Terhune made a crude gesture near his crotch. "Strangle the python."

I laughed out loud at Talin's expression. "Terhune comes from an island far west of here," I told him, "where they still have an occasional bit of old slang. Some of it is rhyming slang, like apples and pears for stairs, frog and toad for road, or Jimmy Riddle for having a piddle."

"That's right," grunted Terhune, "and my bladder says you'd best get out of the way unless you wish me to have an accident." He shouldered Talin aside and flung open the door, admitting a blast of cold air.

The flickering red interior of the room was instantly speared by a shaft of shimmering light, as in the old story about the randy god who visited his imprisoned lover in the form of a shower of gold. Terhune went out, leaving the door ajar to let the bright wild moonlight in.

Talin had barely had time to drift back toward me and the fireplace before we heard the sound of scuffling and muffled oaths. A moment later the door slammed open and a slender dark figure flew inside, followed immediately by the unmistakable bulk of Terhune. He spat in disgust.

"It says a lot for conditions in this kingdom," he growled, "that a person can't even try to piss on a snowbank without tripping over some busybody–and some busybody still caught in the meshes of childhood, to boot."

He lumbered over and dropped a big log on the fire, and the ruddy flames rose up to illumine the trim body and finely chiseled features of Orn's daughter, Diarfa.

CHAPTER 7
THE UNEXPECTED GUEST

"Oh, well," I said, "she may have been sent along by her father to bring us the long-range provisions he promised us..." My cheery voice died as I noticed that she carried no baggage of any kind.

She jerked her perfectly etched face toward me. "Do me a favor and get this ape off me. I can't remember any royal decree making Hunchback Mountain off limits to private citizens."

She wore a wine-colored suit and matching cape. As when we had seen her in the torchlit tunnel beneath the Widow's house, her metallic blue eyes smoldered blackly in the dim light.

"Hey, calm down." I moved forward, but Talin was far ahead of me.

"It's all right," he blurted, going to her, his left arm arcing around her protectively, his right arm trying to move around her in a parallel fashion despite its confining sling.

She slid out of range of his groping left arm and recoiled against the far wall of the cabin. "You're blasted right it's all right," she forced out between gritted teeth. "Touch me again without my permission and I'll rip your arm out of its socket."

Talin retreated slightly and looked at me and Ter-hune. "I think she must be in that snow-dream I've read about," he said, referring to the strange warm daze of drug-like comfort which consumes the person who has lost his way in the mountains.

Diarfa stiffened to display her tall, tightly muscled body. "I am not in any kind of dream. This waystation is less than one day's march from the village. And the snow mad-ness only takes you in the daylight hours, you cretin."

"Oh, be quiet," interrupted Talin, who rolled up against her again. The gods knew what he had in mind, but she did not let him get any further.

She swept her right foot sideways to pull his legs out from under him, while a well-aimed blow from one of her arms shifted his weight so that he fell flat on his back.

Terhune and I exchanged startled glances, but we had both known Diarfa long enough to trust that she would do nothing to harm the boy.

His turkey vulture cloak spilled open, falling into a pool of ink around him. Our vigorous hike up the moun-tain slope had generated enough sweat to make my tan caftan cling to his sinewy body as it tensed to resist her assault.

A clockwork figure clad in burgundy, she descended to her knees and extended one arm so that her hand hovered above Talin's torso. Then she spoke fiercely:

"You're just like every other man I've ever met. Remember the old saying–the Bumblebee of Love flits in the garden of the world, for whose flowers destruction is in his breath. Watch out, my friend, here comes the Bumblebee."

When she finally struck, she swooped down and began to tickle Talin. Like the insect she had invoked, her hand buzzed up and down along his sides, occasionally pausing to scurry into the vulnerable hollow of an armpit.

Her victim was very ticklish, as the young often are. Being partially disabled with his right arm in its sling, he could only spasm and thrash and give vent to a flood of agonized laughter. His helpless giggles, like his rare grin, made him seem more his real age, something I tended to forget when he spoke so maturely.

Lashing his tail in excitement but waiting for my command, Styx crouched on his tabletop against the background of the struggling figures in tan and burgundy, reminding me of the mythic panther who drew the chariot of the ancient god of wine. He made a guttural noise, a ghost of a growl.

I spoke harshly, "Down, Styx!" and he slid off the table and flowed over to the door. I could still see him plainly as he began to coil himself into a ball there, and I realized that the red-gold light from the replenished fire was spreading through the entire room again, staining the air the way wine stains water. It made me mindful of security.

"Diarfa!" I circled the big table and was looming above her in two strides. "Stop those children's games and look at me. I have questions that need answers."

After a brief glance at my expression, she stopped her assault on Talin's ribs. His left eye glinting moistly out of his flushed face, he slumped into the floor and tried to gain control of his cascading laughter.

Diarfa eyed me suspiciously. "What kind of questions?"

"Were you the only person following us? Was there anybody behind you?"

She stood slowly. "How do I know if there was anybody behind me? What does it matter if there was?"

Terhune came around the oval table and plowed into our little group. "Heaven defend us from the brain-dead. We left the Head because we thought someone was after the boy here."

"Yes," I added, "and I'm worried about the light from this fire showing through all these windows."

Terhune was an instant too late in wiping the look off his face. "When we first got here I told you it was dangerous to have a fire, and you said the moon had the mountainside all lit up and nothing would give us away."

"Yes, but if you spend enough time in one place, the moon eventually goes down." I turned back to Diarfa. "Did you see anyone else between the village and here?"

She had become suddenly serious. "No. The watchers were still in front of the inn, and in the baker's yard, when I left, but I went through the tunnel. The Widow Toad was screaming to wake the dead, and her guards were dashing in and out of all the rooms on the ground floor of her house, but they're so used to seeing me run errands and make deliveries to her that they never gave me a second glance. After I got out into the street and left the village I didn't see another soul."

"Hmmm. Maybe we're all right." I narrowed my eyes at her. "Now that you've caused us all this alarm, maybe you'll explain what you're doing here."

Her face rippled, a tidal pool filled with multilegged emotions not quite ready to come to the surface. She made a moue, fluting her lips into a rounded groove. "I was... curious."

"About what?"

"About where you were going."

"Your father knew we were coming here. It was his advice that made me decide to come here. And I'm sure he must have told you what our destination was."

"Well. I was curious about why those men were following you. And how you thought you were going to get away from them."

I looked at the door, still guarded by Styx. His dilated pupils were black holes ringed with green, like the holes left by crossbow bolts fired into a snowbank. Crossbows.

"We could have better weapons, but all things considered this isn't a bad place to go to ground. Temporarily, of course. Once your father gets here with more provisions we'll move on."

"We haven't settled the question of what this child is doing here," Terhune rumbled. "I'll wager her interest lies here on the floor."

Her eyes dropped, involuntarily it seemed, to where Talin had drawn himself up on one elbow. Curiosity and embarrassment were mingled with the tears of laughter on his face, and as usual he appeared uncomfortable being the topic of conversation.

Diarfa was evasive. "I'm sure I don't know what you mean."

"Don't come the raw prawn with me, I'm not that easily deceived. What I mean, Catalan, and I imagine it's occurred to you too, is that this boy has the looks of a young god, and our unexpected guest here must have noticed that the minute she saw him back at the Head."

Talin laughed uneasily; it came out as more of a soft bark. "The unexpected guest–that saying always frightened me as a child." He pulled himself together and unfolded into an upright position again, conspicuously avoiding meeting anyone's eyes.

"I think his looks whammed her in the face like a rolling catapult. She decided she fancied him, and she followed us so she could get another glimpse of him."

Diarfa was breathing convulsively in short, shallow gasps. "Why is it so hot in here?" She whirled away and ripped off her cape, crumpled it into a ball, and threw it into a corner. She was composed when she turned back to us.

"You're insane. I don't fancy him, I can give you my pledge on that."

Terhune cracked his swollen knuckles. "Yah. A truthful woman is a freak of nature, like a cat with horns. You fancy him, all right. And you're mad at yourself because of it."

Our young dervish had lowered his head and was deeply absorbed in restoring his cloak to its former position, where it concealed the clean bold lines of his muscular body. Diarfa's mouth was opening for another retort when we heard it.

Immediately above us the low ceiling of the room began to vibrate with a horrid scrabbling sound, as if some creature was crawling across the roof with unretracted claws. I had noticed as we crossed the clearing to the cabin that the flat roof lay close to the high windows on the walls, with no apparent room for attic or crawlspace, and I could easily imagine such a noise now being created by a squirrel, opossum, or unusually clumsy lynx up there on the slates.

Except that the area of space being taken up by the scrabbling claws indicated a beast at least twelve feet long.

Something very large was on the roof.

CHAPTER 8
THE THING ON THE ROOF

"Outside!"

We practically bolted for the door, where the sentry cat had gone rigid at the urgency in my voice.

"Styx, move!" I roared, and he dissolved out of the way, letting the four of us flood through to the clearing.

Despite my fears, the moon had not yet set. Although lower in the sky, it still bathed this part of the mountainside in enough light to let us see clearly, but we could no longer distinguish colors with full accuracy. Diarfa's burgundy doublet looked dark brown; so did Talin's shaggy red wig. Our shadows on the snow were less intense, more blurry around the edges.

Once clear of the porch, I turned and scanned the roof of the cabin. The thing had crawled as far forward as the edge of the porch roof, directly above the steps, and was rearing its long snaky body upright, its many short legs waving in the air.

I knew it at once for what it was, feeling an instinctive surge of fear and disgust and tasting bile in the back of my throat.

Terhune recognized it too and belched an expletive: "Damn and blast! A dragon!"

It was indeed a young dragon, and we were both surprised for the same reason I had been surprised back at the Floating Head, when Talin had implied that he knew what one looked like. They are rare creatures, not found in this part of the world.

Diarfa was as still as a statue at our side. "Wh-what? I thought dragons were only in myths."

"Don't underestimate the old stories," I told her. "They stem from ancient truths. They are our oldest legacy, they will be our last bequest, flitting from mouth to mouth when the world's libraries are in ruins and the alphabet has to be reinvented."

Terhune spat. "If you're through lecturing, we might want to move to the edge of the clearing. It's coming down."

As we stepped briskly across the snow, with frequent glances over our shoulders, the dragonling started a moist slithering movement down one of the columns supporting the porch roof, and by the time we had reached the far end of the clearing it was on the ground.

It crouched there, occasionally rocking from side to side on its claws. Its hideous red-brown hide looked almost black in the moonlight, wetly gleaming like raw liver freshly ripped from a corpse, reminding me of one of those parasitic wormlike flukes that grow in the stomachs of certain fish.

Diarfa visibly shuddered. "How dangerous is it?"

"Well, when they're this small they usually can't breathe fire yet, but their bite and their breath are already poisonous. It—Watch out!"

Now the dragon was raising its flat triangular head up on its elongated neck. Its crest of horns stood out darkly against the bone-white wall of the cabin, and out of its widely distended jaws sprang a gray tongue as long as my arm. We heard an incredibly loud hissing noise, as if a full cauldron had been upset into a fire.

"We're in luck." Terhune was cheerful, for Terhune. "From the smell, I'd say this beastie has just finished shedding its skin. They always move more slowly then."

Even as he spoke I detected what his more sensitive nose had caught, the rotten-egg stink of sulfur tinged with a more corporeal stench of organic decay.

"I don't care if it's half-paralyzed. If we bolt, we're going to provoke it. You know they tend to go after moving targets." Styx, leaning into my leg, growled softly, and I slapped the top of his head to shut him up.

A faint moan on my other side made me look at Talin, who had gone as rigid as the raised figure on a sarcophagus. His one visible eye had grown huge in anticipation and showed liquid in the moonlight.

"Don't worry," I told him. "We'll spread out to confuse it. As long as we're not clustered in one spot it won't know where to strike."

Terhune spoke. "If we're going to spread out, we should do it now. That little lizard is not going to wait for us to line ourselves up like a walkway cut out of yew hedges. I can see it drooling from here."

We promptly broke up and scattered along the edge of the clearing. Terhune and I marked the outer ends of the crescent, while Talin and Diarfa stood rooted along the inside curve. Then the beast began to move.

As the dragon came clicking across the ground where the snow had been trampled down, it rattled damply like an old skeleton being dragged out of a pond.

With trepidation I saw that it was headed unerringly toward our dervish. Never wavering, never hesitating, it flowed on a collision course with him, and its fanged jaws clashing together over and over as it came.

"Terhune," I shouted, "we've got to do something!"

"There's nothing we can do with the weapons we've got. It's suicide, going up against a creature like that with just a sword. We'll have to leave it to the lad to take his own evasive action."

"But he can't. Look at him, he's frozen with fear. Like a sparrow mesmerized by a snake."

"It's too late. As close as it is now, if we move it'll attack us. We may have to sacrifice the boy."

The dragon stopped within striking distance of Talin and reared up the front half of its body again so that its hideous head was on a level with his face. The corpse-gray tongue stabbed the air, while its many short legs clawed space in anticipation of seizing its intended prey.

Talin gave a piteous mewing cry. From my distant position I could actually see him shaking, his free hand clenching and unclenching convulsively at his side. The creature lunged forward, and an inarticulate shout broke from my lips.

Then there came the sound of a wet explosion, like that of a full wineskin being crushed beneath a wagon wheel, and the dragon blew apart.

Before the flying fragments had a chance to splatter onto the ground, however, they had turned into big blossoms. Feathery three-lobed spiderflowers, those mutant irises that always made me think of brightly clad peasant girls dancing in the air. Even in the uncertain light I imagined I could see their distinctive yellow and maroon pattern as they cascaded down around the still and now silent figure of Talin.

I was the first to move to the boy, while keeping one eye on the lurid spiderflowers that had been bloody gobbets of dragonflesh just moments ago. One of them crawled toward me in a sudden mountain breeze, and its shape and color scheme made it look like some tropical thing that wanted to bite me. I stepped around it.

Talin's face was a pale oval punctuated by a blank stone eye. With a convulsive shudder he turned away from me. When I put my arms around him from behind I could feel him trembling like a spooked colt. His ablutions at the inn had included removing the stubble from his face, although he had not reshaved his head; the sensation of his smooth cheek against my face was strangely erotic.

Our companions came up around us. Terhune was

chomping on his tobacco with placid self-containment, but Diarfa's eyes were enormous.

"What—Was it an illusion?"

"Illusions don't smell that bad."

I made an attempt to speak rationally, while Talin quivered in my embrace. "This makes up for the bandit attack outside of Andor, which ended in a mass transformation that left no clues, no prisoners. It looks as if there is magic on both sides, which supports his story of the Lady Marabar as a player in his game. She is a known enchantress, and has been connected openly for many years with a sorcerer named Tharados."

Terhune spat into the ever-darkening air. "So the melting wax trick we saw in the foothills was the work of the lad's enemies? And this dragon-to-flowers thing came from his supernatural Lady sponsor?"

"I don't know yet. But based on what we just saw, someone with access to magic is definitely protecting the boy."

"Or trying to scare him."

Talin was still shaking in my arms; I could actually hear his teeth clicking together. When I turned his head back toward me, I saw that his eye was glazed ice, and he seemed unable to meet my gaze.

"He's in shock," Diarfa blurted. Then she seemed to pull herself together, throwing her shoulders back and tossing her head like some proud doe.

"Let's get him back inside. If we don't snap him out of this now, we may never get him back at all."

Terhune and I started to manhandle him toward the cabin, while Diarfa strode along and sharpened her tongue on us.

"I must say you've done a grand job of taking care of him so far. What are you going to do to pull him out of this trance?"

"I've got some shotweed with me."

The moon was almost gone behind Hunchback now,

and my eyes were slow in adjusting to the starlight, so the face she jerked toward me was no more than a dark mask. When she finally spoke again, her teeth gleamed faintly.

"I thought shotweed was outlawed."

Terhune grunted as we hauled the boy's senseless body up the porch steps. "Many things are outlawed, but that doesn't stop them from being useful in a pinch. Now be a good bird and hold that door open for us."

We staggered and jerked our way into the still-firebright room. Over in one corner, I spied a decaying armchair that made me think of fat old men swilling brandywine before a fire. I relinquished Talin and dragged the chair in front of our fire; then I looked for my leather pouch while the others got the dervish settled. By the time I returned to the hearth scene, they had him slumped in the partially upright position of an invalid, his bizarrely wigged head drooping on his long neck like a sunflower with a broken stalk.

I rooted around in my pouch and found the hubble-bubble. "Terhune, I'm going to need a more reliable source of light than this fire. It keeps flickering like mad, and there's always the possibility of its burning down to nothing. I have to watch his eye very closely after I use the shotweed."

"Aye. There used to be something here." He disappeared into the shadows and came back carrying an oil lamp with a shade of stained glass. Set up and ignited on the large oval table, it threw red and yellow splashes of light over us.

Diarfa goggled at the apparatus I had removed from my pouch. "What exactly is that?"

"The hubble-bubble is a simple water pipe, what used to be called a hookah. Inside is a reservoir containing a cooling liquid of some kind. For shotweed I tend to use natural mineral water so there's nothing to interact or interfere with the drug itself. The idea is that the smoke passes through the fluid and is cooled before it enters the user's lungs. The process also makes a bubbling noise, hence the name."

Terhune fiddled with the lamp. "Only a blasted poet would use a word like 'hence.' What's stopping you from filling the pipe?"

I started unwrapping my packet of shotweed. It spilled onto the table, a dark green, venomous green mass of stems, seeds, and leaves. As my hands automatically plucked out usable fragments of the herb, I kept a running commentary going for Diarfa.

"The name shotweed comes from chatouie, an ancient word meaning tickled, because the drug applies tiny teasing touches to the subconscious and provokes a rush of memory like a burst of laughter."

A study in indecision, Diarfa glided back and forth between Talin and the lamp. "Yes, I know about liquid speech. It's the stuff of many horror stories in Father's front room at the inn. If he's this disturbed and we induce a state of liquid speech, isn't there a real danger of brain damage?"

"Just the opposite. When he goes into liquid speech, it will trigger the suppressed psychomas that are now blocking his relationship with the real world. The flood of his subconscious will knock down the mental block that stands between him and us."

Terhune mumbled, "The flood of your bullshit may reinforce the block between his situation and reality." I glared at him and he stifled himself.

"Shotweed is not as powerful as some of the liquid speech detonators on the black market, but it's definitely the safest."

"I hope you know what you're doing." Seeing that I had finished filling the bowl of the hubble-bubble, Terhune got a slow fuse going and handed it to me.

This was the tricky part. While applying the slow fuse to the loaded bowl, I snaked the amber mouthpiece between Talin's lips, making sure there were no kinks in the connecting tube, and pinched his nose so that he was forced to inhale through his mouth. The fuse flame dipped and the bowl glowed brighter. I visualized the harsh smoke filling his lungs, filtering into every crevice the way the relentless light from the still raging fire was reaching into the corners of the room. Then his breath came blasting out in a vast exhalation, stinging my nostrils with the smoky smell of burning leaves, and the mouthpiece fell into his lap.

I kept repeating the process, while the pipe gurgled and chortled. Time and smoke crawled along together. Styx coughed.

At the end of the bowl, Talin was still in his own lost world, eyelid drooping, mouth hanging slack. I let his head sag against the back of the armchair.

"Now what?" Diarfa was restless.

"We wait for the drug to take effect." I wanted to keep a close watch on the dervish, so I pulled up another of the massive armchairs. Fishing out a pouch of cavendish, I packed and lit my old briar.

White pipe smoke sprayed out before me, turning dark as it twisted and swirled against the bright background of the fire. Like a dollop of fresh cream dumped into a mug of black coffee, only with the colors reversed.

My companions grew still. I almost felt like a midwife attending a pregnant woman in the last hours of her confinement. Thus in the quiet hours of the night, one house shuts in as many incoherent and incongruous fancies as a madman's head.

Then Talin's eye sprang wide open, a beacon of green and amber, and I saw the pupil enlarging as his head rolled toward the fire. He stared into the blaze and his body stiffened, his brain gripped by the chemical claw I had forced upon him.

Suddenly words gushed from his mouth in a spate. He was vomiting the words like the agonized laughter he had spewed forth when tickled.

"Burning and burning—"

PART II

LIQUID SPEECH

CHAPTER 9
HAPPY DAYLIGHT IS DEAD

Burning and burning in the whitening pyre, the wagon cannot help the wagoner, thongs fall apart, the sinner kens not cold

Fire has been my downfall, dragonfire that left me with one eye, manfire that launched me on this lurid and divinely damned quest

Hanging fire on the eve of an annual celebration, poised on the edge, balanced on the brink, touching my lip to the earthen bowl so that, lip to lip, it might murmur, "Seventeen years!"

Watching from the castle ramparts, perched on the keep's highest crenelated wall, atop an ancient tower like a carved chesspiece

A wagon, a chariot, an empty hazelnut made by the joiner squirrel or old grub, time out of mind the fairies' coachmakers, comes over the hill, carrying my foster parents

I see the King at the reins, vanity driving him as he drives the black stallions, digging his chin into his chest, jiggling and jutting his spadeshaped beard, not knowing he is about to embrace the ultimate spade, the Ace of Spades, traditional emblem of death

Late winter melting into spring, the late afternoon

melting into dusk to mirror the transition of seasons, the air smiling but showing its teeth to prove it still can bite

My Queen, the only mother I have known, jounces at her sire's side, draws about her aging throat her ever present flowered shawl, lifts her crooked nose as if to sniff the feastscented smoke of the kitchen fires working to make a royal welcome home

The wagon sweeping down the hill, the horses' hooves ringing on the pavingstones of the road, I move to turn toward the stairs, my palms scraping across the rough stone of the parapet, my loose sleeves swishing through the crisp light

A sharp dry crack, the sound of a dead tree snapping under nature's fury, too loud to have come from the distant forest beyond the hill

Spinning back, my soft velvets fly out around me, my eyes look not down but up

Heaven's cloudless dome splits open under an invisible sword, the jagged gash shows unearthly scarlet against the bluegray of the quickly darkening sky

From the gash springs tigerlike a tawny bolt of bloodbrown flame, glittering obscenely as it strikes, inconceivable celestial fire

In near silence, the wagon with my parents explodes, a rotten seed pod in a hot hot fire, the flames keening against the everdarkening grayblack

Bonfire of rust, pelt of dead fox, the flash of a clotting wound, the hillside crawling

Redbrown redbrown dirty blood blood in the mud
Father
Mother
Happy daylight is dead

Now comes the flock of hysterical servants, gabbling at me like disturbed wildfowl, their slack jaws flapping, their sleevewings quivering, their eyes scabbing over with the horror of Death, the maggot in the cheese

Your parents gabble gabble absolutely no warning gabble gabble almost inside the walls gabble gabble freak storm gabble lightning gabble hopeless gabble burnt gabble

A last glimpse of the sacrificial cake of clotted gore, the malevolent bonfire on the hill, a bonefire, a fire for burning corpses, as they sweep me off the parapet and drown out my murmur

That was not lightning, that was manmagic, I could tell by the color, why aren't you listening to me

They swirl me down an inner staircase, away from this sigil, this hideous sign of occult power, this monstrous act by which my foster parents have become dirty pillows in Death's bed

The dark stairwell sucks us down as dark thoughts suck me down

Were my parents too ambitious in exploring the limits of their kingdom? Am I too ambitious in exploring the limits of my knowledge? How can I keep from burning when I run after the blazing sun?

Gabble gabble how ever will he gabble gabble inconsolable gabble gabble oh here's his tutor gabble he'll know how to gabble these scholars think alike gabble

My tutor is my reservoir of learning, with his mouth full of wisdom, which he is used to force upon me as an owl feeds her young

"How now, Master Talin, an unfortunate circumstance, but what does the literature of the ages tell us about unfortunate circumstances?"

He does not gabble so much as hoot, his hoots have filled my days with a cacophony of ancient quotations on every subject except music, his personal black beast, he claims that music is the brandy of the damned

Into my nerveless hand he thrusts a whitish bitter mint, horehound, he stretches and twists his heavily corded birdthroat, he gives vent to his words of literary solace

"To clothe the fiery thoughts in simple words succeeds, for still the craft of genius is to mask a king in weeds"

I see his round feathery face shake and vibrate in the magic circle of his torch, and I see strange reptiles and birds coupling and twisting on the mossencrusted stone wall behind his head

Yes, I can play his game

"Death is but a blind, false door to me, and gives no hope of exit final, free"

The fat fool in front of me grunts and slides aside, my quotation has turned the lock that puts him to rest

The throne room, a constellation of underground lights, white lights, amber lights, wall hangings where ship-wrecked sailors drink requital on a reef and scream for succor, where a funeral flame follows and death sunders soul from flesh, where their shades haunt you till their price is paid

The throne enfolds my foster parents' daughter, my shadow sister, narrow head and long neck of a peahen, beak of a nose and peasized brain to match

My birthday a year ago, caught in the winter garden, come into the park that is said to be dead, brittle pine cones, skeletons of shrubs, pressed up against a mannequin of a body, a green stickerbush in the shape of a woman, thank you but no thank you

I see it in her eyes, her painted eyes like hanging lanterns beneath ornamental arches, rejection has made me a passing fancy, a toy in blood

I cannot move, her imminent pronouncement like the green and climbing eyesight of a cat crawls near my mind's poor bird

Torches and more torches, who would have thought the old castle would have had so many people in it

From the far end of the chamber, an arrow's flight away, my irrepressible tutor flutters under a mural of a griffin strangled by a centaur

"Do not hasten to judge Master Talin, he is suffering from anhedonia, an insensitivity to pleasure or pain, an affective disorder, I have prescribed"

No matter what he prescribes, I want sleep, sore labor's bath, balm of hurt minds, great nature's second course, chief nourisher in life's feast

My shadow sister opens her lips, firm and irrevocable is her doom

"Dispatch you with your safest haste, within these ten days if you are found so near our public court as twenty miles, you die for it"

Formication, the itching sensation like that of ants running on the skin

Everything changes, and one by one we drop away

CHAPTER 10
THE UPPER ROOM

They throw me off the caravan when we reach the north shore of the Scorpion Sea, where fat complacent darkskinned men sip red wine on stone terraces overlooking the constantly wrinkling blue waters, shop windows display stuffed dogs and live parrots, bars with slowly turning ceiling fans shelter drinkers with metal hooks for hands

Rumor, a horror, misshapen, huge, with her cloak of tongues and ears erect, beneath each feather on her head a sleepless eye, by day sitting at watch high on a lofty tower to terrify great cities, by night flying gibbering over the shadowed world

Rumor states that the enchantress Marabar is in the city seeking champions for some great quest, some snuffling pursuit through the twisting labyrinth of time and space, some golden fleece of a chance to prove the didos, capers, and antics of a young buck can pull the family jewels out of the fire

The Lady Marabar floats on a balcony above the city square, a sick rose partly destroyed by the crimson joy of which she dare not speak

I must help her, no matter what her trouble I know I have to help her

I wonder if she needs a scribe, with my training I can create new apes clambering up the margins of illuminated manuscripts, unicorns stamping and whinnying at the heads of chapters sheltering convocations of eagles, wedges of swans, an ostentation of peacocks, capital letters soaring like brilliant minarets above the cityscape of the text

Her upper room is rich with green days in forests and blue days at sea, the drunkenness of things being various, white flows the river and bright blows the broom, lurid spiderflowers crawling up the late March windowpanes, the people in the street say they are her favorite flowers, and of course her gramarye, her occult lore, gives her whatever she wants, her seasons are not our seasons

They also say she will not use magic to mend what has gone awry or departed from her striking looks, still she stuns, a rose starting to dry up but not spawning for the last time, strong angular face the color of sunset, stalky green-gowned body, elongated neck like a dragon's tail, long severed yet still hard with agony

Metalgray strands of hair tortured back from the eyes, eyes protected by opalescent lenses, wide mouth pulsing like a jellyfish

"I need a man" she says

Her words are potent, all morning the sunshine has been clogged with mist, now the Sun takes his yellow whip and drives the fog away

The chamber fills with light and my brain fills with light, illumination as nacreous, as pearly as her lenses

Her voice is sherry, smooth and sweet

"You know what it is like to be canvassed, to be tossed in a canvas sheet? Sometimes for sport, say at a wedding? Sometimes in punishment?"

I can only nod dumbly

"Well, I have been canvassed, beaten, trounced, castigated, and *shamed*" (her voice deepens a thrilling octave) "by my Lord Tharados, he who was once my boonfellow and poplolly, my good friend and special beloved"

Her barely controlled venom gives me gooseflesh, my armhairs stand erect like the porcupine against its foes

"My Lord and his aimcriers, his supporters and cronies, have been as prime as goats, as hot as monkeys, as salt as wolves in pride"

She fingers an onyx decanter of burgundy, while her lips knit themselves into obscure designs

"Their sexual escapades have made our palace a dungeon full of spiders, blindworms, and frogs, a cistern for foul toads to knot and gender in"

Shaking hands lift the decanter, spilling wine to dry foxfur red and make rust stains on the tablecloth

Redbrown redbrown dirty blood blood in the mud

"What do you want me to do?" I blurt

She stands frozen, a fountain statue, the wine goblet raised halfway to her fluted lips, her green gown cascading down the slopes of her angular body

"My Lord was always hovering over my wing of the palace, the way a raven hangs over an infected house, until we finally came to an agreement

"Young lovers tumble and frolic like buttoneyed puppies spilled from a basket, but he and I were more in the manner of scavengers and carrion

"He, like the magpie that steals and hoards bright shiny treasures, like the hideous shrike that murders small animals and impales their corpses on twigs, has secreted away from me a most magical talisman of power

"A wargame that mirrors the way he sees everyone in his path

"We are but pieces in the game he plays, upon a chessboard of nights and days, hither and thither moves and checks and slays, and one by one back in the box he lays"

Quoting, quoting from the old poems, but changing the words to fit her situation, what's she doing

"Warrior pieces, castle pieces"

I can see them, crenelated pieces like the battlements where I stood when I saw the death of daylight, in the game they are called rooks

Rook, another kind of blackbird, another feathered scavenger like her Lord, she speaks

"Crowned pieces, the all-important kings"

I can see them too, faces like masks carved from copper beeches, stern brown masks, a hue strange but familiar, almost

Redbrown blood in the

"One army in onyx, the other ivory"

Now the masks in my mind are changing color, one king burning black, his darkening followers around him like a field of pansies freaked with jet

The other king paling as the color bleeds out of him, bleaching, blanching like a skull in a bonefire, burning and burning in the whitening pyre

Everything changes and one by one we

"Listen to me!" Passion makes my Lady's voice thick and intoxicating, a holiday sauce laced with brandywine, her voice is the color of dried blood

"My Lord robbed me of this mystical wargame just as I was learning how to use it to spread good throughout our kingdom—

"You are familiar with the legend of the Grateful Dead? Of the traveler who finds an unburied dead body, disposes of it in hallowed ground, and is rewarded by the spirit of the dead man coming to his aid?"

I nod in wonder

"I helped such a one, and in return he led me to the place of concealment of this enchanted wargame, but my Lord stole it and left me crushed and weeping while he broke it into its three components and hid them again

"Ivory pieces in one hiding place, onyx pieces in another, the board of inlaid squares, mvuli wood and stained sandalwood, in a third cache

"And now he taunts and tantalizes me, like a drunken nobleman waving scraps of meat before an abused kitchen wench

"Find them if you can, he sneers, and they are yours, I will even give you clues

"And so we enter the covenant, he allows me to select one agent for each component of the game, searchers to follow the clues, find the components, and bring them back to me, champions like you"

She claps me on the shoulder and I almost stagger from the blow, who would have thought the old lady had so much strength in her

"My magpie Lord, having secreted his three stolen treasures in their farflung nests, will click his black bill and dispense clues, one bead at a time

"I am graciously allowed two things, I can transmit the clues to my agents, my champions, in any fashion I see fit, and I can give each agent one helper, an assistant, an artful dodger

"The clues will come in sets of three, each clue leading the agent one step closer to the end of his journey, their correct interpretation gives direction and dispatch

"Yes, there is a time limit, I must have all three components of the wargame by the winter solstice, some nine months hence

"Bear in mind—" my Lady seizes my forearm, her voice turns even darker, "the behavior and performance of my agents will be judged as much as their success in finding the components, and my Lord is allowed to send out his own agents to stop you

"I choose you as my champion for the ivory pieces, bring them to my palace on the island of Phuxor by the winter solstice and I will love you as I love the sun

"I will find you lodgings here in this house, go, your assistant and the first clue will reach you by dawn

"Sweet dreams"

The spiderflowers writhe at the windows

CHAPTER 11
A SPECIES OF MAD HILARITY

A jonquil dawn floods my brain, putting light in my head when there is not yet light outside the casement, o my God, what night vision is this

A vast lake or inner sea, the water light green and lightly turbulent, containing multitudes and multiple possibilities, stretching to a far horizon where green and jonquil mingle and slosh like the lake of light behind my lids

A man lies naked on the head of a broken statue, a shattered and ruined idol rearing its great imperturbable face barely out of the water, turning to the sky a blank stone eye as big as the man's head, its nose a mudgreen slab, the man's feet kick against it as he gives his silent screams and tries not to slide down the slope of the tilted face

His long lean body and narrow face are eclipsed by a moving shadow

Swooping down is a giant brown owl, bigger than he is, each tapering yellowtipped wing looking strong enough to crack his skull, its yellow tail long and deeply forked by the V-shaped cleft in its center

Its eyes are dark jewels, pieces of the night caught in feathered folds of yellow, its eartufts are long devilhorns, its horny beak is clacking, asking to be fed, asking for the man's eyeballs and tongue, its claws like hideous hands are reaching for his screaming face

My screams are not silent, they drag me upright with the bedclothes flapping around me, I am naked like the man in the vision, I can see myself because it is suddenly dawn, I can see

Someone is in the room with me

He is between me and the casement, his voice rings like a silver bell

"The devil damn thee black, thou creamfaced loon, where got thou that goose look?"

He speaks gently, formal but playful, like my tutor trying to make a jest

He moves and I see him better, he is small and slender with shoulderlength dark brown hair framing a monkeyface, his simian eyes twinkling and winking down his long pointed nose, in his eyes is a species of mad hilarity

"I speak of the devil purely as a literary character out of the old mythologies, of course, since no one of any intelligence believes in gods or devils, I do hope you're not a True Believer, on the whole I think organized religion does more harm than good, but you were just dreaming of something with devilhorns, weren't you?"

I am so surprised that the spate of noise rushing from my mouth dries up, I clutch the bedclothes more tightly around me, he chuckles silver filigree

"Your eyes are as big as dinner plates, from which I gather that I am correct, but there is no mystery here, just a gift I received at birth, sometimes to catch fragments of what lies in others' minds, unfortunately only fragments and not in a fashion to be predicted or controlled"

I finally croak out a word, "Who"

"There should be no surprises here, the Lady Marabar, that yet unravish'd bride of time," he does something with his smiling mouth that makes me hear the apostrophe in unravish'd, "promised to send you a clue and a helper, she has sent you the clue enfolded in a dream, like a coin baked into a holiday cake, and here am I, the helper"

He executes a deep theatrical bow, like a traveling player accepting the applause of the crowd, I notice that he is wearing motley, the multicolored dress of a king's fool

"Prance is my name but no more questions of a personal nature can I answer, for the bird of time has but a little way to fly, and lo, the bird is on the wing"

Quoting, quoting from the same old poem as my Lady, he must be telling the truth, he knows too much to be lying, where are my clothes

"I have horses ready for the first leg of our journey, on the way downstairs you can tell me about the dream, which will indicate what direction we are to take"

"I don't see how, it was merely this dreadful owl"

"Ah, yes, owly, prowly, howly, owly, browny fowly, little owl, as the poet says, except, judging by the brief glimpse I got of your thoughts, your owl was not that little, rather large, I should say"

Now I am standing, my stars, his bare head barely comes to my shoulder

Bare head, he has no fool's cap, no little belled tentacles springing out of his skull, his hat has been spirited away, perhaps by a mischievous cat, somewhere there is a cat in a hat, now he has me talking in rhymes, time to go

There is no one on the stair, so I tell him of my dream, he is whistling a swirling tune he says is "The Drunken Piper"

Bells jingle as I talk, but he has no belled cap, I see he has tiny bells sewn into his doublet, they punctuate my tale of the swooping owl and the man on the shattered statue

"Ah," he says, cutting off his piping whistle, I see that he knows this place and this owl, at least the scene described does not puzzle him

"So the mute forest has uttered its first bird of the season"

"I don't understand"

"You saw a sea, the sea you saw was the great inland sea of Hroom, known for its giant mutant owls, a few years ago they emerged from the wooded hills to prey on the good folk who populate the sea's edge, tearing open the throats of cattle, carrying off sheep and the occasional child, even killing the odd adult foolish enough to get caught out of doors between dusk and dawn"

Today's dawn fills the courtyard with light that is bright but not the jonquil of the dream, and there are the horses

"What do you mean, the first bird of the season"

"These prowly owly creatures don't come out of the forest until spring, although the local experts on ornithoid behavior can't tell you why, some say they migrate south for the winter and return to Hroom with warm weather, others say they hide themselves in hollow trees and go into a comatose state, sleeping through the snow season without the flicker of a feather"

The house is behind us, we are riding toward the outskirts of the city, the streets are starting to fill with all sorts of people, courtesans and coarse women, perfumed in musk and cigars, returning home from assignations that have lasted all night, fishermen and porters late for work, the everpresent derelicts and beggars

"Bird migration is a fascinating field," Prance never stops talking, "many people once thought that cuckoos turned into hawks in the winter, because the cuckoos left just as the hawks came"

A stream of city dwellers is swirling around our horses now, moneylenders, storytellers, craftsmen, galley slaves in chains

"And of course less than a hundred years ago the high priest of Hroom wrote in a learned treatise that the swallows all flew to the moon for winter, but what can you expect from people who practice theriomancy"

I give him a puzzled look while steering my mount around a nobleman arguing with a ratcatcher

"Fortunetelling by animals, sometimes they cut them up and study their entrails, other times they just let them go and watch their behavior, like the auspex, one who watches for omens in the flight of birds, my personal favorite being cephalomancy, fortunetelling by boiling the head of an ass, though that gets to be a bit of a drain on your livestock"

We pass doors bearing signs for bookbinders, bounty hunters, stonemasons, translators, and interpreters

"Still, dealing with the animals, even if they're dead, must be more exciting than tyromancy, which is fortune-telling by watching cheese coagulate, it all comes back to the link between animals and the divine, that ancient notion that gods tend to have favorite animals and frequently trans-form themselves into beasties to rampage through the coun-tryside with greater impunity, which brings us back to your nocturnal friend on the rock

"The inhabitants of Hroom have decided that some god has become angry with them and is sending the owls to punish them, and conveniently enough the priests have recently come under the sway of this new religion you must have heard of, involving the True Word, its followers have been using traveling missionaries called dervishes to spread the Word of the one True God, and all the oracles seem to suggest that the owls are a chastisement for Hroom's slow-ness in adopting the new religion"

The crowds have fallen behind us and we pass the last buildings of the city and strike out into the open coun-tryside, I can feel the day growing warmer, the sun is higher in the sky now, the eye of the morning, the day's eye, a daisy in the sky

"Personally I take a dim view of all this infallible divination, most of which is done by priests who happen to be demented at the time by benefit of drugs, I never saw a priest who wasn't mad as a hatter

"Speaking of drugs, that small stone farmhouse up ahead, at the edge of the marshes, is a halfway house for addicts, very nice animal paintings on the parlor walls I'm told, and the tool shed out back should be our next stop because we need to find you an ax, how good a thief are you?"

CHAPTER 12
THE HAGGARD HAWK

And so, bearing a stolen ax like a scepter of power, sporting a royal robe artificially distressed with bramblebush and marshwater, I work my way north again in the guise of a woodcutter

"Of course you resemble a workingman about as much as a jeweled egg does a clod of earth, but at least your chest and shoulders are good, the sooner we start you swinging this ax the faster your muscles will build up"

"If you knew you wanted an ax for the woodcutter disguise, why not bring one with you, or buy one in the city?"

"We wanted our departure from the city to be as inconspicuous as possible, disguising something as long as an ax would be like disguising a crocodile as a cat"

"There were all sorts of people carrying all sorts of things"

"Yes, but anyone taking note of you and your not unpleasant demeanor would remember the ax and be able to give a description for those who might follow, tall young woodcutter accompanied by small man of radiant wit"

My pepperpot of a companion glibly talks us into one job after another

"Good day, Grandmother, and might you be needing a supply of kindling, yes we know it's spring, but the evenings are still cool, and then there's always cooking fires that must be fed, a venerable woman like you deserves a hot meal every day, all we ask in return is a fistful of coppers and a mouthful of food, a small price to pay for comfort in your twilight years, tell me now is it so or not?"

Skirting my former kingdom, we creep onward into uncharted territory, mile melting into mile, week into week, spring into a summer thick with vegetable love, and Prance knows the names of all the plants

Lungwort, the erect herb with its blue flowers and hairy leaves blotched with white, the crimson scattering of love-lies-bleeding and other amaranth, the reddishgreen stem and leaves and small yellow flowers of purslane, also called pussley, which Prance snatches up for a future salad

Common weeds such as scurvygrass and the lion's-tooth, called dandelion by regular folk, and common bluebells like the hyacinth, cowslip, and harebell

The yellow blink of a tormentil, a rosaceous herb with a powerful astringent root, used in medicine and in tanning, Prance says it is also called bloodroot or redroot, "its fancy name is the diminutive of an old word for torment, because it is used as a painkiller, you know"

More herbs rise to meet us, the silverweed with its edible roots, the many kinds of lowgrowing speedwell which embrace both the bird's-eye and the veronica, we also tread on bugleweed, stone mint, bearberry, elephant garlic, and rampion

Flowers cry out to us with their brilliant mouths, toad lily, horned poppy, Johnny jump-ups, Bouncing Bet, an Early Purple orchid blooming when and where it should not be, a striped trout lily, prompting a couplet from my companion

"Then lilies, turned to tigers, blaze amidst the garden's tangled maze"

He continues to spout poetry and odd bits of knowledge during our rest stops, forcing words upon me as he forces water and apples upon the horses

"Stumbling on melons, as we pass, ensnared with flowers, we fall on grass, how could such sweet and wholesome hours be reckoned but with herbs and flowers"

I lie back with a saddlebag beneath my sweaty neck and eye our steeds, whose flanks gleam moistly in the humid air

"In the lands far to the east," Prance volunteers, "they believe that horses are a form of magical travel, that they can travel at night because they have eyes on their knees"

Our horses have bony angular legs, knobbed like old walking sticks and tipped with sharp hooves hard and deadly as any iron ferrule, but not a single eyeball to be seen

"So many strange things are to be found in the animal kingdom that nothing would surprise me," my companion babbles on, "like the fact that birds can't smell at all, your average owl can kill and eat a skunk or a stink badger and not mind the stench because it doesn't smell it"

The tiny bells sewn onto his tunic tinkle as he leans forward to fish a couple of apples from his pack, in his sun-browned face his teeth are very white and very small like those of a child, he bites

"Seek-No-Further, an apple not readily available in these regions and certainly not at this time of year, or perhaps you would prefer a Northern Spy," with a flourish he hands me a large yellowred fruit the size of my fist

"Speaking of our friends in the animal kingdom, many creatures we are wont to hunt for food or sport produce their own special excrement, which can be so distinctive that it can be used to track them selectively, I hope you don't mind my discussing this while we eat?"

Poised to sink my teeth into the Spy, I have paused to polish it on one of the patches of my robe not ruined by marshwater, "No, please, go on"

"Hunters in olden times even had names for the

excrement of different animals, the crotels of a hare, the friants of a boar, the spraints of an otter"

Having wolfed down his Seek-No-Further, he settles crosslegged beside me and begins to fill an ancient meerschaum pipe carved into the fullmaned head of a lion, its bowl the yellowishwhite of old ivory, it protrudes from his mouth like a swollen fang, I see the thick blunt nose and sneering mouth of the lion

"The werderobe of a badger, the waggying of a fox, the fumets of a deer, and a multitude of others I would not dream of boring you with"

Why stop now, I wonder, if I were not here you would be talking to the horses

"What can we expect to find when we get to Hroom?" I ask

"With the coming of the True Word, the priests have seized local control, so we shall have to tread lightly, as is common with those passionately devoted to a particular religion they do not smile upon anyone who disagrees with them, in fact the next logical step for them, after recognizing the giant owls as divine chastisement for spiritual lethargy, has been making human sacrifices to the owls, the victims being those who are slow in embracing the True Word, as you saw in your dream"

"That's horrible, but we must follow where the dream points, what's our next step?"

"Ahead lies Giddings Ha-ha, just beyond that is an inn called the Haggard Hawk where we have business"

"Ha-ha?"

"A ha-ha is a sunken fence or ditch with a retaining wall, used to divide lands without defacing a landscape, once we get past Giddings Ha-ha we shall be in the land of Hroom and subject to their laws"

"What business do we have at the inn?"

"I have a thought to purchase a sentry cat, I have studied many philosophers and many cats, the wisdom of cats is infinitely superior"

"Why not steal a cat, the way you had me steal the ax?"

"With a sentry cat, the transfer of ownership must be done with the good will of the trainer, to instill confidence in the new master, you can't just throw a blanket around his muzzle and bundle him off like firewood"

The mention of fire seems to remind him that his lionpipe is not yet lit, he eyes me quizzically and produces from his pack an ornate tinderbox, on its lacquered lid floppyeared young pigs cavort amidst piles of green apples

Green apples, I feel the tingle of a buried memory, his monkeybrown eyes burn into mine and the hot summer air sears my lungs, spreads through my chest like mulled wine gulped too fast, my vision clouds, gnats seem to sing in my ears

Prance's hand is on my wrist, he takes the Northern Spy from me and boosts me to my feet, "If you will not eat now, we must be on our way," his head is wreathed with acrid smoke, he smells like a burning zoo

When did he have time to light his pipe?

Even in the failing light of early evening, Giddings Ha-ha is in an obvious state of disrepair, the road we have been following comes to an abrupt end at a crumbling stone wall being devoured by tanglewood, hart's-tongue fern, and foxglove, while pepperbush and stumpwood have grown tall above the wall to mask the wide depression beyond

Rainstorms have also taken their toll on the ha-ha, carving it deeper into the moldy earth and destroying its original shape, I know this because Prance tells me so, he also points out how the steep sides have changed it from a ditch to a veritable gorge now choked with dog's mercury and the tangle of traveler's joy, any man descending into it would find himself hipdeep in ground cover

"We leave the horses here," he says, talking around the pipestem still clenched between his teeth even though his pipe has gone out half an hour ago, "We'll send someone

from the inn to bring them the long way around, we have
no leisure for such tactics, as I said before the bird of time
has but a little way to flutter"

Balancing pack and saddlebags, he struts over to a tall
monkey puzzle tree that nuzzles the time-eaten wall, high
on its hard yellowish trunk a sturdy branch juts out over the
ha-ha and trails a rope swing into its shadowy depths

"Tie up the horses to whatever is handy, they won't
be left alone for long, then get ready to swing across the ha-
ha, you'll need one hand free for the rope"

I watch him adjust loops and straps on his baggage,
skip up the side of the wall, snatch at the rope, and disappear
over the mossy rim, an insignificant bug swallowed by a
hungry mouth

Moments later I follow him, catching the thick rope
as it swings back from the far side of the ditch, launching
myself out over the greensmelling darkness and trying not
to think about snakes

An easy landing sends me staggering up towards the
top of the slope, where a mad mixture of mustard, worm-
wood, nettles, and catnip comes foaming over the edge from
the meadow where Prance waits

Once past the meadow, Prance points ahead and
announces, "The Haggard Hawk"

Cloaked with the musky aroma of goats and other
livestock, the inn is a goblin's helmet with turrets for horns,
stained glass windows make splashes of blood on its gray-
brown cheeks, animal pens spread down away from it in a
wooden cuirasse, an all-encompassing collar of cages

Dusk closes in around us, cressets in the windows
spring to life as candles and torches are lit, and I wonder if
we have been spotted yet

"Why the Haggard Hawk?"

"It means a hawk caught while migrating as an adult,
as opposed to one captured as a fledgling and raised in captivity, such grown hawks are generally fiercer and more res-
istant to training, I believe the woman who runs this inn

fancies it as a symbol to refer to herself, but that's something you'll have to decide on your own"

A large dark bird floats through the large dark air, we pick our way around ominous headless statues and head for the front door, it yawns at us and leaks amber torchlight

In the woodpanelled entrance hall two robust and florid gentlemen, alike enough to be brothers, are arguing

"I don't care how badly you think we need a sentry cat, I'm not throwing good money after bad to buy an impure animal"

"She's the only breeder for miles"

"It's the wrong color and has no markings"

"The markings may be there but you just can't see them because it's—"

"Black! Black as your hat! Have you ever heard of a black sentry cat?"

The less angry of the two, who is wearing no hat, goes to answer and catches sight of us, he speaks with forced cheerfulness

"Praise the True Word!"

"Praise the True Word," Prance repeats promptly

"And the Snowman who brings it"

Prance's face settles into a polite mask, his eyes are cold glittering pebbles

The man repeats darkly, "And the Snowman who brings it," I can see clouds of suspicion and dislike forming in his redveined face

"And the Snowman who brings it," my companion finally parrots

Each gentleman now wraps his right hand around his own throat and gently squeezes, as if to strangle himself, after a moment they release their grips and stare expectantly at us, the angry one raps out a question

"You don't make the Sign of the Gallows, why not?"

Prance hastens to reassure, "You must forgive us, we are newly come to the True Word and have not mastered all of its joys, that will come in time, the Sign of the Gallows you say?"

"It is to commemorate the selfless sacrifice of our
Prophet, who died on the gallows to save us all from eternal
sin and torment," he seems ready to go on for quite some
time when a reedy voice from the stairs beyond him inter-
rupts

"On your way, gentlemen, either you buy my cat or
you don't"

A tiny old woman, her head covered with a dark
scarf, hobbles down into the torchlight, she is wearing
smoked spectacles, the portion of her face not covered is
smothered in liver spots, from her arm hangs a black
umbrella, closed but not furled, a dead bat in the dim light

Muttering, maybe imprecations, maybe a continu-
ation of their argument, the two men push past us and
vanish into the evening, the old woman turns to us

"I am Rana, I don't suppose you could use a good
sentry cat, she's rather unconventional in color but well
trained and reliable"

"Much have we heard of the excellent service and
quality of goods to be found at the Haggard Hawk, as a
matter of fact we have come here looking for a cat, could
you be so good as to show us what you have on hand?"

"Only the one at the moment, come this way," she
takes one of the torches from its wall bracket and stumps
toward the back of the hall, rocking slightly from side to side
on thicksoled shoes

Trailing at a respectful distance, we follow her down
a long corridor towards a back door, I say quietly to Prance,
"That Sign of the Gallows was rather bizarre, wasn't it?"

"For such folk, ritual is all, it gives them something
to do and keeps them from thinking"

"And what about the Snowman?"

"That name I have not heard and do not know, he
must be the head of this new church, the one behind all
these dervishes that have been flooding the countryside"

The walls of the corridor are covered with all kinds

of paintings of bears, in the light of the torch they seem to perform a strange kind of shuffling dance as Rana passes them, she comes to the back door and waits for us

"Ransom should be right out back, she's not tied up because she's been properly trained"

"Ransom?" I ask

"Because she's worth a king's ransom, I'd trust her with my life"

We emerge into a courtyard with wooden pens on both sides and the cat is there, sitting upright, head cocked alertly to note our coming, she is indeed black, jet black all over, the regulation size for a sentry cat, which means large, looking exactly like the pictures I've seen of wild black panthers

Her eyes are not the standard greengold of any such cat that I have come across, they gleam a deep pure emerald, an unalloyed green that blazes in the torchlight

"She's a sport," Rana tells us, "and by that I don't mean an object of derision, although she's certainly been that"

"I know what you mean," Prance leans forward for a better look at the cat, "an organism that shows an unusual deviation from the normal or parent type, some would say a mutation, I must say she is magnificent"

Staring into those hypnotic unblinking eyes, I let the world around me become fuzzy and distant, I vaguely hear the others dickering over a price, there comes the clink of coins, Prance's hand falls gently on my shoulder

"I've explained about the horses, this good woman will hold them here until our return, we go the rest of the way on foot to keep things simple, we must be on our way"

With an effort I tear my gaze away from that of Ransom, who has not moved, I think to protest, "We've spent so many nights sleeping outdoors, could we not take advantage of being here at the inn, think of a soft bed—"

"Alas, I've just handed over the last of our money, but if our friend can wait for later payment and will trade us a night's rest for a supply of firewood, she must have a great many fireplaces?" he eyes the old woman hopefully

She bobs her scarfed head, the smoked spectacles mirror the torchflame, "Of course, spend the night and tomorrow you can head out and bring me back the wood," she ushers us back inside, throwing a gently spoken command over her shoulder, "Ransom, stay"

A bed, why does that thought suddenly disturb me, make my flesh crawl when it should comfort me, yes, the monstrous act that launched me on this quest, my foster parents have become dirty pillows in Death's bed, reason enough to continue if I find myself needing a reason

As the door closes behind us, Ransom gives a soft cough, punctuation or agreement to my brooding thoughts

CHAPTER 13
THE UNDERGROUND WOMAN

Now we are on a hill near the Haggard Hawk, in the distance the city of Hroom spreads out along the horizon like an angry bruise, beyond it shows the shimmer of a large body of water

Down the hill from us, children of an absent shepherd are playing jackstone with five or six ankle bones from unfortunate dead sheep, tossing them up into the bright morning air

"Of course we must honor our promise to the good lady Rana, I suggest that I make an exploratory foray into the city with Ransom while you spend the day in that wood over there chopping wood for the inn, turn it over to Rana, and meet me at sunset on the steps of the city's main temple, anyone in the street can direct you to it"

I look at Ransom, who is lying on her belly with paws tucked under her and her tail coiled delicately, in the sunlight I notice that even her whiskers are black

"Yes, I suppose you have a greater chance of running into trouble in the city than I do in the wood, take her"

"You must take no offense, but I can move faster without you," he sets off down the hill in an odd skipping run, I cannot help but laugh, he looks more like a monkey than ever, his voice flutes back to us, "Come, Ransom," she rises regally to her feet

I find the wood much like those we have been traversing, many more plants still engaged in a quiet riot to take over the forest, I find delight in reviewing what Prance has taught me of their names

I dodge a clump of devil's club with its pricking thorns, pass flame-of-the-forest trees and the plant known as bloody-man's-finger, see beech trees which the older folk call wolf trees because they ravenously gobble all the nutrients out of the soil

Demented birdsong makes me look up, a family of martens explodes from their nest in a large dark clump of dwarf mistletoe in the top of a tree, I know from Prance that such a clump is called a witch's broom

Still looking up, I stumble and drop the ax, my right foot has caught on something very hard on the ground, I almost pitch over on my face

Nestled in the ground cover is a huge thick ring of heavy bronze, fashioned like a snake biting its own tail, exploration reveals that it is embedded in a partly buried square of weathered stone

They say that curiosity will always kill a cat, but our cat is safely on her way to Hroom, I grip the ring, brace my feet, exert my newly acquired brute force, my strength is as the strength of ten because my heart is pure

And because I have been chopping wood every day since the spring, my disguise has not been a waste of time, I feel the muscles of my shoulders and back flex and bunch up, with a scraping groan the slab starts to part company with the earth around it, my thighs become pillars of matching stone as I push my heels down into the ground and heave

Suddenly the slab shifts, it falls to the side with a dull whump, before me grins a gaping gravelike maw, the mouth of the Beast, from it rises sweet clean air but something makes me hesitate before leaning closer

A flight of ancient stone steps slithers down into the belly of the Beast, disappearing into the flickering half darkness just out of reach, out of sight, out of mind, out of the birddrunk air and into the silent planet

An oubliette, a secret dungeon with only one entrance, through the top, the name from an old word meaning "to forget" because a prisoner could be locked away in such a hole and safely forgotten

I reach for the tinderbox in my pack and stop myself, no need for a torch until I see how much light is down there, the flickering on the walls means manfire and not the organic luminescence called foxfire, the dull steady gleam of fungi in rotting wood would not move like real fire, someone is down there

Within seconds I am through the opening, moving slowly but steadily down the steep narrow stairs, the warmth and brightness of the summer morning receding above me as I round the first turn and edge into a cooler and darker world

Soon I come down into a grand room that slides carpets beneath my feet, a room that throws up wall tapestries to graze my outstretched fingertips, a room that dangles canopies to make a majestical roof fretted with golden fire, candles everywhere, ten thousand thousand white and burning candles, creating a lagoon of light

She stands like a painting, Girl in Orange Gown, the material thick and rich, the sleeves full and flowing, one hand resting lightly on a clothcovered table filled with glass flagons and dishes, a bowl piled high with green apples

Green apples

Her figure is thick and rich like the gown, an opulent figure, I can see it through the bright velvet, her hair is thick and rich and dark, her eyes are dark with the power to cloud men's minds, all that's best of dark and bright meet in her aspect and her eyes

She smiles at me, the smile is on her lips and in her eyes, they crinkle into bright slits of delight, she reaches for a snowgreen apple and holds it out to me

My buried memory stirs, demands to be heard, will not go back gently into the good night of my past, that time of cloudless climes and starry skies

The first poem I ever wrote
Setting
Sun turns the field
To gold, mellowing heaps
Of green apples and the flash of
Your smile

Not bad for a boy of twelve, the number of syllables in each line carefully controlled, two four six eight two, that's a cinquain

I think I am in love with the cook's daughter, a quick bright thing, we meet every day in the orchard, weaving blades of grass into grasshopper traps

One day I write down the poem and bring it, her manner quickens, her eye brightens

Then my shadow sister, she of the park that is said to be dead, catches us in a trap of her own, she tears up my poem, she sends me to my room, the next day I hear that the cook and his daughter have been banished from the kingdom for stealing

So quick bright things come to confusion

Swift as a shadow, short as any dream, the memory folds in on itself and sinks, all I am left with is a

Green apple in a white white hand

(How long since she has seen the sun?)

"Comfort me with apples, for I am sick of love," her voice is light and cool and shot through with filaments of good humor

Framing her heartshaped face, her dark hair catches the light from the candles and cascades over the shoulders of the vivid gown, she moves again and I catch the fresh smell of fruit, not from the apple but from her

She chuckles, she is a lover of laughter, she is a lover of loins, my stars, why am I thinking that

Stars

The candles are ten thousand thousand white and burning stars

My head is tingling from the buried memory, I lurch toward her, practically into her arms, a parched traveler pulled off the caravan by my desire, her eyes are the cisterns where my weariness drinks

"Stars," I gasp, "... I drink..."

She coils the fingers of my left hand around the apple and steals away, her gown is summer rain, it goes away, it comes back, into my right hand comes a silver goblet foaming with pale fire, bubbles winking at the brim

She guides it to my lips, I taste the sparkling sweetness exploding on my tongue, fire and fruit commingling in my mouth, carrying a celestial warmth inside me, into my blood

I am drinking stars

"My name is Zayo, I have been waiting for you"

She has her hands in my hair and her lips on my brain

"Or someone like you"

We sink to our knees on something soft beneath us, she smells of the orchard, we are in the orchard, she is the orchard, her hands move like plants unfolding, her mouth is an undiscovered flower, she is an unexplored cloud forest, I can smell and taste the apples, I can see and taste the stars

Slowly I open my eyes to flickering candlelight, my cheek is resting on her shoulder, the damask is rich, elaborately patterned in waves, you see such waves on the blade of a good steel sword, the purple cloth spreads over the curves of her upper body, a great bruise, what have I seen recently that reminded me of a great bruise, yes, that distant view of the city of Hroom from the hill near the

Hroom

My rendezvous with Prance

How long have I been here

Not orange but purple, she has changed her gown

I bolt upright, staring at the candles, tall and serene, burning placid and selfcontained, they appear unchanged, no guttering stubs melting or flowing down the flagons that hold them aloft

"The candles," I blurt, I feel her stir beside me, her sweet heartface swims up to me through the pale light of the fire, the same color as the sparkling wine

She appears to misunderstand me about the candles, she thinks I need reassuring, "They are still here, they will always be here, they are here tonight"

"Tonight? How long have I been here? How many candles have we used?"

Her mouth curls up at the edges but she does not show her teeth, "Who knows? These candles do not consume themselves, they never need replacing, there is no time in this place"

I whip my head around and search the tapestries, the carpets, the overstuffed chairs and divans, the jasper columns ornamented with capitals of gold, I spy the empty silver goblet and, beyond it, the heavy brown glazed bowl I saw filled with green apples when I came in

It lies overturned, upside down on the green carpet, a tortoise trying to crawl away from me, get into its burrow, but it is too slow, I snatch it up, uncovering a dozen skinny apple cores, already turning tobacco brown, so well gnawed that no trace of sweet fruitflesh remains

Her rich chuckle ripples into my right ear as her arms slide around my waist, "You have a good appetite, I like that in a man, of course you didn't eat them all at one time, we had several meals over the course of our tryst"

When I turn to her, our faces are so close that our lips are almost touching, to speak is to be within striking distance of kissing

"This was not a tryst, a tryst is an appointment to meet at a designated time and place, I don't know who you are"

Her dark eyes widen as if in surprise at my words, she tilts her head to one side, "I'm sorry, I don't mean to be flippant, in my situation I have come to be philosophical and to take things as they come, have some more wine"

My blood is racing, how much time have I lost, I shake my head, "I cannot stay"

Her merry laugh is a thing of wonder, made of little bells and metal filaments and balls of glass, gone almost before I have finished hearing it

"You have to stay, there is a binding spell on this place, no one who enters here can leave, just as I cannot leave," she grows suddenly solemn, her face still, a white mask, her eyes hothouse grapes, "I thought you knew, I'm sorry," and there is another full wineglass in my hand

Dazed, I suck at the tumbling bubbles, feeling the jolt to my insides, I can barely force the words from my mouth, "Why—why are you here?"

"I have had some schooling in magic, nothing on a cosmic scale, spells of concealment, shape shifting, weather control, my father warned me to be careful—my father!" her voice is tinged with bitterness, her lips tighten, the cords stand out like ropes on her ivory throat

"Trafficking in magic, he called it, as if I were engaged in buying and selling, intellectual curiosity is an alien concept to him, ever since the True Word came he has found it impossible to think for himself, here, drink"

Bemused, I find that my glass is empty, this is not a metal goblet but a delicate longstemmed flute, she produces a dark bottle from somewhere and pours shimmering light into the beckoning bowl

"If we were out of this place, I would not need the bottle, I could refill your glass with a spell, but I am power-less here," resignation and defeat hang on her features, no trace of the merry girl of a moment ago

"Who put you here?"

"I... ran afoul of someone unpleasant, someone with powers greater than my own, someone who saw me as a threat, someone who also admired me and wanted to possess me, he comes here every seven days to check on me, to spend time with me, to... use me," her mouth twists and she averts her eyes

"Outrageous," I can only mutter, the pale golden liquid lying heavy on my tongue now, its fire coursing down through my limbs, "what if you are in trouble and need help between visits, what of a cave-in, an earthquake, the invasion of wild animals?"

She stretches a languid, despairing arm and points to a distant corner, "If by some remote possibility I desire his company, I have only to touch that talisman and my master will come instantly"

I stride over, a trifle unsteady on my feet, and look down at a squat black statue of a bandylegged creature, its short arms cleaving to the top of its flat head, its mouth frozen wide open in an eternal scream, its pigeyes glazed in perpetual fear

How can such a pathetic thing hold so much power, how could anyone force such a lovely woman to stay here against her will, how can I stand here and do nothing, as I have done in the recent past

Bonfire of rust, pelt of dead fox, the flash of a clotting wound, the hillside crawling

Redbrown redbrown dirty blood blood in the mud

I am seeing red, a dusky film floats down before my eyes, something is building up inside me, the wine is singing in my blood

Blood music

"This is what I think of your master"

I lift my right foot, I raise it behind me, the voice of Zayo comes bright and shrill, "No!"

I kick the talisman, it shatters with the sharp dry crack of a dead tree snapping, a cold wind sweeps through the chamber, half the candles go out, the long hair at the back of my neck is standing up

Before me is a tall copper urn, the kind used for

heating water to make tea, so large that it is made to stand on the floor, its burnished curved surface shows me a reflection of the chamber behind me, Zayo a purple splash against the now darkened background, her hands two smaller pale blobs caught in the inky flow of her tresses as she pulls her hair in anguish

"No!" I hear her cry again

I feel rooted to the floor, my eyes fixed on the blurry picture shining on the front of the urn, now it shows me a disturbance in the air in the middle of the chamber, the ripple of hot air above a mirage, the birth of a dust devil, a warning to those about to reap the whirlwind

Barely seen particles appear in the air, twisting and dancing around one another, growing in size and color and density as they converge, coalesce, darken, solidify, thicken, become something alarmingly large and unearthly in color, an experiment gone horribly wrong

Suddenly he is here in the chamber with us, suddenly I am free to turn and look at him, study his frightening seven-foot stature, his greenblack scaly skin, his coiling goathorns, his bulbous yellow eyes, his clawed hands

I have never seen one but I know at once what he is, he is that supernatural being known as a genius, shortened to genie in some parts of the world but always genius to those of us north of the Scorpion Sea, some are friendly but this one looks demonic

He crouches slightly on long muscular legs, naked as is the custom of his kind, between his legs swings the heavy club of his manhood, its ridged length marked by pusyellow protuberances, its snout glossy and drooling

I am shocked sober, struck dumb, once more rooted immobile, waves of evil come pouring from him, along with the smell of sour milk

His yellow goateyes roll towards the girl, his dark metallic voice clangs in the silence of the chamber, "What is this, traitress?"

She flings herself headlong at his longtoed feet,

writhing close enough to kiss the horny talons of flint that are his nails, she is moaning, "He is nothing, a mere traveler who lost his way, he means nothing to me"

Now in his hand there is a sword where there was no sword, a heavy saber with a curved thickbacked two-edged blade, he holds it by the blade and thrusts it down pommel first, forcing it upon Zayo

"Take the sword," his voice rings throughout the everdarkening enclosed space, the candles that never need replacing are continuing to go out one by one

She remains prostrate, her face turned away from him and from me, the purple bruise of the gown has become the black of a gangrenous wound as the light grows dimmer

"Don't make me repeat myself," I hear him so clearly, I am so clearheaded, how quickly has the sight and sound of the genius killed the music in my blood

She pushes herself up on one elbow, she takes the sword, she staggers to her feet as if she were the one full of wine, she looks up into the impassive face of her master

"Cut off his head," he orders calmly, a reasonable request, the tone of a husband asking for another cup of tea

Her eyes, already impossibly huge and dark, seem to grow larger and darker, she stares wildly from master to guest, the point of the sword drops downward as the heaviness of the blade pulls her hand toward the floor, there is a strangling noise in the back of her throat

The silence of the tomb engulfs us for a moment, I can hear the candle flames flickering like insects, I think I can hear the apple cores crackling as they brown

At length the genius sighs, his breath hisses out through his monstrous scabby nostrils, he grins and I catch a glimpse of his dirty fangs

"Very well, nothing so simple as execution by steel, I shall remember your disobedience, but now it is time for me to have a little pleasure," he raises one hand and spreads its claws as if to admire them

Something breaks inside me and I lose control, "Wait, you don't need to do anything hasty, I can go back the way I came"

Where is my noble intent to play the hero, my bowels have turned to water and my heart is in my mouth

"I have to meet my friend, he will miss me if I don't turn up, he will be most disappointed," I add wildly, "perhaps he has come back looking for me, perhaps you have seen him," I am babbling now, "a fine fellow, not very tall, brown hair and eyes, looks something like a monkey, always talking"

The genius gives a grotesque parody of a smile, the black centers of his eyes smolder, he gestures with his raised hand, saying, "You have pronounced your own doom!"

Blinding light assails my eyes and blots out the chamber for a moment, raging fire runs coursing through me, the heat of a fever dream, my tongue and groin are burning, my eyes are sizzling, something like boiling oil is dripping from my ears, my hands and feet tingle with bee-stings, a blurry glimpse of the chamber floats back to my consciousness

Tapestries, furniture, genius, Zayo are all receding, at the same time getting farther away and bigger, a difficult trick, everything in view is taking on a brownish tinge as if seen through unwashed muslin, I feel the nails on my hands and feet stirring and crawling and lengthening, my skin itches and prickles, something is happening at the base of my spine

I whirl and look at my reflection in the tea urn, my royal robe is gone, I see a tiny Talin, an impish browneyed face beneath the fur now spreading all over my new long-tailed body

I am a monkey

CHAPTER 14
A VICTIM OF WINE AND MAGIC

My mouth is full of bitter seawater, I am on all fours trying to cough up the lining of my little monkeylungs, the planks of the ship's deck are rough beneath my paws

The air holds the tangy smell of salt, the distant mewling cry of gulls, the closer rumblings of rough men

Now I remember how I came to be here, the genius laying hands on me, roaring something incomprehensible, the two of us flying upward, passing through the ceiling of the chamber, through the earth, as through smoke, rising above the treetops, hurtling over auroral forest and field

The great graygreen greasy sea of Hroom bursting upon us, opening like a vast eye under the rising sun

The genius releasing me, as an eagle drops a tortoise upon rocky ground to break its shell, but I am now above water and not earth, the turbulence of the green waves rushes up and as I am plunged into it, I recall the magician in the old story who vows to discard his powers, "Deeper than did ever plummet sound, I'll drown my book"

Vague waterlogged memory of clinging to a floating spar, being swept into the side of a moored ship, being fished out in a net, now to be enmeshed in the more dangerous net of the sailors' superstition

"Having a monkey on board brings ill luck to a vessel"

"Throw him back into the sea"

"Knock him on the head with a hammer"

"Let me shoot him with an arrow"

"Let him be," comes an authoritative voice just behind me, I peer up and around to see a tall thin woman in captain's dress, her white hair is chopped short, her black eyes snap in a narrow shrewd face, I fling myself forward and grasp tightly hold of her leg

She pats my head, "This creature has sought my protection and he shall have it, let no one molest him or interfere with him"

A young seaman appears at her elbow, "Captain, the priests are here from the city, they have some sort of message from the High Priest"

On the moment the deck behind the boy is filled with men in black, the one with the greatest height and largest beard carries a scroll of parchment

"Praise the True Word," he intones

The Captain repeats politely, "Praise the True Word"

"And the Snowman who brings it"

After the slightest of pauses, "And the Snowman who brings it"

The bigbearded priest clutches his own throat in the Sign of the Gallows but rushes on without waiting for a response, "Most courteous greetings from Ludon, High Priest of the True Word in the city of Hroom, he asks if each personage on board would be so kind as to write a line or two on this scroll, using his best hand"

The Captain takes the scroll and unrolls a portion of its crackling goldyellow length, eyeing the spidery inktracks scrawled across it

"You see," the priest goes on, "our High Priest's secretary, an eminent calligrapher, has recently died, and he is anxious to find a replacement with a similar talent, one capable not only of handling his personal correspondence, but also of making glorious copies of the True Word for the edification of the masses"

As he pronounces the last word, his eye falls upon me, cowering and shivering almost at his feet, and his prominent nose wrinkles in disgust

The Captain takes the scroll and the accompanying pen, a big black cigar of a pen, I spring up and snatch them from her grasp, chattering eagerly in the only tongue I have in my possession at the moment

"Stop him, he'll throw the scroll into the sea," cries a priest, but the agitation of the crowd is stilled as the men see that I am holding the pen and paper with great care, I have spread the parchment open on my knee and have the pen poised above it, ready to write

"Let him do what he will," orders the Captain, "if he scribbles or makes a mess I will have him punished, but if he really can write, as I hope, for never did I see a monkey with such a clever air about him, I shall adopt him as my son"

Someone holds out an inkpot, I dip the pen and dash off six couplets I know by heart, praising the beauties of nature, using a different script style for each, best first to catch their attention, time to explain my predicament later

The leader of the priests takes back the scroll and goggles at what I have written, declaring that it eclipses everything else on the parchment, no need to take samples of the hands of anyone else on board, I must go at once to the High Priest

By now, having eaten nothing but a dozen apples in twenty-four hours, and still drugged by the aftereffects of wine and magic, I slide into a daze and am barely conscious of being lifted down into a small boat

Now I find myself half swooning over a low table richly spread with all manner of delicate meats, my small body has been wrapped in a robe of honor, the hands of attendants are holding my head up and introducing savory bites into my mouth

Across from me sits a large blackrobed man with a square head, black hair and eyes, chalkwhite skin, a broad mouth filled with too many wolfteeth, he shows them in a mirthless smile

"I am Ludon, the High Priest of Hroom, you are in the main temple of the city, do you understand what I am saying to you?"

I nod as calmly as I can, fighting my natural hunger and sense of urgency, eating rapidly but trying to show care and moderation, as soon as I feel stronger I gesture to the writing materials at the end of the table

I take a peach and write on it some verses in praise of his hospitality, making him speechless with astonishment, then I do the same on the side of the glass from which I have been drinking, making him mutter, "A man who could do as much would be exceedingly clever, and this is only a monkey!"

He strokes his stubbleblue chin and I see the flashdance of many rings, more than one on each finger

"You're a remarkable creature, you could be very useful as a demonstration of the True Word and the marvels of our Prophet, you could make us a great deal of money"

I want to ask him what the True Word is, is it written down, has anyone ever seen it, but I cannot speak

A jewelencrusted door opens and a longnecked longlegged heron of a man strides in, "Your Worship, your daughter has just returned"

Ludon rises slowly, his heavy robe rustles, he is now a thick dark pillar so high above me that to see him I must raise my head like a turkeycock drinking rain

Zayo sweeps through the door, wearing the purple gown and an enigmatic look

"Father"

His voice a growl, "I thought that you were in captivity, being punished by the Prophet for your impious deviltry"

"No, I was in captivity, being punished by a genius

for my refusal of his advances"

"Do not dare to argue with me, the Prophet has many tools through which he does his work, if he punishes you it is for your own good, to turn you back to his ways"

"How can I be turned back to the ways of an imaginary god when I never followed them to begin with?"

They are standing eye to eye, she has not seen me, though I sit directly between them, I am entranced with wonder and do not move

"By what means did you elude your divine chastisement?"

"A boy stumbled upon my prison, I knew that he could not save me but I was charmed by his beauty, the genius came and transformed him into a monkey"

"This monkey?" With the air of a street performer revealing a hitherto concealed object, he directs her gaze down to mine

She cries out in delight, "It must be, oh, how glorious that he is safe"

"Continue, how did you escape the trap of our Prophet's judgment?"

"Stop saying that, he is not my Prophet and should not be given credit for anything, by forcing your misguided beliefs on others you show yourself to be a man of little worth"

"Well? Must I beat the truth out of you?"

Her face slowly darkens, almost becoming one with her hair and gown, her voice lowers, "I would not advise it, Father," rises again

"The genius took the monkey up through a portal of magic he opened in the roof of my prison, in his haste he failed to close the portal again, I found that the binding spell preventing me from leaving was gone and my powers had returned sufficiently to let me follow through the portal and fly here"

"So still you persist in using this vile insidiousness?"

"If I had not used this vile insidiousness, I would still

be languishing underground, but now I must make haste to restore this fine young man before the genius discovers my escape and returns"

Ludon reaches down his large white hands to grasp me, but she is quicker in her youth and snatches me up in her arms

"You will not stop me, Father, I am going to the courtyard, I must use the fountain there to bring him back"

She rushes out into a long corridor, it seems to me, at my small size, that we are moving at great speed, before I have time to think we are spinning down a spiral staircase past fine paintings of birds of prey, onto an inlaid blackand-white floor, past a bronze statue of a panther devouring a hare, suddenly out into brilliant sunlight

We are in an inner enclosed court bisected by a small canal, an upper gallery runs around it and a fountain shimmers in the center, she puts me down on a marble bench where I can feel droplets of spray from the fountain moistening my fur

Zayo murmurs a word I do not hear clearly, a gold goblet appears in her hand, she dips it into the turbulent waters of the fountain and fills it, telling me, "There is no time to lose"

Even as she raises the goblet to her lips, the air begins to darken slowly, the earth trembles, there is something very powerful, very far away, that is coming in fast

CHAPTER 15
"I BURN! I BURN!"

As the sunlight continues to fade and die, and the bench vibrates and jumps beneath me, Zayo drains the goblet in one draft and stands quietly with both hands at her sides, her eyes halflidded, her lips halfsmiling

"Ah, I can feel it working, I'm getting stronger again," she looks down at me and sets the empty goblet on the bench, "I can temporarily increase my powers by drinking from this fountain so that for very short periods of time I am a match for even this genius that torments me, he was only able to imprison me because he caught me unawares in a moment of weakness and surprised me with his binding spell"

Now the court is dusky with shadow, the air itself is throbbing, I gibber in fear as I see Ludon appear in the doorway

His daughter gives him a cold look and stoops to place one hand on my head, "It is time to turn you back, a simple—" Her words are overpowered by a thundercrack and the genius is here before us, even more horrible than before, his hands like pitchforks, his legs like the masts of a ship, his eyes like torches

"Illmet and unwelcome!" intones Zayo, stepping

back from my bench and leaving a clear area all around her

"So, you were not content with your comfortable palace underground," in the open courtyard his voice is not so clangorous, still it is inhuman enough that I feel my fur bristling and standing up as if I smelled a dangerous predator

Perhaps I smell two predators, for in this moment of terror I catch sight of Ludon lounging in the doorway, leaning sideways, his arms crossed, his face set in an expression of idle curiosity as his daughter stands on the brink of destruction

"I fear that your continued defiance must be punished, you no longer please me as a plaything," the genius begins to raise both clawed hands

"Hold, dog! None of your otherworldly spells, so unimaginative, so easy, like using a club to squash an ant, consider the challenge of dealing with me on my own terms"

He lowers his hands again, his eyes smolder in the dimness of the court, his mouth works silently

"I challenge you to a shapeshifting duel, here and now, one that will allow us to combine power with cunning, to defeat me in this way you will need intelligence as well as brute strength, I don't believe you can do it"

"Very well," grates the genius, "you well deserve the end which now awaits you"

His features begin to melt and run, like an image seen through a rainflooded window, he drops to all fours, his head and neck darken, his mouth and jaws swell, his green-black scaly body rapidly toasts to a golden brown, now he is a colossal blackmaned lion ready to spring

Zayo darts in on the beast, skipping aside from the widely distended jaws reaching to seize her, she plucks one of the coarse dark hairs from his mane and murmurs two or three words over it

In an instant the manehair becomes a longsword, with one bold slash she cuts the lion's head from his body and sends the furry orb flying across the cobbled pavement

The tawny headless body collapses and dissolves into a stinking crackling puddle that is soon gone, seeping out of sight with a disagreeable sucking noise

The lionhead bounces once, rolls, comes to rest some distance from us, flattens itself into the pavement, turns black all over, sprouts a long curved tail with a stinger at the end, four pairs of jointed legs, a pair of jointed mouthparts, and two large lobsterclaws, the biggest scorpion I have ever seen

With a dry scrabbling motion he scurries toward us, as he comes closer I notice that his flat spiderhead has no real face but that protruding from its sides are the bulbous yellow eyes of the genius, they roll and glare as he clicks his claws together and swings his stingered tail back and forth

Zayo throws the longsword over her shoulder, it vanishes in midair, she presses her arms to her sides, begins to narrow and elongate, her purple gown turns into a bright enamel skin, her limbs shrink and vanish, her head becomes flat and triangular, her mouth widens and shows fearsome fangs, she falls to the pavement as a huge snake

With indented glide, she moves to meet the scorpion, feeling before her with her forked tongue as if eager to make contact, quicker than the eye can follow she hurls herself upon the creature and closes her teeth upon him, they grapple and toss as the scorpion stings her over and over on her scaled nose

Now something is happening to the snake's prey as he wriggles in her mouth, he is growing, changing color again, changing shape, stretching her jaws until she is forced to drop him, he crouches and hisses, an ugly grayishyellow weaselly creature, a long brindled body with a tapering tail, a mongoose, he stiffens his short legs and dances towards the snake

The transformations are happening more swiftly as the duel proceeds, I blink and the snake is a slategray timber wolf, looming over the mongoose, overlaying his shadow with hers, his hissing with her growling, their muzzles almost touching, their drool intermingling on the pavement

They bite and snatch at each other, locked together in a waltz of death, two plague victims engaged in a final fling, coupling in the halfdark, dancing till they drop, circling the fountain, never letting go

The wolf relaxes her jaws to get a better grip, the weakening mongoose curls up in a ball of dun fur and is rolling away, escaping, shrinking, becoming richer and brighter in color, now a fat redorange pomegranate, now swelling up to the size of a pumpkin, still leering with the yellow eyes of the genius, like the big head of a harvest festival sundoll

The giant pomegranate rises into the air, floating up to the level of the gallery above us, glaring like a malevolent goblin, then comes crashing down again to smash into bits and scatter seeds and bloodpulp all over the courtyard

Instantly the wolf is a white chicken, running and scratching and pecking, swallowing the seeds as fast as she can find them, ignoring the red fruitflesh that cakes the cobblestones like the offal outside a slaughterhouse

The bird can find no more seeds, she flaps her wings and makes a frantic crowing sound, she makes signs to us with her beak but we cannot help her, I turn my head and notice Ludon leaning out from the doorway, his brows knit and his mouth pursed

I follow his searing gaze and see one last seed lying on the edge of the canal that flows through the court, with a desperate squawk the chicken sees it too and goes hopping toward it, just as she reaches it and pounces to pick it up, the seed rolls into the canal and becomes a goldfish

She flings herself into the water after him, from my perch on the bench I catch a glimpse of the drenched whitefeathered bird assuming the slender body, long snout, and spiny fins of a pike and zipping after her prey

For many long minutes they chase each other up and down the canal, uttering horrible cries that are muffled by the water, until I lose track of them and an ominous stillness falls upon the courtyard

When the surface of the water is finally broken, up comes a long snout, but it is not the snout of a fish, up comes a flat triangular head, but it is not the head of a snake, up comes a crest of horns, but they are not the horns of the genius, up comes a grinning longfanged mouth and the blazing yellow eyes of our enemy

The horrid head continues to rise on the elongated neck, up comes the long snaky body, the many short legs clawing the air, the wet gleaming skin redbrown, almost black, the unmistakable raw liver look of a

Dragon

Tendrils of smoke are curling from his nostrils and his open jaws, his reptile face is masked with cunning and hatred, I can feel the furnace heat of his breath from my crouched position yards away from him

Impossible to tell how much of him remains coiled underwater, but when he stops emerging from the canal his head reaches above the galleried walls of the open court, he bends his neck and stoops slightly to eyeball me

Suddenly Zayo is between us, she is in her rightful form, back in the purple gown, which is bonedry and undamaged, I note with astonishment that tendrils of smoke are also curling from her nostrils and mouth

"Very well," she trumpets, "you force me to fight fire with fire, though nothing is more dangerous in my experience, you well know that when the weapon of fire is used none can survive its peril"

Now the dragonhead comes swooping down toward her, smoke rolling from the eyes as well as the nose and mouth, a spate of bright flame gushes from the distended jaws, and from the mouth of Zayo leaps a ball of fire to meet it

She seems to be wreathed in flames, a burning coal ringed with smoke, flame pouring from her, while the dragon continues to spit and vomit his own fire down upon her head, and dark clouds cloak the inside walls of the temple

I am in agony lest I be burnt alive, I cast sidelong glances at the water in the fountain, finally a squeal of terror squirts out of me

Zayo turns to look at me, the dragon hisses in triumph, his mouth hangs open as if in obscene laughter, I see the tombstonegray tongue just before a sheet of fire descends to envelop her, they are locked together in a mass of flame and a curtain of smoke hides them from view

Without warning the dragon bursts through the smoke, blowing fire in my direction, he is overtaken by Zayo, blowing fire in his face, so that flames fall upon me from them both, her fire passes through me without doing any harm, but a monstrous gobbet of dragonflame as big as a man's hand strikes my right eye

A firebeetle burrows deep into my skull, gnawing at the soft tissue, the pain goes straight through to my brain, shrieking the entire length of my monkeybody, convulsing me, while to my other eye the world is drained of all color and is nothing but shades of gray

The next thing I know, I am hanging over the edge of the bench, my breath coming in ragged gasps, I raise my head, color is slowly seeping back into the clouded vision of my left eye as the smoke slowly seeps out of the courtyard

"Victory! Victory!" Zayo is shaking but still standing, at her feet lies a great heap of ashes

"He is gone, he will trouble us no more, but time is fleeting," she rushes to my side, seizes the goblet, fills it from the fountain, pronounces a quick spell, empties it over my singed head

I feel a quiver, a falling sensation, I am a man as I was before, except that I am now naked and blind in one eye

Ludon has come out into the courtyard, followed by the heronlike man, she turns to him

"Flames, these tormenting flames, I have gained the battle but it has cost me dear, his fire has penetrated to my heart and I have only a few moments to live"

I try to speak, but she will not permit it, she stops

me with a gesture

"If only I had found and eaten that last pomegranate seed in time, it was the last gambit of the genius and I could have stopped him, but instead we had to resort to fire, and now I am undone"

Smoke is still leaking from her body, every time she speaks a puff comes from her mouth, she closes her eyes, black sparks spring out on her face and hair

"I burn! I burn!" she cries, she flares up, a woman-torch, and where she stood there is a column of cinders that collapses in on itself and falls to the pavement

Ludon turns on me a face of stone, "We had our disagreements but she was my daughter, I never intended for her to give up her life, I'm sure the Prophet would not have asked that of her"

I am drugged by my pain and still not seeing clearly out of the one eye still left to me, I know not what to say

He continues, "You distracted her during the final confrontation, she looked away from him because of the noise you made, that is how he was able to overcome her, you have killed her, you do not deserve to live," he lowers his voice so that only I can hear, "and, of course, now that you are no longer a versifying monkey, you are worthless to the True Word"

He turns to his aide, "Surely this is a sign of our Prophet's displeasure, we must take the proper steps to appease him, it has been some time now since the last ceremony"

He looks at me again and his eyes are black ice

"Take him away and lock him up until dawn, we will give him to the owls"

CHAPTER 16
SACRIFICES AT DAWN

One hour before daybreak, when the streets are silent and deserted, when even sound appears to slumber, and profligacy and riot have staggered home to dream, they drag me from my cell and march me out onto the front steps of the temple

I am still naked, I am sick with pain and guilt, I cannot stop thinking of beautiful Zayo going up in flames because I lost control of myself at the wrong time, I also remember Prance and our missed rendezvous and imagine Rana back at the Haggard Hawk, stumping up and down her back hallway, peering through her smoked spectacles at her pictures of bears, wondering where I am, waiting for the wood

They bustle me down the steps and along the street, moving at a brisk pace, past a jumble of buildings gleaming white in the starlight, brothels, gaming houses, rich mansions, a convent, a closely shuttered mental asylum, somehow I know the true nature of each house we pass, though the occupants are unseen

As we near the waterfront, the deep whang of a gong resonates in the empty streets, it sounds again and again, people begin to appear in doorways and windows, they cluster on roofs and balconies, they are carrion crows attending the last faltering steps of a dying animal

By the time we reach the docks, the gong is deafening in my ears, there is a whisper of light low in the sky, the spectators are thronging the streets, jamming them, lining the water's edge, I know them by their dress

Harlots, hangmen, witches, corsairs, charlatans, acolytes, slaves, gladiators, ploughmen, weavers, pilgrims and nomads from outside the city

A tall figure in a black hooded cloak catches my eye, the hood is raised so that the face inside is blotted out by intense shadow, the hands are tucked into the big sleeves of the cloak out of sight

As my guards sweep me past the figure, the darkness inside the hood flares briefly, I get a glimpse of glowing red spots, circles within circles of bright spots shining in the concealed face

Here am I, reduced to one eye, while this creature appears to have more than he could possibly want

We break through the swelling crowd, we are at the water, Ludon stands against the rising sun, an obsidian column backlit by early morning fire

He stares intently at me, he opens his mouth but an aide tugs at his sleeve, "Your Worship, the city's special guest has been given breakfast and his animal has been fed"

Behind them is Prance, in grand multicolored apparel and looking as if he deserves it, flanked by the black sleekness of Ransom, who licks her chops, moistens a velvet paw, and applies it to the side of her face with solemn majesty

"Watch carefully, sir storyteller," the High Priest tells my friend, "and you will witness the power of the True Word, its grandeur and—" the rest of his sentence is drowned out by the next tolling of the unseen gong

I see Prance rub his hands together, his light voice reaches me as the loud metallic vibrations begin to subside, "Ah, yes, owly, prowly, howly, owly, browny fowly, little owl, as the poet says," he is still playing the fool

Ludon grunts, he turns back and leans into me, his manner is soft with menace, "I suggest that you use the time you have left to contemplate what you have done to my daughter, and whatever you do," his right index finger is raised, pointing into my face, "give us a good show"

He stabs his finger deep into the empty socket of my right eye, roots around, scrapes his nail against the bare bone on the inside, shreds the exposed nerves and fragments of singed flesh, a howl of pain leaps from my mouth, a dark blind shuts down over my brain, I am gone into darkness

Now I am lying naked on the head of a broken statue, a shattered and ruined idol rearing its great imperturbable face barely out of the water, some one hundred yards from the shore

It is my dream, the first dream, the one that I was having when Prance first came to me in my room in the seaport where I found my Lady Marabar

I am the man in the dream, I look down at the statue face beneath me and see the blank stone eye as big as my head, the mudgreen slab of its nose, my feet kick against the ridges of stone as I try not to slide down the slope of the tilted face

I throw my head back and search the dawn sky, the same jonquil dawn that flooded my mind with a lake of light in the dream

Distant specks are moving above the trees on the far shore, getting higher in the sky, growing larger as they come closer to me, I fancy that between the measured crashes of the gong I can hear the flapping of great wings

The mute forest has uttered its first birds of the season

My face is throbbing, my damaged right eye is burning, I swing my blurry left eye toward the shore, I can make out the black pillar of Ludon, the rainbow splash of Prance, the ebon stillness of Ransom on the edge of the milling crowd

A shadow sweeps over the water, I look up again, swooping down is a giant brown owl, bigger than I am, each tapering yellowtipped wing looking strong enough to crack my skull, how did it get here so quickly

It sails over me, a deliberate miss, banking and curving to turn for another pass at me, I see the long yellow tail, deeply forked by the V of its central cleft

I hear conversation on the shore, sometimes sound travels so well over water

"Your Worship, I would beg a boon," Prance's voice comes belling across to me, "allow me to substitute myself for the boy, finish the ceremony, let the boy go"

Ludon's answer is rough, lowpitched, cut off by another shattering blow on the gong, "I fear that will not be possible—unless the boy is willing to—"

Suddenly the owl is upon me again, just as foretold in the dream, its eyes are dark jewels, pieces of the night caught in feathered folds of yellow, its eartufts are long devilhorns, its horny beak is clacking, asking to be fed, asking for my tongue and one remaining eyeball

I lose control and start to yell, its claws like hideous hands reach for my screaming face

It sweeps past me again, I am buffeted by the wind of its passage

A small boat glides to the side of the statue, I look down and see Prance clambering up to me, he is more urgent and agitated than I have ever seen him

"Ludon has agreed to consider releasing you and letting me be taken by the owl, if you agree to become a dervish and travel the countryside in support of the True Word"

I look at him the same way I would look at Ransom were she to begin spouting poetry, he shrugs his narrow shoulders

"I know, a dishonorable task and one that would bring more harm than good, to you as well as to others, but if we are lucky this debate may be nothing more than a delaying tactic, behold!"

Between us and the shore, a dark wedge has appeared in the water, coming toward the statue slowly but steadily, it is Ransom's head, she is swimming out to us, swimming her heart out

"If we can deflect the attack of this owl, we can use the boat to get to the other shore and be on our way, no sacrifice, no deal with Ludon, no new dervish to join the ranks of the Snowman's minions"

Now Ransom is climbing the statue face, clinging precariously to the slick spraymoistened rock with all her claws, she is bigger than I remembered, a fair match for any bird of prey

The owl is still circling, soaring effortlessly on its broad wings, Ransom stops just below the nose of the statue and fixes her gaze on it, she lashes her tail twice and makes a noise deep in her throat

Prance is burbling in my ear, "If something goes wrong, not that it will, and you have to follow through on the agreement, it is not such a bad idea for you to temporarily take on the role of dervish, it would be a good disguise and a way to travel safely, no need to preach the True Word or collect any money for the Snowman once you got away from the immediate environs of Hroom"

"What could go wrong, we have Ransom here now"

Between the strokes of the gong, we hear Ludon speaking again on the shore, "Sir storyteller, I feel obliged to tell you that your mysterious appearance at our temple aroused my suspicion, coming as it did at the same time as the arrival of your young friend there"

Ransom starts the smooth liquid movement that will raise her up onto her haunches, but her hind legs appear to falter, she slips on the stone

"My nasty suspicion lingered all through the night," Ludon goes on, "all through my breakfast, which I had just before I gave orders to have your breakfast prepared, and it seemed to me that you might try to interfere with our ceremony"

Ransom's hind legs collapse and hang down beneath her, twisting backward as if broken, she scrabbles with her front claws, now she loses the use of all four legs and begins to slide down the statue face

The High Priest's growl crawls over the water, "I'm afraid I had to poison your animal"

Ransom seems bewildered and distressed, she shakes her head in impatience as she splashes back into the sea, she is crying piteously as the green water closes over her bright green, glazed eyes

She is gone

The distant gong is still driving its torture into my head, I think that I will go mad

Ludon's smiling voice reaches us one last time during one of the intervals between clangs, "By the way, I accept your offer"

Prance's face is just above mine as he leans over me, pushing words out through his obvious dismay, "Very well, what must be, must be, let me perform this last service, it is the only way to save you, it is what I am here for"

The owl slams into him with enough force to knock him off his feet, his back arches and his face contorts as the claws close on his neck and chest and he is lifted into the air

It beats its long wings twice, slowly and powerfully, and begins to rise into the brightening jonquil dome where its companions are circling

True to the end, Prance is still speaking, but I can no longer understand him, the metallic waves of the gong crash over me as he goes up with the owl and the distance between us lengthens

Father

Mother

Why is it that everyone I come close to is destroyed, some day you must explain it to me

The speck that is Prance dwindles and disappears
I am left behind, doomed to become a dervish
I am left maimed, I am left with one eye, I am left
staring up at that owltorn, that gongtormented sky.

Part III

The Garden of the Frenzied Contessas

CHAPTER 17
A MOVABLE FEAST

The fire was in its death throes when his voice finally dried up. Cold morning light spilled in from the high windows, showing us his white drawn face with its eye glaring; as we watched, the beacon of green and amber slowly closed and his body sagged sideways in the decaying armchair that had carried him on his wild night's ride. I wondered if his wig might fall off and catch fire.

Seated around him in a semicircle, we stared in silence at each other, I speculative, Terhune familiarly phlegmatic, Diarfa inarticulate with horror. Styx was keeping careful watch over the oval table, where oil lamp, hubble-bubble, and my tobacco pipe were scattered like medical instruments after an operation.

Footsteps crunched across the snow outside, came up the steps, and became the stamping of boots at the door. I heard Orn's treble voice giving one of our universal pass-words, "Plummy and slam!" Still we said nothing.

He dithered in, laden with enough food sacks to keep a rebellion going for six months. His hair and bird's-nest beard were flecked with fat snowflakes, and he was shaking out his favorite umbrella, the one with the handle mottled like the beaded throat of a tropical lizard; he always used an umbrella when it was snowing. As usual, he was sensitive to temperature and light. "Why is that fire going out? Ah, the boy. How is he?"

"We won't know until he comes to. We had to use shotweed on him. What have you brought us?"

"Shotweed? You of all people should know how dangerous—"

"We had to do it, Orn. I'll explain later. What have you brought us?"

"Um." In closing the umbrella, he managed to drop most of the sacks and had to stoop and paw through them, occasionally sticking his nose inside to take a good whiff for the purposes of identification.

"Smothered chicken. Medlar-jelly. Brandysnaps..."

"Quite a feast. A little fancy for our purposes—"

"Craneberries. Squantersquash."

"Orn, we don't know where we're going—"

"Pot cheese. Bonnyclabber. Smearcase—"

"Or how long we'll be traveling—"

"Sunshine salad. Finnam haddie, that's haddock smoked with green wood—"

"Orn—"

"That thin oatmeal cake they call farl, not the tastiest morsel but it'll do if you're not one of those fussgrapes who toy with their food—"

"Orn—"

"Cathead biscuits, they're good for traveling because they're dry and will last forever. No offense," he swung around to Styx with a rueful face, "they don't have any cat parts in them, it's just a name."

Seeing that he had finally run down, I asked pointedly, "Anything to drink?"

He thumped a couple of the sacks. "A flagon of balderdash. Though why anyone would want to drink a mixture of beer and buttermilk, I can't imagine. But Terhune seems to like it. And some of my October ale. I keep a live toad in the barrel to improve the flavor, you know."

"Many thanks," I managed. "We're not sure what our next step is—"

"They're not here!" The cry came, clear and vibrant, from the armchair by the fireplace. Talin was sitting up straight, blinking at the cold sunlight filling the room.

"Why is it day so soon? What happened after we got here and lit the fire? I don't remember a thing."

"You went to sleep, lad," Terhune said as gently as he knew how.

"Yes, I know. I just had another dream. The last one, about the poem and the porcelain hills, was just to point me in the right direction. What's on the other side of this mountain?"

I was relieved that he was all right, so relieved that I was trembling. "A small valley with natural hot springs. The hot water overflows and heads south, as a fairly large stream, staying so hot that it never freezes even in weather like this. A half day's march before you reached that pass where you were ambushed, you must have gone over it on a wooden bridge."

He nodded. "Yes, I remember thinking how odd that it wasn't frozen."

"It keeps getting bigger and bigger, until it becomes a river. You could sail all the way down to the sea if you wanted to."

"Never mind about the sea. I've seen it. Is there a strange building at these hot springs?"

An expert on local history, Orn spoke up. "To be sure. Back in my father's day there was a rich old coot, no doubt he was—"

"Coot!" Terhune thundered. "Why are we suddenly surrounded by birds? Everyone in the lad's story either looked like a bird or was about to be eaten by one."

Diarfa jumped in. "Not Prance. Prance looked like a monkey." She had wiped the look of horror from her face and was in complete control again.

Talin's eye narrowed in suspicion, darting back and forth between the two speakers. "What do you mean, my story? How do you know about Prance? What happened during the night?"

"You talked a bit in your sleep," she said drily.

"All right, daughter. That'll do. Now, as I was saying, this rich old... um, gentleman, no doubt as mad as the moon, took it into his velvet-head to build some kind of retreat at the hot springs where the wealthy could escape the rigors of daily life, get away from the ninnyhammers surrounding them in the city. The waters, you see, were supposed to have restorative powers if you bathed in them." He coughed.

"The week before the work was finished–my father loved to tell this part, he used to laugh until he choked–the owner got drunk on brandywine, fell off the roof into the springs, and drowned. They form a rather large, deep pool."

Talin leaned forward in his chair. His eye was gleaming with excitement and youthful enthusiasm. "Yes, I saw it in my dream. There was a square pool with steam rising from the water, open to the sky but with roofed verandas on all sides. Slick ceramic tile in patterns of pink and black. It looked partly ruined."

"Aye, that's it," confirmed Terhune. "That earthquake we had a while back probably did some damage. Not that the place was ever in the best of shape. Most of the builders trained in the last fifty years don't know bee from a bull's foot about quality workmanship."

Diarfa was drinking in the boy with a steady gaze. "What about this dream? What do you think it means?"

He almost lunged at her in his eagerness. "You don't know about the dreams, but I can tell you about them! I'm on a special quest, and I'm being sent clues about the pieces of an old war game I'm supposed to track down. They're not here, they're down at the hot springs, I'm sure of it!"

"Calm down." I was starting to hand food around. "Diarfa and Orn don't need to be told everything. They'll be going back to the Floating Head, I imagine."

Her spine stiffened almost imperceptibly. "I never knew you to turn down an extra pair of hands, as long as the person knew what she was doing. Remember when I helped you with that poisoned honey mystery?"

"All right," Orn interrupted, "I'm no sapskull, I can see where this is going." He was seething; I could smell the garlic bursting from the pores of his face. "What makes you think I'm going to let you tag along on this ragtag expedition to nowhere? You're a lovely bell-bone of a girl, the kind that rough men are wont to snack on like a sweetmeat, and this trip is headed for dangerous ground. I swear it is, or I'll eat my head!"

"I'll go if Catalan will have me. He knows I'm good with a dagger and have a sharp mind. Do you have any particular plan for stopping me?"

It was an old argument, one I had witnessed too many times to doubt the outcome. Orn subsided, muttering, and took a swig of his October. "I don't suppose anyone would object if I came along as well? There's plenty of food. We'll just take it with us. A movable feast."

Terhune stood, the leather of his garments creaking, and headed for the door. "I'll visit the snowbank again before we go. I wish this cabin had a jordan."

"Chamber pot," I translated for Talin. "All right. We'll go look at the hot springs. All of us. Sticker, we're moving."

He jumped down from the table and glided across the hardwood floor, his unretracted claws clicking like a dog's toenails. Orn was anxious to leave, plucking at the food sacks and fiddling with his umbrella. The two young people, now that the question was decided, sat and looked thoughtfully at each other, as if sizing each other up. It was too much for Orn.

"Come along, now. It won't be morning forever. You, daughter, pick up that balderdash, that's a good girl. Don't just sit there with your teeth in your mouth!"

We were on our way before you could say, "Cathead biscuits."

Chapter 18
Cannibal Saliva

"They kept me in Hroom until the worst of the damage to my eye had healed," Talin was saying, "weeks and weeks, I lost track. Of course nothing could grow me a new eye or bring back my sight on that side, but scar tissue eventually formed and it didn't hurt so much."

He must be a fast healer, I found myself thinking. He had already removed and discarded the sling put on his arm by the doctor in Andor.

We were in a very small, very old graveyard in the foothills on the north side of Hunchback Mountain. From the shelter of the toppling tombstones we could look down into the valley of the hot springs, where a ruined structure was visible through a curtain of lightly falling snow. Orn's umbrella, open against the snowflakes, resembled a giant dead mushroom springing up out of the graves.

"The Wine of Life keeps oozing drop by drop, the Leaves of Life keep falling one by one," Terhune intoned. I looked over at him, since he was not in the habit of quoting poetry, and saw that he was reading the inscription on the headstone in front of him.

I checked out the stone at my elbow. "God touched her with His finger and she died."

"Mother's not dead, she's only sleeping," added Diarfa. She peered at the unwalled collection of graves around us. "Isn't this an odd place for a graveyard? With no villages or houses or anything nearby?"

"There was a village on this side of the mountain, but the earthquake took it," I told her. "Took the living and left the dead untouched."

"That's what I was supposed to do, take the living for all they were worth," Talin went on bitterly. "When Ludon decided that I had mended as much as I was going to, he had them shave my head and eyebrows, gave me a robe and a traveling pouch, made me take the standard vows, and turned me loose in the open countryside. I was to collect offerings from anyone I ran into, while spreading the glory of the True Word, and turn over the money whenever I hit a town that had a temple in it. It all gets sent down south, to some central gathering place, to be checked out by someone called the Snowman."

"Yes, I remember from your story. And did you spread the glory of the True Word?"

"Heavens, no. Once I got away from Hroom, I followed Prance's advice and tried to use the role of dervish as a disguise. I wandered randomly, not talking to anyone, working at odd jobs to earn my meals. I kept waiting for another dream to point me in the right direction for my quest. And finally it came, the one I told you about, with your poem written on the sand. That's what brought me to you."

Idly I scraped at the snow on the stone before me. "But you told me that the people watching you knew that you had become a dervish, that they were looking for someone who had taken the vows and shaved his head. That was the reason for the wig, you said."

"Yes. I finally figured out that I was being followed, that they knew who I was and what I looked like. So I took a second disguise, returning to the appearance of someone with a regular head of hair." He fluffed up the tangle of curls in his hideous wig, which he had stubbornly refused to abandon. "Not that it did any good. It looks as though I've been tracked every step of the way, probably followed right here to the very hiding place of the playing pieces."

"Someone's down there," Terhune interrupted. He jerked his head in the direction of the ruins below us.

I squinted and caught a glimpse of several miniature blue figures moving in and out of the shelter of the crumbling walls. "All dressed in blue? Like a uniform?"

"That's not their clothing. Unless I miss my guess, it's their skin color."

Diarfa gasped. "Blue skin?"

"If they're who I think they are," Terhune went on patiently, "they stain themselves with blue dye they extract from a plant called woad—"

"From the mustard family," Orn put in.

"To frighten their enemies into submission. It's a trick that goes back for centuries, but as far as I know they're the only ones who still do it."

"Who are they?" Talin was leaning forward, straining his one eye to pierce the gradually thickening snowfall.

"The cannibals of Ugor."

"Cannibals!" This gasp came from Talin.

"Aye. They're a western people, though. I'm surprised to find them this far from their normal stomping grounds."

I searched my memory. "Weren't most of them killed off by some kind of disease a while back?"

"A virus called kuru, transmitted through the eating of human flesh. It ran through the entire tribe, killing the women and children first, then the men, by destroying their brains and their ability to move. The name kuru means 'trembling,' which is the first symptom. The virus is slow and can take up to a year to kill an individual. You can only get it by consuming the infected brain of a victim. The problem is that their funeral rites involve eating the corpse of the deceased."

"Who do they prey on?" Talin wanted to know.

"I can take this story from here," said Orn. "When they ran out of neighbors to chomp on, they took to the rape and pillage of estates. Then, when they had gone through all the tasty humans they could find, they took to foraging in the wild, picking up old bones, cutting them to pieces at the joints. If they found any worms or maggots, they would scald them over a fire to force the vermin out, boil the bones, drink up the liquid, and then grind the ends of the bones in a mortar and slurp up the paste. Lately they've been eating their horses' guts and ears, any kind of wild bird they could grab hold of, bears, venison, beaver, tortoises, frogs, squirrels, dogs, skunks, rattlesnakes, the very bark of trees. Not the sort of people to mingle with."

"But if we think Talin's war game is down there—"

I froze as something cold, hard, and rough touched the back of my neck. A guttural command sounded in my ear: "Splang squee hojo cola solo isbister kushkush." A blue hand reached around to unbuckle my sword.

I saw that a man had materialized behind each of my companions. All of them were below average height, gaunt, rawboned, skeletal, stripped to the waist despite the weather, smeared with dull blue dye that looked hastily applied. Their hair was dark, long, and tied back behind their heads, and their eyes were black diamonds that burned through the falling green-white snow. All of them held crude stone-tipped spears, capable of inflicting wounds that would be painful and quite possibly deadly.

We picked up our bags of provisions and started to march downhill. When I looked around to check the status of the rest of the party, I noticed that Styx had disappeared.

Outside the main entrance to the ruined structure housing the hot springs, a vast goathide tent loomed before us. The falling snow and the general darkness of the day made it difficult for me to see the tent poles, so the shelter seemed to hang in the air like a leathery creature, part bird, part bat. It exuded the smell of moldy smoky leaves.

We stooped to enter, most of us being taller than our captors, and the hide flap slapped shut behind us. A torch blazed on a tripod in the center of the enclosed space. In front of the tripod squatted a low shrine bristling with ivory carvings of warriors. The playing pieces of the war game.

They were cut in the likeness of kings, queens, holy men, mounted warriors, and foot soldiers, and the ever-moving torchlight turned them to rose quartz and made their tiny faces twist and grimace and gape, their glassy essences like angry apes. They stood at attention but in random arrangement, with no playing board and no opposing army in sight.

Talin, hunting bird that he had become, lunged forward toward the shrine, but his captor had him firmly by the collar of his cloak and jerked him to a standstill. We were all forced to drop our bags of provisions and sit on the dirt floor. They did not bind our hands or feet, but at all times the flint spearheads were inches from our throats.

I took a closer look at our captors. The one standing over me had the flat-nosed, smashed-in face of a bat. His skin was wet and slimy from the snow, and I could see where the dull dirty blue dye had come off in flecks. His face looked rotting, ready to fall off. The black diamond eyes never left me. I saw that he was holding my sword and that it was unsheathed.

They appeared to be waiting for something. They stood over us for what seemed to be hours, their spears as unwavering as the phalluses on those statues designed by some cultures to have their stone erections rubbed for good luck. The fluttering doorflap revealed that the wind was rising, the snowfall was turning heavier, and the day was turning darker.

Suddenly Terhune thrust one huge paw into a food bag. The cannibal next to him, a wiry wolfish man with an ugly snout and a wide mouth, jabbed him in the neck with his spear. Terhune grunted and froze, sitting still as the blood oozed up from the cut. Then slowly, defiantly, he pulled out the bottle of balderdash, a heavy stone flagon with a square black base and an ivory stopper the size of a baby's fist. It looked like an ink bottle designed for giants. He started to work on its contents, pausing for an occasional eruption of a belch. His captor watched him with no expression.

A sinister corvine shadow, like that of a carrion crow, went running up and around the tent walls, moving in erratic bursts. Diarfa gave a startled yip and instinctively clapped her hands over her head. Her overgrown rat of a guard nicked her throat with his spear and then drew back slightly, still watching her. "There's a bat in here," she blurted. Then she wiped at the blood on her throat.

Orn jerked as if he had been jabbed himself, then he made a visible effort to recover. "Puh! No need to get yourself all aflunters, daughter. They want to keep us alive. For the time being."

"I'm all right. It's not the first time I've been stabbed. I just got startled by the bat."

"If you weren't gravel-blind, you'd see that's just a bangsash."

"Better gravel-blind than totally stone-blind," retorted Diarfa, squinting at the large nocturnal bug buzzing between her and the torch. "It's almost as big as a bat, and it's scrimy and dirty and disgusting. Look at those antennae, they're like feathery ears—Oh!"

The bangsash, one of the few new varieties of mutant moths still active in cold weather, had finally blundered into the flame of the torch. With a crackling burst of sound and an eye-popping burst of dead white light, it went up like a paper lantern set ablaze. The image of a paper lantern made a tickling glisk in the back of my mind. Then I was distracted by the stink of the singed insect. Even in the stench of the tent it stung my nostrils.

Terhune rolled over onto one elbow, tipping his bottle to his lips while using his other hand to toy with the round ivory stopper, and the point of his guard's spear followed him. "Ye gods and little fishes, but it smells in here. There's a noxious choking gas called firedamp that is sometimes exhaled by goats when they're sick. They must have had a whole herd of sick goats in here for a week before we got here."

"It's the drugs they smoke when preparing for special events," said Orn. "Their experiences in the wilderness have made them experts in all kinds of wild herbs, so they know just what to consume to whip themselves into a fighting frenzy or to chill themselves into a near coma for a sacred rite or ceremony. You must have heard of their seizure salad, a secret combination of plants and tubers and flap-dragons—"

"What?" I asked.

"Raisins soaked in brandy. They throw all these ingredients together and eat themselves into this strange state of joy mixed with sorrow, what they call merry-go-sorry. At least that's how it translates from their language. They put themselves into it just before they're ready for a special feast."

"Like us." Diarfa's eyes were stained with disgust.

"Yes, indeed," agreed Terhune, now sprawling on his back and trying to keep the bottle balanced on his burly chest. He seemed oblivious to the spear still poised above him. "Of all edible creatures, the Ugor consider other human beings to be the most esculent. Would you like to hear how they prepare and eat human flesh? Of course you would."

She opened her mouth to protest, but her father beat her to the punch. "He's fap, daughter. Nothing will shut him up now."

"Let's not have an argybargy. I'm getting drunk is what I'm doing. I'm thinking that there are enough of us here, especially considering that some of us are big strapping fellows, to stretch the meat supply out to an octave. Reason enough to get fat-witted."

I did not like the way things were headed. "Terhune, we need to do something to get out of here—"

"I am doing something. Can't you tell?"

"Yes, you're getting pie-eyed and talking a lot. That's helpful. We need to—"

He plowed right through me. "The cooking is done in pits with steam made by pouring water over hot stones, or sometimes the flesh is cooked in bamboo cylinders in the hot ashes. The children help in both the butchery and the handling of the cooked meat. By that time, of course, we'll be long gone, suffering a sea change into something rich and strange."

He and Diarfa both had blood on their throats, and all the cannibals were watching it as it dribbled down. The bat-faced one directly above me opened his mouth to cough wetly. I thought of the disease running through their people.

Talin spoke for the first time since this exchange had begun. "I don't like this. I wish I had my ax. I don't want to be fishified and discandied in some kind of grotesque outdoor barbecue. Do they boil us alive?"

"Yes and no. Their spiritual beliefs are crude but unwavering. The victim must suffer no pain and therefore must be unconscious. They grow a plant that is highly psychotropic; when they chew the leaves, a natural chemical in their saliva reacts with the herb to create a powerful toxin. Rather than swallow this themselves, they force-feed it to their victims to sedate them. Then it's into the pit, as fast as lightning. If you hear someone talking about cannibal saliva, that mixture that forms in their mouths is what they mean."

"What do you mean, force-feed?" Diarfa was fingering the wound on the smooth skin of her throat.

Terhune's belly laugh almost overturned his bottle, but he caught it in time. "It's passed from mouth to mouth, the way some owls and pigeons feed their young. And it's probably on its way to us as we speak."

Two of the cannibals flanking the doorflap had produced panpipes. They put them to their mouths and produced an eerie piping sound, like wind blowing mournfully through a hanging skeleton.

Now the other cannibals, those without instruments, opened their pursed mouths and set up a mournful keening dirge, which seemed to rise and fall with the wind outside.

Terhune howled along with them. "Ladies and gentlemen, we are privileged to be in the presence of the Kings of Ululation! Not a consonant to be heard for love or money. Vowels stretched and tortured like catgut in a violin factory. That's probably where they get their inspiration, from their sentry cats crying to be fed."

"Inspiration, you know," said Orn in the schoolmaster's voice he adopted upon the most inappropriate occasions, "actually means the act of breathing in, the taking in of something valuable for the body or the mind."

"In that case, here's the last inspiration in this bottle," and Terhune took a final mighty swig that did alarming things to his Adam's apple. "Just in time, for unless I'm mistaken here comes our master chef."

Without warning, a new figure came cranking in, unnaturally tall and skinny like one of the wicker men burned in symbolic sacrifice on certain islands in the west, the almost featureless head a dead ringer for the carved pumpkins seen on autumnal nights in the same region. His scrawny neck, painfully thin wrists, and knobby ankles were adorned with rings of small bones.

By rolling and undulating and pushing with hands, feet, and buttocks, Terhune managed to rise to his knees and raised his bottle in a mock salute. He chuckled explosively. "At last our fearless leader. How pleasant to be in an aristarchy, where the most outstanding and best qualified hold the power. I for one have been growing weary of sitting under the blades of your boggling bum-bailies."

The newcomer had no eyebrows to contract and was clearly keeping his thin-lipped mouth tightly closed for a specific reason, but he did bend his long neck sideways to eye this strange captive more closely.

"Too bad you're not a granivore, a creature that only

eats grain," mumbled Terhune. "Or better yet," he spurted out a mixture of balderdash and laughter, "a grannyvore, a creature that only eats grannies!" He swayed on his knees and clutched the bottle to his chest.

Orn was becoming agitated to the point that I thought he might actually pull most of his beard out. "Are you barking mad? We're in enough trouble without playing the fonkin and clowning around. If I have to be cooked up like a slab of venison, I'd rather have it be as painless as possible."

"Oh, don't worry, me bucko, I think this ancient anthropophagite has brought a mouthful of something very special for the first one of us to go. Probably the fair Diarfa, since the Ugor consider all women to be either flirt-gills– that's a floozy to you and me–or kickie-wickies–that's the wife, or trouble and strife as they said when I was growing up–and they don't intermarry with non-Ugor. Purity of the species and all that."

The skeletal figure moved one of his bony hands to his side, where a rather large and nasty knife was hanging, but at that point Terhune seemed to cross the indefinable line between control and helplessness. He began crooning, "Wait now. Don't woo. Don't wobble. Smoke them spoggers. Gimme a fried hat." His head rolled crazily from side to side.

As the others stared at him, the tiniest of movements on the other side of the torch tripod caught my eye. A slit appeared in the far wall of the tent, and through it slipped a few inches of a chocolate velvet nose and one green-gold eye. Styx had found a back door to our prison.

Ignoring Terhune's drunken babbling, the head cannibal let his hand drop back down from the knife and turned to Diarfa, who scrabbled backwards until her back was up against one of the tent poles. Placing his clawfingers firmly on her shoulders, he leaned down in her face and opened his mouth, revealing it to be brimming with a yellow-green mush like a particularly virulent strain of baby-shit. Diarfa moaned.

"Wait now. Don't woo. Don't wobble," Terhune continued, still working on getting the stopper back in the bottle.

The cannibal's mouth, its vile contents now starting to drip from the corners and over the lips, edged closer to Diarfa's mouth, which was open in horror and ripe to receive its toxic sedative.

A loud velvety growl exploded from the slit in the back of the tent. The warriors turned their heads. And their spears.

Terhune suddenly shot bolt upright, sober as a surgeon, and grabbed the head of the spear being held by his wolfish captor, snatching it out of the man's hands.

With perfect accuracy he threw it at the torch and knocked it over, plunging the tent into murky gloom.

CHAPTER 19
SNAKE OF WATER, SNAKE OF SMOKE

The fallen torch lay on the dirt floor behind the low shrine of the war game, where it sputtered and threw out just enough light to show us to the enemies around us. In two long strides, Talin reached it, snatched his shaggy red wig from his head, and crammed it down onto the dying flame. It seemed to twist in his hands, becoming a dark smoky tangly thing, a giant spider on fire, an orange-legged jungle tarantula.

The guard beside me was swinging my sword up when I slammed my fist into his bat face. It felt exactly as if I were hitting a pantomime doll. I snatched the sword from his nerveless fingers, gave him a hard shove that made him stagger backward, and plunged across the dark tent.

Orn was piping, "Out! Out, you boobies!" In seconds, his frenzied thrashing movements had scooped up his precious umbrella and one of the food bags and turned him into a moving target.

"Out the back," I cried, "there's another flap behind the tripod." I pushed through the narrow opening in the goathide into a cold howling twilight getting worse with every heartbeat. The moldy smell of the cannibal drugs was behind me as I found myself immersed in snow and wind, reeling down a short corridor into the ruins of the old building. The walls of the passageway were slick pink and black tile, as in Talin's dream, and I banged into them and bounced from side to side, just as the bangsash had blundered its way around the confines of our prison tent.

In front of me was a lone spearman, running in the same direction that I was. Overtaking him, I swung my sword down from my greater height, missing his head but splitting open his entire back. A lot of little black things fell out, some of them wriggling as they landed. I jumped over his body and pelted onward.

Orn caught up to me, grinning like a raccoon. "Fopdoodles and fleaks, all of them," he puffed. "Don't understand anything but violence. Where are the rest of us?"

Styx was a brown streak weaving back and forth before me, making strange woodwind sounds in his throat. Looking over my shoulder, I saw that Terhune was covering ground quickly, the spearhead of a small phalanx completed by Talin and Diarfa. All of them had objects in their hands, but I could not identify specific weapons.

Into the head of the passage behind us flooded a manswarm of the blue devils. "Keep moving," I cried. "They'll kill us if they have to, even if it spoils their ceremony."

Terhune touched the arms of the young people flanking him and slowed their headlong rush forward. "We're nearly at the end of the passage, and you may have forgotten what's there."

The words were hardly out of his mouth before Orn and I, squeezed shoulder to shoulder by the narrowing walls of the corridor, oozing and oiling our way along the snow-wet tile, popped forth like greased pigs and plunged into the hot, steaming water of the central pool. Even with my height, the water was up to my chest, while Orn was flapping and splashing, trying to keep his mouth above the surface without dropping what he had rescued from the tent.

"You slimy scroyle," he sputtered. "What do you take

me for, a flish? A hellbender, one of those mudpuppy sala-
manders? You're no bullyrook of mine, no pal of mine!"

Terhune and the young ones stopped at the lip of
the pool, where Styx was already crouched with flattened
ears and narrowed eyes. "This is not good. Not with that
ravenous scarecrow of a cannibal king coming to bemonster
us. We need transport."

The water was very hot, just about as hot as I could
stand it, and the steam was scalding my lungs and burning
my tongue and nasal passages. I could smell sulfur. The
droplets running down from my wet hair into my mouth
tasted faintly metallic.

Orn was still clucking and complaining as he continued to splash about. "It's like I'm licking horseshoes! This
is worse than being put to sleep and roasted. At least then
we wouldn't feel anything."

I looked around. The verandas on all four sides of the
square pool were teeming with warriors, hooting excitedly
and banging their spears against the handrails. They were
backlit by dozens of torches, making the surface of the water
writhe with shadows that reminded me of spiders. Bats.
Giant moths. And pumpkins with carved mouths that
opened and closed malevolently.

Diarfa was joining Styx in taking quick catlike
glances around the area. "You said that the springs overflow
the pool here and form a stream that heads south. Did
anyone ever use that for traveling? Maybe there's a boat."

"If there is, it would probably be waterlogged and
rotted after all these years," Terhune said, squatting and
peering out over the torch-dazzled water. "Unless they left it
neaped high and dry, run aground and under cover."

With a mewling cry, Styx rose to his feet and went
loping around the pool to our left, melting in and out of the
shadows. The sentry cat nosed his way through a curtain on
the far side of the pool, a dusty curtain of baubles, bangles,
and glass beads. Probably a shrunken head or two woven in
there somewhere. Even though the warriors on the verandas

were growing louder, we could still hear the cannibals from the tent coming up behind us. Styx was swallowed by the alcove beyond the curtain, and then the men from the passage were upon us.

Diarfa, Talin, and Terhune, who held only the food bags and no weapons, scrambled along the tiled edge of the pool, barely keeping ahead of the spears being thrust at them. It was clear that the Ugor wanted to recapture us alive, to prepare their feast in the manner to which they were accustomed.

Orn and I struck out through the hot smoky water, using clumsy breaststrokes. Our timing was such that we five human victims came together at the same moment Styx emerged from the curtained alcove, all of us clustering on or around a wooden ramp that plunged from the alcove down into the pool.

In a movement quite graceful for one of his bulk, Terhune spun around on the warriors at his heels, raised his arms in a parody of religious ecstasy, and screeched, "Ia! Ia! The Goat of a Thousand Young! Shut your cakeholes, you colstrels and rutterkins, the ceremony is about to begin!" Although he had exhausted his drunken act back in the tent, he still stood as a prime example of a dangerous madman.

Our enemies slowed their advance and huddled shoulder to shoulder, keeping their spears raised while eyeing us. I was swinging my sword in an arc, hoping to hold them at bay. From time to time they slid their eyes towards Terhune as he continued to rant. Some of them moved their lips and made gestures in the air.

"So what if they think you're as mad as the seven seas," Orn grumbled, giving a few practice slashes with the tattered remains of his bumbershoot. "This cannot be anything more than a delaying tactic. We're all dead meat."

"Yes? Then perhaps you can tell me what this ramp was built for? And what we should find just inside this tastefully curtained storage room? Gold ingots? Shelves of bibelots? A dray of squirrels repairing their nests for the worst part of the winter? Or maybe *this?*"

With a savage swipe of his arm Terhune smashed aside the glittering curtain of beads, thrust himself just inside the alcove, slamming Styx out of the way, and dragged out a bulky structure that jammed temporarily in the doorway. I lent a hand in pulling it to the top of the ramp, where the torches revealed it as a crude raft of knotty pine planks, just large enough for five humans and one sentry cat.

Terhune gave a gargantuan shove to launch the raft towards the pool and leaped on board, as momentum and gravity kept the craft sliding down the ramp and into the water. The rest of us tumbled after, down the ramp and onto the raft.

"How are we supposed to guide this thing," Orn snapped. "My brolly and your sword are the closest things we have to oars, and they're both too short to touch bottom. We're just going to float around out here, another movable feast like one big food bag, until they throw down a torch and the whole raft bursts into flames. I can imagine the greediguts up there licking their chops right now."

"You're determined to complain until you're blue in the mouth, old man. The people who built this craft weren't total idiots." Terhune reached down to the base of the railing on his side of the raft, unhooking and lifting up a long pole which he plunged over the side and into the violently bubbling pool. His shoulders and arms bunched up as his muscles worked, and then we found ourselves in slow motion, leaving the base of the ramp and gliding over the surface with the stately majesty of a royal barge setting out for a pleasure cruise.

"The corridor from the main entrance brought us in on the north side," I pondered aloud, "so I would head for the far side if we want to find the outlet to the stream. It flows south to the sea, as we said before, and it's our best bet for making an escape."

Orn begrudgingly agreed, apparently fixated on rolling his sodden umbrella into a tightly furled weapon.

"Otherwise, with their fondness for pyromania, our starveling friends will lob a few fireballs at us until we start roasting, tow us ashore, and prepare to chow down. They can even garnish us while we're cooking, if they want to drop some love apples off the verandas onto us."

Despite the heaviness of the load, the raft was picking up speed as Terhune continued to work his pole. The square enclosure rang with the shouts of the warriors and flashed with the flowering flames of more and more torches as reinforcements arrived from the interior of the ruined building.

A splattering liquid cry from the end of the corridor caught my ear, and I turned in time to see the cadaverous Ugor chief spitting out his mouthful of cannibal saliva mixture onto the snow-covered tiles at the lip of the pool, looking for all the world like a sick man vomiting. Then I felt a rough undulant bump, and with a bone-jarring surge the raft sprang up out of the pool and darted into a deeper darkness. And so we beat on down a stream with a strong healthy current, borne forward into the future, while behind us the cannibal-haunted stronghold receded like a small country estate set ablaze by malicious marauders.

Diarfa leaned over the railing to see what could be seen of the water carrying us to safety, although as we moved out of range of the torches we found ourselves in dusky darkness. There was just enough light for me to make out my companions and to notice that it was still snowing, but the dimly glowing flakes seemed to be smaller and slower in their descent.

"This is what my granny used to call owl-light," Terhune grunted, shoving without complaint on his pole. "Just before it turns completely black."

Talin recoiled against the railing where he had been slumped since our wild embarkation. "No more owls, please. Not of any kind." He sounded tired and defeated.

"I always like to pass on bits of information that might come in useful at a later date. Owl-light is the best time for batfowling, you see. You catch birds by blinding them with a light and batting them down with a stick. Handy if you're desperate for food and there's nothing to be found on the ground."

Diarfa gave up studying the stream and turned on him. "Except we don't have a light. And, just out of curiosity, why is it called batfowling if you do it to catch birds?"

"I do not know and cannot guess. Maybe for the same reason our people call bats bawkie-birds. They're all creatures of the air, don't you see."

"Damn and blast, but I hate to get my beard wet." Having painstakingly rolled and packed his bumbershoot into a long thin package like a walking stick, Orn pressed a point near the handle and it snapped back open into a black blossom over his head. "A remarkable device. Spring-loaded, so it opens by itself. I bought if from the Widow Toad."

"Speaking of springs," his daughter said slowly, "I've been wondering if these hot springs are phreatic or vadose." I saw her teeth gleam faintly as she grinned.

Orn glared. "Daughter, I can't imagine where you get your propensity for showing off your arcane knowledge."

"Inherited from you, I imagine. And it's hardly an idle or an academic question. They're both underground waters, but vadose just sit immediately above the water table, while phreatic come up through wells. A vital difference if we're thinking about how strong this current is going to last and how far it will take us."

I had been watching Talin's moroseness with some concern, and the banter on the raft was starting to get on my nerves. "As I mentioned in the graveyard, this stream turns into a good-sized river that flows all the way down to the Scorpion Sea, so there's no need to worry."

"No need to worry!" The words fairly exploded from Talin, as he pushed himself away from the railing and rocked slightly to keep his balance on the undulating surface of the raft. "We practically had the prize in our hands, the playing pieces were right there in front of us, and we had to leave them behind. Hardly cause for celebration."

"No one got boiled up and devoured," I retorted. "If you ask me, that's a grand cause for celebration."

"Speaking of devouring things," I saw Diarfa's smile reappear in the rapidly thickening darkness, "I wonder what's left in these food bags we were so careful to bring away with us. Father?"

Orn sounded puzzled as he rooted around among the bags, operating out of necessity by touch and smell alone. "Well, back at the waystation before we started we ate the brandysnaps, the craneberries, the pot cheese, and most of the smearcase. A sort of snack for the road, don't you see. It looks to me as if we still have the bonnyclabber, the sunshine salad—although I can tell you right now that's going to go bad by sunrise—the Finnam haddie, and the squantersquash. I didn't let anyone touch the farl or the cathead biscuits, because they last forever. Oh! And I saved the medlarjelly to put on the smothered chicken. Except..." He scrabbled among the bags, now totally invisible on the bottom of the night-enshrouded raft. "I don't seem to be able to lay my hands on the bag with the chicken in it."

Diarfa's laugh was so full of bright light that I almost imagined I could see it spreading out from her mouth in a luminous cloud. "What I have in my hands is the bag that used to contain smothered chicken. But now, for some strange reason, it contains smothered kings, queens, holy men, mounted warriors, and foot soldiers."

Talin's cry of joy was almost as bright as her laugh. "You got them! You saved them!"

"Well." She seemed to shrug, although by this point even silhouettes were hard to see. "I thought the big lug guarding me was something of a milksop who only needed a little distraction to bemadden his senses, and I had the bag of chicken right there under my hand, so I emptied it over his head. So this fellow got chicken in his hair and calipash sauce in his eyes, and I also gave him a shove that sent him ass over teakettle–"

"No foul language out of you, my girl! Haven't I threatened to fine you any time I hear such billingsgate coming out of your mouth?"

"There are worse words than ass, Father. I also put one copper coin in the ginger jar on the bar in the Head every time I swear, but I also take a coin out every time I hear you swear, and last time I looked the jar was empty."

"Humph." Orn appeared to be moving his umbrella from side to side, as if to check how heavily it was still snowing.

"So here I am running right past that little table with the figurines on it, and I've got this empty sack in my hand, so..."

"You're a marvel! You're a goddess!" I thought I heard Talin move towards her, but it was now too dark to see anything. An awkward silence fell upon the raft, broken only the vigorous gurgle of the stream.

Finally Diarfa asked, "Can we take them out and look at them when we get more light? Tomorrow, when the sun rises? Is it safe to handle them?"

"Oh, yes. They don't have any power unless they're combined with the other components, the onyx pieces and the gameboard. That's why the Lady Marabar is so keen to get the whole game back in her hands. And even then, you have to know the right incantation, I think."

"In that case," I advised, "I think we could all benefit from a little rest. And sleep, if such a thing is possible after what we've just been through. Terhune, wake me after a couple of hours and I'll spell you on pushing that pole."

"Aye. There should be enough room for four of us to lie down as long as one of us is standing and steering, even though we're steeved in here like goats in a pen. And ever since I got a lungful of that goat stench back in the tent, I've been feeling more and more captric. It wouldn't surprise me if I woke up tomorrow and found myself turned into a goat." He gave a short bleating laugh and turned his back on us, and we fell onto the rough pine planks like drunkards.

I was on watch at the guide pole when the sun came up. During the night we had come a long way from the springs, it had stopped snowing, and the stream had widened into a full-fledged river, but the water was still hot enough to fill the air with smoky steam, turning the snowbanks on the shore into shimmering mirages. Here and there I saw clumps that had succumbed to the heat, melting and sliding partway down the banks, fat green candles left too long alight. We burn our candles at both ends, I thought, they shall not last the night.

Diarfa was sitting crosslegged in front of me, eating great double handfuls of the sliced fruit that made up most of the sunshine salad, scooping it straight out of the bag. Talin was sprawled out beside her, mummified in his cloak, his lips slightly parted, his eye jumping beneath its closed lid in some early morning dream. The fuzz on his head was continuing to grow out, its coppery gold so breathtaking in color that I could not decide what I would rather look at, him or the rising sun.

"Bring the playing pieces to my palace by the winter solstice," Marabar had told him, *"and I will love you as I love the sun."*

Ahead of us the river swooped in gentle curves, bending around dead trees and outcroppings of rock, stretching into the distance, a vast snake of steamy water and sinuous movement. I remembered Talin's description of the shape-shifting duel between Zayo and the genius in the inner courtyard at Hroom, and how he had spoken of the serpent's bright enamel skin and indented glide. Our raft was riding on the back of a hot-blooded reptile, slithering toward the sea.

Emptying the bag of sunshine salad, Diarfa licked her fingers and then mischievously trailed their spit-slick tips down the side of Talin's face, making him sputter and twitch as he fought his way up out of his dream. She laughed at him. "With deadly abundance of rich robes I caught him fast, as the poet says. How did you sleep?"

He made a show of disgust, but even with his nose wrinkled, his eye squinched shut, and his mouth in a grimace, his face was a work of art. "Terribly. These planks are rough and sticky, and the bark sticks to your skin. The whole raft needs to be sanded or something."

"If this were a real ship, manned by real sailors, they'd be all over it with holystone. It's a soft sandstone they use to scour wooden decks. Some say the name comes from the notion that it's made out of old tombstones."

Orn poked his head up out of a tangle of woolen garments; his flyaway hair and uncontrollable beard were pointing in all directions. "More likely, daughter, that when men use holystone to work on a deck they have to be on their knees, as in prayer. Pass me that food bag, that's a good girl."

"Sorry, Father, but I have a date with destiny. It's time to take a look at these playing pieces." With Talin watching intently, she drew open the mouth of the canvas sack and groped inside, examining each piece one at a time and then handing it to him. Thus the figures made their way around the circle of travelers until we had all examined them. All except for our slumbering giant Terhune, whose half-naked body was bellied up against one side of the raft like that long oval mound of unstratified glacial debris they call drumlin. Trust him to resemble something prehistoric when he slept.

Good omen or not, Diarfa managed to pull them out in the correct order in which they were supposed to be placed on the board, descending from most important to least powerful.

The King was a strong middle-aged man with a sturdy crown, long hair, bangs almost in his eyes, and a neatly trimmed beard. His carved robes were thick and rich and cascaded down over chain mail. He stood in a broad stance, his sword planted firmly before him with its point between his feet, its enormous length placing its hilt just under his chin.

His Queen was surprisingly much younger, very tall and very slender; under her lighter diadem, her hair ran around her head in tight braids and trailed down her back in a pigtail. She wore a classic but simple gown and an expression of beatific serenity.

The Bishops were toned-down versions of their sovereign, heavy in hair and beard, their robes accessorized not by chain mail but by crosses big enough to kill a bear in hand-to-hand combat. Although neither King nor Queen appeared to have feet beneath their long garments, the holy men showed glimpses of sandals. A nice touch of ecclesiastical modesty and piety.

The Knights were much smaller men, shrouded in chain mail and conical helmets, brandishing swords as they clung to the saddles of their rampant steeds. The horses seemed to take up an inordinate percentage of the size of each piece, rearing up and stabbing the air with their front hooves.

Next Diarfa passed along two Rooks, sometimes called Castles, tall and slender towers with crenelated battlements on top and slitlike windows on the sides.

Smallest and most expendable were the Pawns, the true worker bees of the army who got out into the fracas and did their job simply and well. Short and nondescript, they displayed helmets, chain mail, small shields, and even smaller swords. Ready to die for their superiors with not the slightest change of expression on their hard ivory faces.

When all the figures were back in the bag, Talin's eye glazed over, and he began to mutter. "That day I met the Lady Marabar in that upper room, she recited a quotation. What was it? Yes. 'We are but pieces in the game he plays, upon a chessboard of nights and days, hither and thither moves and checks and slays, and one by one back in the box he lays.' Now I know that these pieces are part of a game, but I'm beginning to wonder just how big this game is that we are playing."

Without using his hands, he rose smoothly to his feet in one strong motion and reached for the bag in which the figures now nestled. Diarfa backed away from him, almost falling over the whalelike lump of Terhune's still sleeping body.

"Talin, you're talking very strangely," she said. "Why don't you have some breakfast. Look how high the sun has gotten already."

We all glanced to our left, where the rising ball of fire was losing some of its redness and becoming brighter, more yellow, more powerful. It made me think of the bright power we might be carrying on this raft.

Then I was startled by a resonant pop, like the sound produced when a bottle of sparkling wine spits out its cork. I turned to speak to Talin and found myself staring at the empty spot where he had been standing.

Chapter 20
The Hungry Hag

"Wh— Wh—" Diarfa was bereft of normal speech, dropping the bag of figurines and spreading her hands out into the empty space our new friend had just been occupying. Orn started muttering into his beard.

Terhune gave a mighty wild boar snort, rolled over, and sat up, trailing loose clothing around him like an exiled king set adrift in foreign waters. "All right. What's the trouble?"

I had still not found my voice, so Diarfa blurted out in one breath, "We were looking at the playing pieces and then Talin just vanished, right off the raft!"

"Mmmm." Idlly he reached into the nearest food bag and started chewing on the first thing he retrieved, which happened to be a piece of farl. "No big surprise, really, as we've had magic involved in this business from the very beginning. Used by the players on both sides, as it appears."

"But was this thing triggered by our touching the pieces?" she wanted to know, darting her eyes at the dropped bag on the deck and then looking up at him again.

"Probably not directly, or every cannibal who fondled them would have ended up being transported bang into the parlor of the culprit responsible for the spell. I'd say it was more like an alarm to alert the spellcaster that they had been found. You know how you can pile up a stack of bottles in front of your door when you go to bed at night and you'll hear them fall over if anyone opens the door. Like that. Then you take whatever action you think appropriate. In this case, the spellcaster took what he thought was appropriate action."

"But we all touched them, not just Talin." Diarfa was bewildered. "Why take just him?"

"Because," I had finally gathered my thoughts together, "he's the official agent acting for the Lady Marabar. With him separated again from the pieces, there's no guarantee they'll ever make their way back to her."

"Unless we take them to her ourselves," she shot back defiantly, strength seeming to flow into her as she bent and scooped up the bag.

There was a long pause. "Yes," I said finally. "Unless we take them to her ourselves."

"What?" Orn was outraged. "What are you thinking, Catalan? Why should we finish up a business that's none of our business? As long as I've been your landlord at the Head, I've never known you to act so addled. Have you been drinking medicine or taking drugs from a spurious quacksalver?"

I stared ahead at the bright rushing water of our path into the future and did not answer.

"Leave him be." Terhune was rooting for more farl cake and talking with his mouth full. "The lad's been whisked off to an unknown fate beyond our imagining, what some call a wanweird when they don't know what else to call it, and we all need time to think. Our present speed and course will bring us to the inn called the Hungry Hag by early afternoon. A good opportunity for rest, hot food, and unhurried cogitation and planning."

"I've heard of that place." Diarfa licked her lips and then looked guilty. "Their specialty of the house is a confection of grated almonds, sugar, and egg whites, made into a paste and molded into different shapes. It's called marzipan."

"Sorry to contradict you, daughter, but I've been dining on that, in places fancier than the Hungry Hag, since before you were born. It's called marchpane."

"Marzipan."

"Marchpane."

"What sort of shapes?" I asked, to shut them up more than anything else.

"It used to be always animals, but I've heard that with the coming of the True Word some places are making lots of little figures of the Prophet, seated on a throne, complete with crown and scepter and that ghastly hangman's noose around his neck." Orn shuddered. "Who knows what we'll find at the Hag."

Diarfa asked, "Do you think we can pick up any clues about what might have happened to Talin?"

Her father eyed her sharply. "A moment ago you sounded a lot more interested in sweetmeats than in sweet love."

"I'm sorry. I'm hungry. Do I have to apologize for being hungry?"

Terhune came and took the guide pole from me, and I settled down beside him with Styx's head in my lap. "You've been to the Hag before," he stated, not a question.

"Many years ago."

"That's where they have that famous garden out back, where you wrote that poem everyone liked so much, about the lanterns hanging in the trees."

"Just a different rhyme scheme from what I usually use. And an experiment in repetition. It seemed fresh at the time."

"What garden is that?" Diarfa asked.

"The Garden of the Frenzied Contessas."

"My stars, what a mouthful. Will we get to meet the Contessas?"

Terhune spat tobacco juice over the side. "Everyone

who comes to the Hag meets the Contessas."

Like many people of literary bent, I tended to look at old houses as heads or skulls or helmets, but the Hungry Hag was merely a large rambling country structure of stone and brick, with many stories and many chimneys, continuing to draw trade because it was the only commercial establishment for a hundred miles.

And because of the Contessas, of course.

And because of its specialized clientele.

The freshly fallen snow around the scarred door was untouched, indicating that we were the first visitors of the day, even though it was well past lunchtime. It reminded me of the old murder puzzles, in which a body is found strangled to death on a beach with no footprints in the sand.

No one responded to our knock, so we pushed through into the entrance hall. "No door whore," muttered Terhune, causing Diarfa to look at him oddly.

Bird paintings jostled each other for space on the walls of the entrance hall. I recognized the purple-black majesty of a boat-tailed grackle; the sultry beauty of a brace of black-crowned nightherons; a tragopan, that Eastern pheasant with hornlike appendages and brilliant plumage; and the common turkeylike gamebird variously called woodcock, timberdoodle, bogsucker, or twister, depending on where you were.

Gamebird. The thought made my stomach rumble. As if on cue, Orn went scuttling across the floor and through an open door, saying, "This way, daughter. The time has come for fresh food."

I followed them into the large barroom I remembered from years earlier, a black box running the entire length of the building, featuring black lacquered floor and walls, a black ceiling of hammered tin, a long bar of solid ebony, and one wall made entirely of glass that I knew gave access to the fabled Garden. The only sources of light at the moment were the weak winter sunlight washing in through this wall and the fireplace opposite the bar, where a single log smoldered on a low four-legged set of iron fire-dogs.

Orn and Diarfa, wasting no time, were already belly-ing up to the bar across from a pale, greasy creature clad in black and sporting an excess of silver jewelry. His dark hair, lacquered to his skull, matched the decor of the room and shared its tendency to soak up all the available light.

"Greetings, friends," he hissed. "Think the rain will hurt the rhubarb?"

Diarfa raised her finely etched brows. "I beg your pardon?"

"Just an expression. Always pleased to have new guests here. My name is Maggot. I have a nickname that rhymes with it, but I don't use it in mixed company."

He grinned mirthlessly and showed a set of teeth slightly yellower than the set of ivory figures we had left behind on our raft. As I approached the bar and got a closer look at him, I noticed that his skin had a decayed, worm-eaten quality and that acne covered his face in the pattern known as coppernose. Named by name and not by nature was an old saying that did not seem to apply here.

"So! What can I offer you travelers?"

Father and daughter spoke at the same time.

"Marzipan," said Diarfa.

"Marchpane," said Orn.

They glared at each other like gamblers caught playing identical top cards in a game of cooncan.

Maggot made a dismissive gesture; his pale hands were sea slugs on the dark top of the bar. "Surely you'll want something wet first. I have a lovely liquor made from deer's blood and opium, if you plan on taking an afternoon nap. On the other hand, if you're thinking of partying straight on into the night, a snakebite black is always a good choice. Cider, lager, and black currant, with a little bit of sulfate mixed in to keep the metabolism revved up for a guaranteed minimum of twelve hours."

While my friends engaged in silent debate about their choice of beverage, I looked around and suddenly noticed that a knot of youths, old enough to shave but not old enough to drink, stood in the corner farthest from the glass wall. I thought of the lack of footprints out front and wondered where they had come from.

They were long and lanky and disturbingly attractive, holding poses that sang the body electric, expressing that insolent adolescent eroticism that no boy can carry into manhood. The physically exquisite, charmingly naughty puppy you feel compelled today to hold and to stroke and to kiss is doomed to turn tomorrow into a shambling, loutish lummox of a dog. So it would be with these boys. So it would be with Talin. Nature's first green is gold, and nothing gold can stay.

One was holding up a teddy bear and pretending to lick it in a very private place. Another loudly offered to kiss a companion in the same place. I believed him.

My eyes met Terhune's as he joined me, and I shrugged. "We've seen worse."

He grunted. "You've done worse."

I felt my face flush. I was glad that Talin was not there to hear.

"Why am I the only woman here?" Diarfa asked.

"Some men, daughter, prefer the company of other men."

"Or boys." Terhune carelessly avoided my gaze as he studied the gaggle of youths across the room.

"You are not the only woman here," Maggot assured her. "Now that you have arrived, there are six women. We have five regulars who are always here."

"I do not see them."

"Four of them are statues in the garden out back. The fifth is our proprietress, the Hag herself."

"I never heard that there was an actual person called the Hag," Terhune said softly in my ear.

"There wasn't, the last time I was here."

A green baize door beyond Maggot banged open, accompanied by a strangely familiar laugh that sounded like tearing leather. Into the narrow space behind the bar waddled a fat old woman with a bald head and bulging eyes. It was the Widow Quod.

"Ah, speak of the devil. Here's our proprietress now."

She reared back on her stumpy legs and rolled her eyes at us, leering slightly. The stains around the long curved crevice of her mouth gave her lumpy face crimson wings, showing that she had been munching on her favorite treat, raw tomatoes.

"Welcome, welcome. So nice to see new faces. You can't have too many strangers drop in, I always say." Her ancient voice came creaking and crackling out of that horror of a face, while the jiggling of her folds of flesh filled the air with her usual excess of white powder.

New faces? Strangers?

"Don't you know us, madam?" I asked formally.

"Don't believe I've had the pleasure of laying eyes on any of you before."

Something was very wrong here.

"We've just come over Hunchback Mountain from the village of Andor." Orn was tormenting his beard and studying every inch of her, noting the twisted hands clutching her long skirt, the fingers shaped like spatulas, the naked bumpy head like a small boulder. "You don't, by any chance, have any close relatives living in Andor? A sister? A cousin?"

"Oh, no. Everyone else in my family has been rotting in the ground for decades. Thin blood. I've been running the Hag alone for years. Now, whom do I have the pleasure of addressing?"

"My name is Catalan. These are my friends—"

"Catalan!" She stiffened, and her protuberant eyes bulged even farther than I would have thought possible. "Not the poet Catalan?"

I nodded.

"What an amazing coincidence. We got a new guest in this week, and all he can talk about is that poem you wrote out in our garden some time back, the one about the lanterns. He can't stop quoting it. He keeps jabbering about how he wanted to see the place and how could he find you and meet you and so forth. And here you are!" She laughed again.

"Really? My fans tend to pop up in the most extra-ordinary way, and seek me out with the most extraordinary motives. Where is this gentleman?"

"He's sitting out back in the Garden. I told him it was too cold, even though it is a sunny day, but he's from the southern shore of the Scorpion Sea and says for someone used to a hot climate the cool air is very refreshing. If you'd care to step this way—"

She flung open the baize door, gestured with one claw, and vanished. "How can she look and sound just like the Widow and yet not be the Widow?" Orn wondered.

I looked at my companions and shrugged. "Let's go."

The Garden was not really a garden, growing neither vegetables nor flowers as I recalled, but merely a walled grassy area where guests could retreat to sit on stone benches and contemplate life in serenity and silence. At the moment, of course, it was an expanse of unbroken snow ("Come into the park that is said to be dead," indeed), except for one trail of footprints leading off to a bench in a far corner, against the back wall separating the Garden from the forest that had grown right up to the Hungry Hag and threatened to engulf her. At the bench, a tall figure was standing with his back to us as he looked over the wall at the trees on the other side of it.

Diarfa spotted the Contessas at once and cried out in surprise. At the center point of each of the four walls enclosing the Garden, the glass wall of the barroom and the three others of stone, stood a remarkable sculpture of dark bronze. We walked over to the nearest one, which we probably could have seen from inside through the glass wall if we had looked.

She was a noblewoman of moderate height, dressed in fine clothes that would have been made of rich material if she were a real woman and not a statue. She had on a large hat that curved around her luxurious metal hair and partially shielded her face, and on her fingers were carved rings with huge stones. However, despite her apparent high station in life, she appeared to be in spiritual agony. Her handsome features were contorted in rage or despair, her entire body was writhing with some deep emotion, and her arms were raised, her hands clenched into fists as if to pound against the wall before her. A glance around the Garden confirmed my memory that the other three, although not identical, were similar in theme and appearance. Noblewomen tortured into a frenzy, driven to such desperation that they were prepared to beat against glass or stone rather than accept their fate. Whatever that was.

"I've never seen anything like it," Diarfa said.

"The sculptor always refused to explain the work," I told her. "The only thing he would reveal, after he had finished, was that this area would be called the Garden of the Frenzied Contessas. For years people have enjoyed coming here just to look and speculate about these women and what they are doing and thinking."

Movement caught my eye and made me look over at the corner bench, where the tall figure had suddenly turned to face us. He was bathed in the pale dandelion wine of the early afternoon sunshine, and even from this distance he looked familiar. I started heading toward him in great loping strides.

It was Talin, but again there was something terribly wrong here. In the few hours since his disappearance, he had somehow contrived to make himself beefier and thicker around the middle, and his face was heavier, coarser. He had lost the long clean lines of a predator, so that now he reminded me not so much of a proud eagle as a dumb ox. His one visible eye was flat and yellow, his hair had grown out even more, and his jaws were smeared with darker stubble than I remembered.

I stopped before him, almost unable to speak. "Talin," I finally gasped, "where have you been? What have they done to you?"

He answered in a deep, growling voice, not the voice I carried in my memory, and I heard the rough accent of the southern seacoast.

"Who the blazes are you, you arrogant figsucker?"

At the same time, I noticed that the flat yellow eye glaring at me was his right eye. He was wearing his patch on the wrong side.

CHAPTER 21
THE LANTERNS SWING IN FORESTS BLACK

The cloak this young man wore was more form-fitting than the one that had disappeared with Talin, emphasizing the change in body type. Although Talin's frame was muscular, it was toned and well-proportioned, the broad shoulders narrowing, suddenly and thrillingly, to a slender waist, whereas this fellow's bulging overmuscled body made him look blown up like a poisoned dog. I had heard that there were those who took drugs to achieve that effect. Warriors, bodyguards, assassins. I wondered which category included this stranger.

The others came rushing up around us, and I felt Styx lean against my leg. He knew that something was wrong and gave his ghost of a growl.

Wide-eyed, Diarfa looked as though she had seen a ghost herself. "What happened to you? You look..." Her sentence trailed off helplessly.

"Who are you people?" he retorted. The voice was definitely deeper, more bass than light baritone. "Can't a man stand outside enjoying the cool afternoon without a bunch of mad folk stampeding about him?"

"Talin?" The girl was almost crying, and rightly so. This was like finding a loved one who had been trampled by wild horses, his face and body destroyed, his right mind departed.

Orn, who was nobody's fool, laid a hand on her trembling body. "Daughter," he said with uncharacteristic gentleness, "this is not Talin."

"Well, who is he? Who are you?"

"My name is Agib," he shot back. "And you?"

"Diarfa. My father Orn. Our friends Terhune and—"

"I don't need a list of names for every lovestruck maiden and her aimcriers this side of the Scorpion. You can take your band of supporters, with and without fur, and march yourself back into the inn. Who told you I was out here, anyway?"

She was looking at him as if he had hit her in the face. "The woman who runs this place. She thought that you would want to see us."

"Oh, that blob-tale, that buzzing tattle-tale. She could talk the hooves off a sounder of swine, she could. You'd think, if she's trying to run a business, that she'd respect the privacy of her guests."

I decided that it was time for me to take over. "She says that you have been asking about me. I'm Catalan, the poet."

He started and had the grace to look ashamed for a second, until he got himself under control again. "Why didn't you say so?" he demanded truculently. "I've been trying to track you down over this poem you're supposed to have written here at the Hungry Hag, here in this garden. It's very important to that I'm in the right place, that you really did write it here. I don't want to find out that it's some silly legend, that I've wasted my time, that I'm in the wrong place."

He fixed on me a ferocious look, both hunting and haunting, one that would have awakened terror in a less seasoned man.

His manner did not make me inclined to help him, but of course I was curious. Here was a near dead ringer for our missing Talin, and like Talin he was seeking me out because of one of my poems. Coincidence was not the word for it.

"I did write a poem here in the Garden, some years ago. I gather that you've read it?"

He closed his eye and knitted his brows in concentration.

> "The lanterns swing in forests black.
> In pools of dark they do not sink
> But gleam on moss and rabbit track.
> The lanterns swing in forests black,
> Like buoyant beacons bobbing back
> And forth upon a sea of ink.
> The lanterns swing in forests black.
> In pools of dark they do not sink."

"Yes, that's the one all right. As you may know, they have a custom here on warm nights, when there are more guests out here in the Garden; they light paper lanterns and hang them from the branches of the trees on the other side of this wall. Sometimes they light up the whole forest that way. It can be quite striking."

His eye sprang open and blazed at me. "Then it's true? You did write that here in this spot?"

"Of course. Why is that so important to you? Exactly who are you?"

"I've been sent here. That poem came to me in a dream. It was supposed to be a clue in a game I'm playing, a sort of quest, for an old bird named Marabar. She wants me to get hold of some playing pieces for a war game. The black pieces, that is."

"Oh my god. Another one." Diarfa's voice was now tinged with horror.

"What did you expect?" Terhune spat tobacco juice. "You knew from the first boy's story that there are other agents."

"Yes, but... How many Talins are there? Are they all going to be coming after us?"

I cleared my throat. "After me. So far they've been coming after me. I feel involved, to say the least. I want to hear this one's story."

She was now bold enough to grab one of Agib's sleeves and start pulling him toward the inn. "Let's go. If it's anywhere near as long as Talin's story, I want to be sitting next to the fire."

We all moved together, in a ragged clot of cloaks, headed back for the relative comfort and warmth of the black barroom.

"I only took this quest for the money," Agib began.

PART IV

THE JAWS OF DARKNESS

CHAPTER 22
ALONE WITH HER IN A ROOM FULL OF OWLS

I took this quest because of the money.

I grew up in a small kingdom on the southern shore of the Scorpion Sea. They told me that my real parents were murdered right after I was born. I was raised by the king and queen, in a palace overlooking the water. They were petty, small-minded people, who gave me shit if I was wearing clothes that weren't clean. They complained if I wasn't wearing the right shoes when I appeared in public. As for me, I couldn't be bothered. Life's too short to look in the mirror. I'm glad they're dead.

They were drowned in a boating accident last spring. I felt free for the first time in my life. No one to criticize the way I looked. No one to tell me what to do.

I was free in another way. The crown went to a distant cousin. No surprise, really. I was not a blood relation and no one had ever promised me anything. I did not even feel that I belonged in the kingdom. I don't know where I come from–where I was born, I mean–but I stood out in the streets. My fair skin and fair hair were smothered by the dark skin and dark hair of my adopted countrymen. I was happy to get away.

I wanted to explore, to wander wherever my feet or my head or my heart took me. But I knew that it would not be inland, where the sand is reclaiming overworked croplands. That place is a desolate place, dry and treeless and barren, where every plant stings or sticks or stinks. My path lay out on the sea.

But it takes money to buy a boat. It takes money to hire a boat. I had very little money.

Then I heard that a stranger was in the city, a noble woman of wealth and power, they said. They said that she wanted to hire a man to be her champion, to do some great deed for her. They said that she could be found in the marketplace.

It was the first day of June, and it was hot and bright. They told me to look for the vendor selling pastries cut in the shape of that new Prophet. It was that religion, the True Word, that had filled our streets with their holy men begging for money. I thought that it was all harmless idiocy.

The vendor had set up his stand near the marketplace, in front of an old shuttered store that looked abandoned. He answered me by mumbling into his dirty beard and pointing at the doorway. I pushed through the curtain of wooden beads.

The front room was streaked with dusty sunlight that stole through the curtain and the shutters. There were shelves and small tables cluttered with trinkets. I saw owls of pewter and owls of clear glass. I saw owls of brass and owls of painted wood. I saw owls of stone and ceramic cups fashioned into owls.

Behind a table a tall woman in green waited. She looked old. Well, older than my foster mother had been. Her face was strong and sharp and pink. Her hair was long and gray and fastened up on top of her head. Her eyes were covered by little goggles in soft colors that ran together, pink and blue and gray. They made me think of pearls and the inside of seashells.

"I need a man," she said right away.

"I am a man, and a strong one." It was true. No one could call me weak or skinny. I had done what had to be done to make myself strong. I knew that, if something happened to my foster parents, all my other protectors would flee or die.

She looked around. "Do you like owls?"

"Not really."

"Nasty things. Have you ever seen one feed its young? Filthy, too. I cannot imagine why people think they are wise."

"Some people think they know everything."

"My Lord Tharados is one such. He's a difficult man. He hasn't been normal for years. His first Lady died in childbirth, and he never really recovered from the shock. He has never treated me with the respect that I deserve."

"What else can you say about him?"

"He is disturbed and desperate and dangerous. He is a quiet predator. He likes to hurt." I saw her lips tighten. "He has stolen from me a magical board game. He has broken it up into three parts, the white playing pieces, the black playing pieces, and the board itself. He has hidden each of these components in a different part of the world and challenged me to find them."

She made a strange motion with her hands, and in them appeared a small bag of soft leather. There were objects inside that had sharp edges poking against the thin sides of the bag.

"These are the fabulous Jewels of Opar. In any city on the face of the planet, they can be bartered for anything you desire. They are almost beyond price." Her voice grew thicker and deeper. "Find the black playing pieces. The ones made of onyx. Bring them to my palace on the island of Phuxor by the winter solstice, and I will double this payment."

I reached out my big hands and surrounded her hands and the bag. "Done. Done and doubledone."

She pulled back her hands and left the bag with me. "Good. Go to the inn called the Drunkard's Dream and take a room for the night. During the night a dream will come to you with the first clue about where you must go. All of your guiding clues will come in dreams. By morning, you will be joined by an assistant who will help you interpret the clues and carry out my quest. Go."

She swirled around and glided into the dusty shadows. And I was alone in the room full of owls.

CHAPTER 23
AT THE DRUNKARD'S DREAM

The Drunkard's Dream was a collapsed ruin of a building. It was gray and ugly and there was nothing dreamy about it. A minor thug named Fisk gave me a room and told me that I would have to pay extra if I stayed past noon the next day. I sneered at him and pocketed the key.

I woke up in my room with a very strange dream in my head. It was about a brass statue of a young boy sitting on a horse. He was holding two baby ducks and strangling them. I decided not to worry about it until I had talked with this assistant I had been promised.

It turned out that he came to my room with breakfast. He was a little brown man with long hair and a pointy nose. He only came up to my shoulder, and he talked funny.

"My name is Trance. A salubrious name, I hope you'll agree, as only in a trance will we divine the truth about our quest."

A little sentry cat was perched on his shoulder. It had the regular cocoa body and darker markings on the face, ears, paws, and tail, but it was only the size of a big rat. I stared at it.

"Ah. You've noticed my friend Smogley. She's small,

but wise beyond her fourteen years. Oh, you may suspect that she is a mere kitten because of her size, but if you were knowledgable about sentry cats you would know that they are born colored solid cocoa and then develop their markings as they grow. No, she's just the way nature intended her to be. A little drowsing cat is an image of perfect beatitude, as the poet says."

I shoveled heaps of scrambled eggs into my mouth. "I dreamed of a brass statue of a young horseman strangling baby ducks. What does it mean?"

"Oh, my, my, my. *That* brass statue. Well, we're going to need a boat. Let's go."

He wasted no time. We went out of the city plagued by robbery, forgery, blackmail, rebellion, illicit sex, murder, perversions, dirty politics, economics, and power. The city where I grew up.

By midmorning we stood before our very own two-man boat. As someone who had grown up pampered in a palace, I knew absolutely nothing about boats. I left it to my new assistant, the monkeyboy, as I had started to think of him.

It was a hot day, but the water looked cold. It was blue and green. There were white birds wheeling above and shitting down upon us. Trance said that he knew where we were going. Somehow I trusted him.

He turned his head and spoke to the cat Smogley there on his shoulder. "You remember the brass horseman, don't you, Smudgepot? The baby ducks?" Then he turned his head back again, so that his ear was up against her tiny chocolate velvet face. In a moment he said, "She remembers. She reminds me that it is atop the dreaded Bent Mountain. She is useful because she tells me things."

I had heard nothing. I stared at her brilliant eyes, part green, part gold, and they stared back at me. She worked her claws, opening and closing them where they sank into the shoulder of his multicolored doublet. She lashed her tail. I looked away before she did.

Trance scuttled up the gangplank. "We need to set sail this morning if we don't wish to estivate here in this harbor. I've seen to the supplies."

"What in the harbor?"

"It means to spend the summer somewhere. As any schoolboy could tell you in my day. I say, Smudgepot, what are they teaching in school these days?"

"I didn't go to school."

"Ah. Well, select a bed and stow your personal effects. We'll be sailing for at least twenty days and twenty nights."

"What? What will we do for such a long time?"

He smiled. "I'll talk to you."

CHAPTER 24
THE STRANGLER OF BABY DUCKS

The little shit would not shut up.

"The woman who hired you is the Lady Marabar, in case she forgot to mention it. Many people fear her magical powers and say that she is a witch. Interestingly enough, women used to tie holly branches onto the ends of their beds to stop themselves from becoming witches during the night. Sheer nonsense, of course. I've known her since before the Flame Wars."

The cat Smogley stayed clinging to his shoulder, blinking out at the cold rippling sea. From time to time he reached up and stroked her head.

"The smallest feline is a masterpiece. The cat is the only animal that accepts the comforts but rejects the bondage of domesticity. People sometimes butter a cat's paws because when she licks the butter off, she feels at home."

It turned out that his idea of food supplies was a bottomless provisions bag that kept filling itself with an endless amount of ham biscuits. He handed them to me as he talked. Sometimes he offered one to Smogley, commenting, "She's a hungry patchwork pussum, aren't you, Smudge-pot?"

He scanned the surface of the sea as we drove across it. "Too bad there are no sea turtles. We could catch one and eat it. You know, while nesting, the female turtle secretes a liquid from her eyes. Since they live in salt water, they must eliminate salt from their bodies all the time. What they cannot excrete by urine they eliminate through their tear ducts, which also keeps sand out of their eyes while they are nesting. And of course it has given rise to the popular story that they are crying from the effort of giving birth. I'm sure you've heard it."

"I have now." I chewed on another ham biscuit.

"Science is a fascinating thing. I once knew a doctor who prescribed a tonic of ground beef bones in wine. It was for some respiratory ailment. Not to be confused, of course, with theriac, a paste formerly used as an antidote to snake poison. Made from sixty or seventy different drugs pulverized and mixed with honey."

"Not to be confused, of course." He did not seem to notice my sarcasm.

"There was at one time a primitive people across the sea, who chewed on a hallucinogenic cactus they called the flesh of the gods, but missionaries came among them and banned its use, calling it the devil's root."

He delved into the bottomless bag and fed Smogley another ham biscuit. I noticed that he never ate one himself.

"The original ancestor of our modern sentry cats was once called an unnatural nightmare kind of cat. Harsh judgment, don't you think? As the old proverb says, those who dislike cats will be carried to the cemetery in the rain."

Smogley suddenly shook herself with a little sneeze.

"Another proverb says that a cat sneezing is a good omen for everyone who hears it."

I thought that I would rather hear his cat sneezing than listen to him much longer.

Finally we came within sight of a great cliff of black rock. "Is that the dreaded Bent Mountain?"

"I believe so."

"And why is it dreaded?"

"It is magnetic and holds the power to draw all things of iron to it. All the ship's nails will dart from her and cling to the cliff. We will be hurled into the mountain and shatter to pieces."

"What? Are you mad?"

He was very calm. "It must be done if we are to reach the brass statue of the duck strangler. It stands at the top of the mountain. Legend has it that so long as the strangler stays upon his horse, all ships that pass below shall be destroyed and all their sailors drowned. Until he has fallen from his horse, no mariner is safe."

I stared in shock. "What have you done to us?"

"Your dream tells me that your destiny is to topple the statue."

The current drove us swiftly along. All the nails flew out of the ship and dashed themselves against the cliff with a horrible noise. We were flung into the raging sea. I grasped a floating plank and was driven ashore by the wind. Trance soon joined me. Smogley still clung to him.

We were at the foot of a set of narrow steps carved into the mountain. "This is it," Trance told me. "It is your destiny."

I thought that he was mad, but there was no going back. We climbed the steps.

At the top was the brazen statue of my dream. The chubby boy sat astride his horse and squeezed the necks of the baby ducks in his fists. I stared.

Trance said, "Dig up the ground here. You will find a bow of brass and three arrows of lead, engraved with talismans. Shoot the arrows at the statue and the rider will fall into the sea."

"How do you know this?"

"Smogley has told me so. Then a boat will appear bearing a man made of brass. Whatever happens, do not speak to him. He will take us on the next stage of our journey."

The cat looked at me and did not contradict him. I clawed at the ground and pulled up the bow of brass and the arrows of lead, just as he had said. I shot the arrows into the sturdy body of the young rider. With the third shot he toppled from his horse and crashed down into the sea, taking his dying ducks with him.

As I looked down where he had fallen, I saw the boat coming with the man of brass. His metal skin gleamed in the sunlight. He gestured to us and we hurried down the cliff steps.

Chapter 25
A Horrific Holmgang

It was a small boat with no sail. We sat behind the brass man as he pushed off from the cliff and headed back out to sea. Silently, I watched the muscles in his metal back ripple as he rowed. He wore no clothes, and I could see no hair on his body, but on his head were metal ridges and bumps that looked like sculpted curls. His ears stuck out from the sides of his round head.

He would not look at us or talk to us as he rowed. After the excitement of our ship's blowing apart, the sea was perfectly calm again. I was getting hungry. The provisions bag was gone.

The brass man was a strong and tireless rower. In an hour we had left the black cliff of Bent Mountain far behind us. Soon a sandy island appeared before us. It was long and curving and filled with trees. I could see coconuts and smell fresh water.

"Fresh food and water!" I cried, my hand falling upon the smooth hard brass shoulder in front of me. "You've brought us to fresh food and water! Thank you!"

He whipped around, turning upon me an expressionless face with two uneven eyeholes and a jagged mouth cut into it. The metal mouth gaped, and I saw bristling fangs.

He dropped an oar and reached for me with a dark hand that had its fingers fused into a pincer-like claw.

In my ear, Trance said calmly, "I told you not to speak to him."

The metal hand hit the side of my head and knocked me sideways out of the boat, and I saw a painful brightness in the air that was suddenly swallowed by the darkness of the sea.

I came to lying on the hot sandy beach. Four eyes looked down upon me, two brown and two green.

"Our brass friend is gone," Trance said. "He was in our debt for what we did to the statue on the mountain, but only as long as silence was unbroken. Some people are funny that way."

I struggled to my elbows and looked around. Inland, I could see fruit trees and a little waterfall. "What is this place?"

"A lovely place, even though a bit arenaceous for my taste. I never could abide sand. Convenient, though, if you're going to fall out of a boat."

"You saved me? You got me up on shore? All by yourself?" He was little more than half my size.

"Well, Smogley here was a great help. Now, what I propose is that you rest while I scout the other end of the island for something more interesting than fruit. Islands have all kinds of things you can eat."

"Like what?" I asked cautiously.

"Boomslang. That's a poisonous tropical tree snake, but the poison dries up when you cook it. Giant bird-eating spiders. Screaming pheasants. Fire fox. There's a monkey-eating eagle that fries up quite nicely—"

I rolled over violently. "Stop right there. I'm sure there's plenty of fruit we can—"

Anchoring a few hundred yards down the shore was a magnificent ship. I could see men swinging down from its deck and landing knee-deep in the surf.

"Let's hide and watch," I said, uncoiling to my feet and loping toward the nearest trees. Trance scuttled along behind, the cat hanging on and uttering little yelps of displeasure.

From the trees, we spied on them as they unloaded a great store of provisions, everything from bread, flour, butter, and honey to freshly killed sheep.

"They appear to be staying for some period of time," murmured Trance. "I hope we won't be witness to a holmgang."

"A what?"

"Holmgang. A duel carried out on an island. To avoid disturbing the peace where they live, gentlemen frequently retire to some remote spot to fight their duels. Sometimes they spend the whole day there. When they do it on an island, it's a holmgang."

The sailors formed a line and carried the provisions up across the beach and into the trees, a good distance away from us. They were followed by more men with piles of beautiful garments. Then came men carrying fine furniture.

Finally from the ship came a decrepit old man, leading by the hand a boy about my age. He had a finely shaped head covered by a cap of black hair. He was the color of coffee with a lot of cream in it. He was smooth-skinned and wide-eyed and perfect. He was the best-looking boy I had ever seen.

"We need to follow them." I surprised myself with the strength of my feelings. Without even looking at Trance and his cat, I started to pick my way through the underbrush.

Soon through the trees I could see a rough rock face covered with moss. The men carrying the provisions and furniture were disappearing into it. I stopped dead in my tracks as I came out of the trees and watched the old man and the boy also go right up to the rock face and vanish.

"Ah. I know exactly where we are now." Trance appeared at my side. "That's a well-known cave in these parts. The Devil's Oven. People who have to keep something out of sight for a while like to use it. It's not a good permanent hiding place, you understand, because everyone knows about it. But for temporarily tucking a tidbit out of danger, there's nothing nicer."

Soon the sailors came back, empty-handed. One by one they went back down the beach and onto the ship. At last the old man tottered out and returned to the gangplank. The ship weighed anchor and sailed away. They had left the boy in the cave.

My assistant spoke. "Smogley and I will go scout the other side of the island for interesting things to eat. You make friends with this boy. You two appear to be of the same age, and we may need each other's help." Then he and the cat were gone into the trees.

I found a narrow opening in the mossy rock wall. Wedged in it was a solid mass of wood, probably a dining table. Because I had done what needed to be done to make myself strong, I was able to flex my muscles and pull the table away from the opening. It was dark inside.

I found a passageway and followed it into the rock. It took me to a large room richly furnished with carpets and tapestries and low tables. The boy was sitting on a pile of cushions, surrounded by flowers and bowls of fruit and candles.

He looked up and saw me and his large amber eyes grew even larger. He was startled and frightened and began to get to his feet, but I gestured to him to be still and he sank back down on the pile of cushions.

"I will not harm you," I told him. "I come as a friend."

"Greetings. I am Droo."

He was as I had seen him outside, glorious, clean-cut, clean-shaven, innocent, untouched, undamaged.

"I have been cast upon this island with no boat to carry me away again," I said. "Why have you been left here, walled into this cave as if buried alive?"

He motioned for me to sit beside him and offered me some fruit. "I am the only son of a wealthy jeweler on the island of Aidan. As he is the master of many argosies and caravans, he has always rejoiced that he had an heir to whom he could leave his fortune. Recently he had the notion of consulting the sages and wise men of Aidan to discover what lay in my future."

I bit into a peach. My eyes never left his face. "What did they say?"

"They studied the entrails of many animals, and they all said the same thing." He flushed slightly under his rich, coffee-colored skin. "They saw a vision of a young man, a boy. They said that he was..." Now he was blushing violently. "They said that he was a youth of blinding beauty named Droo." He smiled uncomfortably. "They meant me."

"They were right," I blurted out without thinking. I crammed more fruit into my mouth.

"They said that if the brass statue on top of Bent Mountain was ever toppled into the sea, then I would be killed on my eighteenth birthday, at the hand of a false prince named Agib."

I almost choked on the fruit. To hear my name in a prophecy about someone else, and to be painted as the murderer of such a boy as this! False prince I might be, as I was raised in a royal household but did not share their blood. Topple the brass statue into the sea I might have done. Agib might be my name. But I was certain the prophecy would not come true. Still, I remained silent about my name.

"Alarmed, as he knew my eighteenth birthday was approaching, my father made plans to hide me here in safety until the fatal day was past. As for myself, I have no fear, as this false Prince Agib is not likely to come here looking for me." He smiled again.

"Do not worry. I will stay here with you and protect you from all harm. The day will surely come when both of us will return home in safety. When is your birthday?"

"Tomorrow."

I took on the duties of his servant. As the day passed I lit more candles and burned incense in hanging braziers, and we ate and drank in tranquility. I was the one who prepared the food and set it before him.

We whiled away the hours with sport and merriment. He had a quick wit and an easy smile. I liked to make him laugh. I liked to look at him.

We had no timepiece and could not see the sun, but somehow it felt like evening when he declared that he wished to wash himself. I brought a basin filled with warm water from the low fire in the corner.

I held my breath as he disrobed. Because of his dark coloration, I had feared he might have a hairy body. To my pleasant surprise, his firm smooth chest was not blemished by a single hair.

I shook my head. Why did I care what he looked like? I held the basin while he dipped a cloth into the water and rubbed his face and chest. I could not stop looking at him.

When he was finished, I slipped out of my soiled cloak and rubbed myself all over with the wet cloth. I saw him watching me.

"I've never seen anyone with your coloration," he said. "It's quite striking. The golden hair, just barely touched with red. The ivory skin. No one in my country looks like you."

"No one looks like me in the city where I grew up. Maybe I'm a monster," I joked.

"The world does not produce monsters so fair to look upon," he murmured. I felt a strange quivering in the pit of my stomach. I put the bowl down.

"Do you like to wrestle?" I asked. Before he could answer, I sprang upon him and bore him to the ground.

Although he was smaller than I was, he was wiry and agile. I had trouble beating him. I decided to use a trick I frequently used on boys when I wrestled. It is cruel but effective. Most boys carry this secret weakness of which they are horribly ashamed. Using it to torture them was my hobby. It was my only chance of intimacy with other males.

I locked my legs around his. With one hand I held both his arms above his head. Then I used my other hand to tickle him, on his flat stomach, all along his sides, up under his arms.

He was so terribly ticklish that he could not take it. He twisted like an eel and nearly laughed his lungs out. His struggles excited me.

Suddenly, despite my greater strength, he surged up and threw me over so I was pinned on my back beneath him. Our faces were inches apart. His amber eyes swam into mine. We were perfectly still for a space of five heartbeats.

"Come here, my golden one," he whispered. Our heads came together and we rolled. His lips were soft against mine and his muscles were hard under my hands. It was more wonderful than words can express. It was something I had been waiting for my entire life.

The things that we did then were things that I had never done before, but I had thought about them a million times, as often as I had put food and drink into my body, as often as I had filled my lungs with air. They were new to us, but they were right for us. They were what our bodies had been made for.

It felt so good that I did not think I could stand it. I had to bite my lip to keep from screaming with ecstasy. In the end the pleasure was so intense that I passed out in his arms.

I think that it was morning when we woke up, entwined on the floor of the chamber. I looked down at our bodies, one dark and one light, nestled side by side. We looked like two opposing pieces of the board game that was the object on my quest.

"Do you think that it is day yet?" I muttered sleepily into his shoulder.

"Yes. I feel older. Today I am eighteen. Once this day

is past, it will be safe for me to come out of hiding and return to Aidan."

"Do you look forward to returning? Do you like your country?"

His face grew somber. "It is changing. The island has been invaded by dervishes, those wandering missionaries of that new religion. The True Word. They collect money and make speeches on the street corners. They have very narrow views of what is proper in life."

Lazily I poked a finger into the cleft in his chin. "What do you mean?" I had never paid attention to them and what they represented.

"They claim that they speak for their Prophet in telling people how to behave. They preach the strictest and most traditional moral standards. Too strict and too traditional, some say. For instance, they would condemn what we did last night. They say that such intimacies are unnatural and immoral and must not be permitted."

"A good thing we did not wait to ask their permission."

"What I find staggering is the arrogance of it, that someone could think he could tell two consenting adults what they should or should not do in the privacy of their boudoir."

"Some would say that we are not yet adults."

He shook his handsome head. "Your chronological age is merely a number. It doesn't necessarily mean anything. I knew what I was doing last night. Did you?"

I looked deep into his amber eyes and slowly nodded. "Yes," I whispered, "yes, I said yes then, I will say yes again, yes."

His bright smile was my reward. "Good. Now bring me a melon and some sugar, that I might eat and refresh myself."

I caressed his face and stood. I found a fine melon among those remaining in the piles of fruit. I picked up an open bottle of wine and drank long and deep from it. It made the room feel fuzzy. When I came back to him, he had draped his naked body along a low couch covered with bed clothes.

"I could not find a knife," I said.

"Look on that shelf above me. I think there is a knife up there."

I stood beside him on the couch and reached for the high shelf and found a monstrously large knife with a sharp blade. In stretching to grasp it, I lost my balance. My feet were entangled in the bed clothes. I fell right on top of Droo and the knife plunged into his chest.

The blade slipped into him as easily as into a wine-skin. It turned inside him as I fought to get off the couch. I pulled it out and a widening pool of blood started spreading down his bare torso.

His eyes and his mouth were wide open with shock. His voice sounded very far away as he said, "It is the prophecy. It is my birthday and I have been killed by another's hand. You never told me your name."

I watched his life drain out of him as dirty water empties from a bathtub when the plug is drawn. I could do nothing. Death came quickly.

I threw the knife aside and sank to my knees and stared at him.

I could not think.

I could not speak.

I could not cry.

Chapter 26
Greed and Grabbiness and Grandiosity

In an icy rage I wrecked the place. I tore down tapestries and broke candles and smashed plates. I hurled tables against the rocky inner wall of the chamber. I ripped open cushions and filled the incensed air with their feathers. Then I picked up the bottle of wine and went back down the narrow passageway to the entrance.

The bright sun struck me like a blow to the face. I left open the mouth of the cave, a gaping wound to match the gaping wound on the dead boy inside the Devil's Oven. As if he had been waiting for me, my monkeyboy Trance emerged from the trees with his cat still on his shoulder.

"Good day. What of the boy?"

"He cannot help us. He is gone."

"Ah. Well, I have news. Once you get away from this end of the island, the land rises gradually to crest as a volcanic cone, smaller than a mountain but larger than a molehill, as they say. Smogley tells me that this is the Jaws of Darkness, dangerous but dormant. A sleeping volcano, if you will."

"Does that mean we should get off the island as soon as possible?"

"On the contrary. There appears to be some kind of

structure on top. I think it must be connected with your quest. I think that we have been brought here for a purpose. Destiny, you know."

"What kind of structure?"

"Difficult to tell without climbing the Jaws. It blazes like a fire in the sun's rays. Perhaps we will find there the prize that you seek."

I was still angry. "What sort of clodpate would put a building on top of a volcano?"

"The ways of humans are sometimes baffling. Aren't they, Smudgepot?" He smiled sideways at his little cat, and in that moment he seemed to be in allegiance with the beasts rather than with the people of the world.

I wanted to get away from that accursed cave. "Very well. Lead on."

We were climbing a rocky slope. The trees had shriveled to stunted thorny growths and eventually disappeared. I stopped every hundred yards or so and swigged straight from the wine bottle. I was feeling warm and buzzy in the hot sun.

As usual, Trance passed the time by talking. He was an uncontrollable fountain of words.

"Interestingly enough, an ancient kingdom far to the south had a pantheon that included gods of silver, gold, and wood, and each was portrayed with a cat sitting on its shoulder. Watch out for that boulder. It looks unstable."

I guzzled wine and did not respond.

"As you can see, the soil is becoming drier and stonier and, even though we are climbing higher into thinner air, you can feel the heat increasing."

I did feel warmer and warmer, but the heat was coming from inside me as I worked my way through the bottle. I stared straight ahead and tried to ignore my companion's prattle.

"There. If you look where I am pointing, you can see the structure I mentioned."

I gazed dully upward and saw a blaze of light in the distance.

"I suppose it may be symbolic, placing a fiery house upon a little mountain of fire. The flaming giant inside this cone is sleeping, but occasionally we can catch a glimpse of him. Behold."

There appeared on our right a narrow crevasse that had smoke pouring out of it. From this point, the trail we had been following split into three steep and rocky paths snaking up the slope in different directions.

Trance reached up and stroked Smogley's head. "It's too bad little Smudgepot here isn't black. It was once thought that if a black cat was turned loose at a crossroads, she would lead you to buried treasure."

I drank the last of the wine and tossed the empty bottle into the smoking crevasse. "Damn you and your blasted cat lore and your blasted cat. Why are we doing this?"

He managed to look hurt and superior at the same time. "You agreed to take on the quest of the Lady Marabar. It is your own doing. Everything that has happened to us has been of your own doing."

I thought of the dead boy Droo, lying in his own blood back in the ruined cave. A powerful feeling surged through me, part drunkenness, part anger.

"No! Everything that has happened has been your fault! You have led me into danger and destruction and death! I don't need you!"

I reeled toward him and put both hands on his bony little chest and shoved him hard. He went flying backwards and teetered on the brink of the crevasse, an expression of infinite sadness on his face. At the same time, the earth rumbled and moved beneath our feet.

He fell into the crevasse and disappeared in the thick smoke. I heard Smogley give a despairing mewing cry. The earth rumbled again and the opening closed up into a solid sheet of rock. They were gone.

Dizzy and hot and blurry-eyed, I chose a path and continued to climb. I could not think of anything else to do. With the dead boy's wine thrumming in my head, I could not think at all.

I soon found myself at the top of the slope, on the edge of a smooth vast tabletop of rock. Before me was a lofty castle of red copper that gleamed in the sun. I could see hideous metal gargoyles crouching on the roof and clinging to the sides of the windows.

As I watched, a door three times my height swung open. Out came a tall gaunt older man with a craggy face, bushy eyebrows, and a thatch of dark, graying hair. He was followed by ten youths. They were all tall, well-built, and handsome, and they all had shaved heads. I recognized them as dervishes.

Their leader saw me and approached without surprise. "Praise the True Word," he croaked.

I knew enough to repeat, "Praise the True Word."

"And the Snowman who brings it," he continued.

"And the Snowman who brings it."

He made the gesture I recognized as the Sign of the Gallows. In a daze, I imitated it.

The young dervishes swarmed around me and chattered in a friendly fashion. I wondered what unnatural godspell had placed them here on top of a volcano, far from any people they could hope to convert.

"I am Rorecros," said the older man. "Come inside and make yourself comfortable as our honored guest."

They led me through the big door and through an endless number of large empty rooms, while I gave them a wine-soaked and rambling version of my story. I did not mention Trance or the boy Droo.

We came at last into a central hall, furnished with ten small yellow couches in a circle around a bigger yellow sofa where Rorecros immediately sat. The dervishes took their places on their couches and indicated that I should sit on the carpet.

"You are welcome to stay here and rest," their leader told me, "but you must ask no questions about anything you see."

He left the hall and came back with a platter of hot meat and a golden goblet. I stuck my nose inside the goblet and found a golden liquid with a delicious smell of oranges. I ignored the meat and greedily drank down the drink. It smarted on my tongue and burned my throat and stomach. I felt my giddiness increasing.

"You have come at a special time," said Rorecros. "Once every month, we conduct a retreat on the other side of the Jaws of Darkness. We must do penance for our past sins. You will excuse us as we prepare."

He went to a closet and brought out eleven basins covered with yellow lids. He and the youths uncovered the basins. I saw that they were filled with soot and ashes and powdered charcoal. Pulling up their sleeves, they all blackened their faces and heads, smeared their robes, and beat their breasts, crying, "This is the fruit of our greed and grabbiness and grandiosity."

I was seeing this through an orange haze, and my tongue was heavy in my mouth. "What do you do?"

They looked at me with reproach. "We must go," they said in unison. "Beware of temptation." They rose and filed toward the door of the hall.

Rorecros tarried to speak with me. "Ask no more questions. I may tell you only that we must stay here in this desolate place, as guardians of this castle, because each of us has failed the test you are about to undergo."

"Test?" My brain was clouded and I was having trouble sitting up straight.

He produced a ring of keys from inside his soot-smeared robe. "This is the treasure house of the True Word. The money collected by our brother dervishes is sent to the Snowman, but all other objects of worth are collected here for the future glory of the Prophet. While we are gone on our retreat, you are free to use these keys to explore all the chambers of the castle. But do not enter the Yellow Door. That is forbidden. If you ignore this warning, as we ignored it in the past, you will forfeit all peace and happiness, as we have."

Again he reached inside his robe and drew out a stone flagon. "This will keep you refreshed while we are gone." He pushed it into my hands and strode to the door, where the last of the ten youths was just going out. I was left alone with the bottle and the keys.

I sipped from the bottle and found that it contained the wonderful orange drink. I looked at the ring of keys. I left the hall and came upon a row of large doors. The first key I tried opened the first door.

I stepped into a high-ceilinged chamber with pictures of birds on the walls. I saw pie-billed grebes and laughing loons and green herons. The room was paved with colored marble inlaid with gold and silver and decked with precious stones. From the ceiling hung cages made of sandalwood and aloe, in which turtle doves sat and sang. I drank from the bottle and listened to the birdsong.

I tried the next door. I found a court planted with roses, jessamine, daffodils, hyacinths, and anemones. Squatting among the flowers were large stone dogs, black and gray, with flat squashed faces and curling ears. I drank from the bottle and smelled the perfume of the flowers.

I tried the next door. I found an orchard watered by crystal brooks. Apples, plums, and quinces hung in clusters from the boughs and the air was filled with the twitter of birds. I drank from the bottle and smelled the fruit.

I tried the next door. I found a vault stacked with pearls and rubies, sapphires and emeralds. I drank from the bottle and ran my hands through the piles of gemstones.

"I am the richest man of all my time," I thought. "What other forms of wealth lie in these chambers?"

I staggered out into the hallway and hammered down another mouthful of the orange drink. I squinted through eyes that now felt blood-red. The row of doors stretched before me. At the end, in the shimmering distance, gleamed a huge sun-yellow portal.

"The Yellow Door," I muttered. "I am forbidden to enter the Yellow Door." I reeled down the corridor, pulled by the sight of that glowing panel. It was like a hook in my mouth, tearing and tugging me to it. I stood before it and drank from the bottle.

"Who are they to tell me what I can and cannot do?" I said aloud. "If this is a treasure house, perhaps the treasure I seek in my quest is inside here. If not, perhaps a treasure grander than I can imagine. And I deserve it. I deserve such a reward for the trials I have gone through."

I drained the last of the orange drink and threw the bottle aside. I fumbled with the keys. I found one that fit the Yellow Door. I opened it

Out came a thick aroma, like snow and vanilla and moonshine. It was so strong that I fell swooning across the threshold. I shook my head and looked around me.

I was in a large vaulted chamber, lit by tapers, scented with aloe and ambergris and musk. Great braziers stood on all sides, burning incense and honeyed wood. Among them, before a manger of clearest crystal filled with sifted sesame, stood a magnificent horse, black as midnight.

It was the handsomest and best-shaped animal I had ever seen. It was richly bridled, and its saddle was of red gold. The long stiff hairs of its tail were woven into an array of hard blades. Folded over its sleek shoulders was a pair of great dark wings.

"This is mine," I thought. "This is my prize. This is my way off this awful island."

I led the horse out of the chamber and down the long corridor. We passed through the central hall and the empty rooms beyond it and came to the tall outer door. We stopped on the flat tabletop of rock in front of the castle.

The earth grumbled and shifted beneath us, as if angry with my actions. I stumbled and put a hand on the horse's back to steady myself.

The beast looked at me with great dark eyes. I climbed into the red gold saddle. The large wings spread out on either side of me. They flapped in long strong strokes, and we rose into the air.

As we went up, a terrible rumbling filled my ears. I looked down and saw the rock splitting open. Dark smoke began pouring out. The Jaws of Darkness were opening.

The horse beat its wings more rapidly and we coursed up and away from the moving mountaintop. Looking back, I saw the copper castle crumpling in upon itself, and then everything below us was hidden in smoke.

We soared out over the sea. Our speed increased. I felt dizzy and closed my eyes and clung to the horse's thick neck. I lost all sense of time.

Finally I felt us going down again. I opened my eyes and saw that we were above a rocky coastline. A group of dervishes stood watching us approach. Not the young dervishes from the Jaws of Darkness. Older dervishes.

The horse drifted slowly down to a landing on the rocks near them. It gave a violent shake that threw me from its back. As I lay sprawled on the ground, it lashed my face with its coarse tail and struck out my left eye.

Half blind and fully drunk, I writhed and moaned on the rocks. The horse rose into the air again and flew away. The dervishes came around me.

They were led by a figure in a dark hooded cloak. I stared up through my one undamaged eye and thought that I saw many fiery eyes floating in the darkness within the hood. I could not speak.

They took me to their temple and shaved my head and made me one of them. I was too sick to protest. For weeks I lay in bed and thought about my fate. It appeared to be my destiny to make mistakes. Little mistakes. Big mistakes. I had been told so all my life.

And now, as I lie awake at night, the voices of my foster parents stab my brain.

"Your hair looks a mess. Come here and I'll brush

it."

"There's stubble on your cheek. Didn't you shave today?"

"That doublet is soiled."

"There's a hole in your breeches."

"Why are you wearing those shoes? There are better ones in your closet."

"Why do you insist on trying to think for yourself? You are in this world to live up to our expectations."

Shitty people smearing me in their own shit.

I'm glad they're dead.

PART V

THE SMILE OF SNOW MELTING

CHAPTER 27
THE MOST MARVELOUS TRICK IN THE WORLD

We stared at each other across a large round table littered with the ruins of breakfast. We were in a private dining room where paintings of birds made splashes of crimson, brown, and gray on the walls. Red-shouldered hawks, sand-hill cranes, cedar waxwings.

Yesterday we had come in from the Garden of the Frenzied Contessas and heard Agib's story. He had talked through the afternoon, and the unappetizing Maggot had brought hot meat pies and cold ale. Then he had reeled upstairs to the room he had taken, and we had agreed to take rooms of our own.

Now we were alone and able to discuss him. Terhune chewed on his tobacco and ruminated. "Does anything about what we have seen and heard strike you as interesting or odd?"

I chuckled. "Aside from the fact that Talin and Agib appear to be twin brothers who don't seem to be aware of each other's existence, no. Aside from the fact that both of them have been enlisted as champions in this game between the Lady Marabar and her Lord Tharados, no. Aside from the fact that each of them has been given what sounds like an identical sidekick, whose primary purpose seems to be luring his young charge into an ugly and destructive situation, no."

Diarfa leaned forward, her brows knitting earnestly. "Yes, what about those helpers, Prance and Trance? If Talin and Agib are twins, what about them?"

Terhune took out an ivory toothpick and worked it between his front teeth. "Even twins have certain physical differences, as we have seen. From what we've heard about these so-called assistants, they sound perfectly identical. They talk just alike too. I have my suspicions as to their true nature, but it's still too early to make a guess about them. I want more information."

The door sprang open and Agib exploded into the room. "I've had my third dream," he blurted out.

"Your third dream?" Orn asked.

"Yes. The first one, the one about the statue of the duck strangler, took me in the right direction away from my home. After I lost my eye and was made a dervish, I had the second dream about your poem, about the lanterns in the trees. That brought me here to the Hungry Hag. Now I've had my third dream. It will take me to the prize I seek."

"Tell us about it," I said.

He pulled up a chair and sat down. "A magician was squatting under the open sky. A rope came snaking up out of a basket in front of him and went straight up. There was a small boy there. The magician used blows and threats and forced the boy to climb the rope, up, up, until he was lost from sight."

A shiver crept over me. I recognized this story.

"The magician called to the boy to come down. He refused. Muttering curses and brandishing a cutlass, the magician climbed up after the boy and vanished from sight."

"The most marvelous trick in the world," I murmured.

He looked at me. "What did you say?"

"Nothing. Go on."

"Blood-curdling screams came raining down from above. A boy's arm fell to the ground. Another arm. A leg. Then the boy's head. The magician's assistants gathered up the pieces and put them in the basket."

Diarfa was staring with her mouth open.

"The magician came down the rope, gore dripping from the cutlass. He snapped his fingers and the rope fell to the ground. He went to the bloody basket and reached inside and pulled out a hand. Attached to the hand was an arm. Attached to the arm was the boy, smiling, alive, and well."

Agib leaned back in his chair and looked at us. "So what does it mean?"

"It is the Marvelous Rope Trick," I said. "A traveler named Ibn Batula wrote an account of it six centuries ago. He saw it done on an indoor stage in a sultan's palace. Scholars believe that there had been a hidden overhead platform to which an assistant tied the rope after it had been pulled up by a black thread against a black backdrop. Pieces of clothing, stuffed with straw and soaked in animal blood, were stored there ready to be tossed down at the proper moment. The boy crept back on stage in the darkness and climbed into the basket to wait for the magician to come down the rope and take him out."

Agib frowned. "But..."

"It's supposed to be done under an open sky with no props. No one has ever been able to do it. Until now."

Diarfa said, "What do you mean, until now?"

"Several miles southeast of here, in a valley called the Madman's Head, they celebrate the winter solstice with an outdoor festival called the Dark Carnival. There are games and diversions and entertainments. I have heard that this year a magician will attempt to perform the Rope Trick out of doors."

Agib rapped the table. "That's it! That's where the dream is telling me to go."

Orn pulled on his beard. "Um. What else do you

know of this festival?"

"The centerpiece is the largest weeping willow in the world. I wrote a poem about it—"

"Yah," Terhune drawled, "is there any notable site in the world that you haven't written a poem about?"

"It's used in a showpiece by a performer who calls himself Professor Salt—"

"Professor?" interrupted Orn.

"An old-fashioned title they used to use for those who ran these traveling freak shows and carnivals and whatnot. His trick is to somehow coat the whole willow in ice and then slowly make it melt, forming fantastic shapes, until the tree is revealed again. He calls it the 'Smile of Snow Melting.'"

Terhune was skeptical. "People pay to see this?"

"Oh, people are always fascinated by the slow destruction of something beautiful."

Agib stood. "Very well. I'll go to this Dark Carnival. Thanks for the information."

I eyed him thoughtfully. "It's safer to travel in a group. We'll come with you."

"To what purpose?" Orn sputtered.

"Agib's quest is a part of Talin's quest. If we pursue his part of it, we may find Talin again."

Terhune spat tobacco juice. "You're besotted. You're deciding with your dick."

Orn made one of his exploding noises deep in his beard. "That's right, Terhune. Don't bother to apologize for your crudeness."

"I never apologize for my crudeness."

I cleared my throat. "The heart has its reasons which reason knows nothing of."

Diarfa said, "I go where Catalan goes."

Orn begrudgingly added, "I go where my daughter goes."

"All right, damn and blast you all." Terhune surged to his feet. "Let's settle the bill. These games and diversions and entertainments had better be pretty diverting and enter-taining."

CHAPTER 28
THE DARK CARNIVAL IN THE MADMAN'S HEAD

"So you think this brother of mine might be down there?" Agib asked.

We were coming down into the valley known as the Madman's Head. It was a bright day, and the sun burnished the snow-green slopes and the trunks of leafless trees. Here and there short bushy evergreens huddled together, like squat old men in bulky overcoats.

"Maybe yes, maybe no. You now know as much as we do." On the journey south we had told him everything. He had seemed especially interested in the notion of having a living family member.

Also on the journey south, we had all but exhausted our food bags, even though at the Hungry Hag the resourceful Maggot had insisted on loading us down with stacks of squid sandwiches. A particularly loathsome combination of bread and sea creature, with suckered tentacles hanging down the sides, impossible to eat without painting your face with ink. It had been a long journey.

As we came down through the trees, I caught a glimpse of the sea of people already filling the valley. "My stars, look at the crowds."

"Aye," agreed Terhune, and it's still a few days left

until your deadline of the solstice."

"My deadline? Whatever happened to 'one for all and all for one' and all that?"

"I think it fell by the wayside when you started deciding with your—"

"All right, all right, I know what I'm deciding with. Just shut up and follow me."

Soon we were passing among food stalls where a multitude of hearty delights could be purchased. Charred beef on a stick seemed very popular. Folk also could be seen carrying lightweight dishes of custard, smothered with some kind of dead or comatose multijointed creatures. Large insects or small shellfish, I did not know and could not guess.

Soon more stalls gave us the opportunity to purchase books, bookmarks, hats, knives, pendants, and ornately carved walking sticks. I was more interested, however, in an organized event that was going on directly ahead of us, in a small amphitheater carved out of the hillside.

It was an instrumental concert of a very old piece. The audience was, for the most part, young, well-scrubbed and enraptured; as I stood watching, though, within the space of two minutes I saw a bottle and a firecracker thrown into the air. Studying the crowd more carefully, from my vantage point above and behind them, I noted that they had brought with them wine, beer, shotweed, cheese, oranges, balloons, sparklers, fireworks, and other toys, and that many of them were in costumes of some kind. They were all wearing angular party hats made out of orange paper.

"He makes sweet music with the enamell'd stones, giving a gentle kiss to every sedge he overtaketh in his pilgrimage," a deep grave voice intoned in my ear. I turned and saw a wasted vampire of a man, with deep-sunk eyes and lips pursed as if he had just sipped an unexpectedly too-dry wine.

"The name is Falcone." He was wearing a tornado-colored jacket and one of the orange paper party hats. He surveyed the concert below us.

"It's interesting. This lot thinks that they are rebelling, on the cutting edge by being here at this performance. They think they invented the word rebellion. When this obscure piece was first performed at a country house party one hundred years ago, a critic called it 'a crass monster, a hideously writhing wounded dragon that refuses to expire and, though bleeding in the finale, furiously beats about with its tail erect.'"

I looked at him. "Indeed." I glanced back at the rest of my party, hovering uncertainly behind me.

"Oh, yes. I come every year because they fascinate me. Pimping, whoring, begging, lying, poisoning, stargazing, free-thinking. I like to think of the festival as an exotic bird of brilliant plumage, the individual celebrants its separate feathers; in the morning it rustles to life and, as the sun's rays warm it, soon rises screaming into the swirling air of the valley."

"Indeed," I repeated politely. "Where do they all stay? Where do they sleep if they stay for more than one day?"

"Oh, they all stay for the whole festival. Let's see. The one inn on the edge of the valley, over there," he gestured with his chin, "is the Vile Aroma. Its accommodations, as you might guess, are somewhat limited. They fill up pretty fast. The nearest villages would be Deep Storking in that direction," another chin jerk, "and Toddler Stout," yet another point of the compass indicated by a twist of his head.

"So where do most of them stay?"

"If you were to head due east of here, you would soon run into a small army of tents. Not terribly warm at this time of year, but cheap and portable and capable of letting you bed down close enough to the Carnival to hear the vile squeaking of the wry-neck'd fife. As the poet says." He smiled without mirth, and folded himself into the milling crowd as the concert came to an end.

Trailed by my companions, I circulated among the celebrants. I saw a youth emptying a battered tin coffeepot into a friend's battered tin cup while chanting, "More coffee in cup, more body in grave." His friend was combing his hair with a fork.

I heard a theatrical troupe discussing their dress rehearsal for a nude scene. The play was *The Virgin of Menace.*

I saw an old woman selling a waxy concoction proclaimed by a sign as *Aunt Tabitha's Amazing Coconut Glass Doorknobs.*

I saw two ancient black men sitting in ragged wool caps, planted like darkening mushrooms, playing chess with old wooden playing pieces. Not remotely what we were looking for. One of the black bishops was missing, so they were using a peppershaker in its place.

I heard fragments of conversation. "We're being driven by hunger, and he's got a big whip."

"What's your name?" "Miles." "Where you from?" "Oh, nowhere you'd've heard of." "Oh, you're Miles from nowhere, eh?"

"May a duck kick you."

"Over there in the woods, at the base of the large old oak tree, there's an open drug market."

"He'll tell you stories that will make your arms fall off!"

"We'll feed you chicken livers and bury you in the dirt." "I'd rather have you feed me dirt and bury me in chicken livers."

Finally an awe-inspiring sunset sprawled its magenta and pink the length of the forested western horizon. "Let's check out this Vile Aroma," said Terhune.

"You heard what our erstwhile friend Falcone said. They'll be full."

"Oh, you know how persuasive I can be." Suddenly he had his sword out and was fondling the blade. I laughed and we headed back up the slope toward the edge of the Madman's Head.

Chapter 29
The Slow Destruction of Something Beautiful

The next morning we were back on the festival grounds, well-slept and well-fed.

"The Vile Aroma was better than I thought it would be," commented Diarfa, looking at the hurly-burly starting up again around us.

A pack of youngsters came pounding past us. "Don't roast!" one shouted exuberantly. "Paint them chimneys!" cried another.

"You'd think they'd get more business if they changed their name," Orn said.

Terhune had bought a jar of tobacco from a stall and was filling one of his ancient pipes. "You know as well as I do that you get the name when you inherit or purchase the establishment, and it's bad luck to change it." He tilted the jar to get at its redolent black-and-almond contents; I watched shreds of the tobacco slither slowly downward to follow the jar's sideways tilt, like moist earth crumbling from the edge into a newly dug grave. I shivered.

"What's happening this morning?" Diarfa asked. "There seems to be a more diverse crowd than we saw yesterday."

She eyed a nearby mother who was crooning to her

small child, "I'm going to draw him a poppy. Draw him a floppy big poppy to copy."

"I don't know," I answered, "but something's up. Look at that line over there at that breakfast stall."

"The morning hours have gold in their mouth, to quote the old proverb." The deep grave voice was familiar, and I was not surprised to turn and see the cadaverous Falcone. He looked as if he had not slept.

"Good day. Do you know what's happening this morning?"

He turned his dark eyes on the bustling crowd. "Professor Salt is giving a special preview of his tree trick. The event proper will be on the solstice, of course."

Terhune struck a light and began to puff away on his pipe. "I still find it hard to believe that people come to see ice melting on a big tree, much less pay for it."

Falcone regarded him for a moment. "Every common bush afire with God, but only he who sees takes off his shoes. As the poet says. You may have heard the story of this Prophet of the so-called True Word. Right before they hanged him he said, 'I set myself on fire, and people come to watch me burn.' He was speaking metaphorically, of course."

A young man wandered by, muttering to himself. His eyes and hair had a mad air about them, and he flicked his tongue out as he walked.

Falcone shook his head. "Sin is sweet in the mouth and bitter in the belly. If some of these young folk don't stop experimenting with these hallucinogenic drugs, their brains will turn into dead bats hanging from the inside of their skulls."

"Well, that's a cheery thought," was Orn's rejoinder. "Where is this Professor going to be doing his demonstration?"

"Down there at the end of the valley. Just beyond the amphitheater, the land flattens out and there's a big open space. That's where the tree is."

"I remember," I said. "I was here some years ago for the Carnival. I don't recall it being quite so big or so busy, though."

"Clutch your memory about you like a scarf," Falcone intoned. "Make your thoughts a flight of starlings." He whipped around and disappeared into the growing crowd.

"What a strange man." Diarfa looked after him. "Well, shall we go look at this big tree?"

The weeping willow was jaw-droppingly, ineffably huge. It filled the clearing and the sky, its long ropy leafy branches springing outwards in graceful arcs, making spider-scrawls against the bright blue of the morning. The celebrants jostled and elbowed each other in their eagerness to see.

Professor Salt had a short barrel-shaped body, very long arms, and a dour drooping hound dog's face topped by a mop of mineral-gray hair. He made a gesture in the air and said something that sounded like "Saka shemok'heba." Instantly the entire tree was encased in a gleaming coating of ice, clear enough to still reveal the fresh green leaves, heavy enough to bend the branches downwards and change the tree's shape. The crowd gasped.

The Professor turned and eyed the audience, as if trying to assess their reaction. He smiled and turned back to the ice-imprisoned willow. He made another gesture and cried out, "Baha mokshe-casa!"

Before my eyes, the icy tree began to melt and run and blur itself into a series of fantastic shapes. It presented a series of visions that could only come from my nightmares. I saw daggers and fog and masks. I saw a fleet of black frigates on fire. I saw mighty warlords twisting in agony on the torture rack. I saw the deadly insects known as bee-wolf wasps. I saw a horse the color of the sun, stumbling and falling with a broken leg. I saw steeples swimming in amethyst and dissolving into stone powder. Finally the mighty tree collapsed in upon itself in a gossip of flames and the icy coating was gone.

I blinked and shook my head. Suddenly Agib was at my side. "So what did you see?" I asked. I knew that everyone sees something different.

He grinned ruefully. "Sorry, but I wasn't here for the show. I found something more interesting over there." He tilted his head toward the far side of the clearing.

"And what might that be?"

"Mud wrestling. There's a shallow mud pit over there. The contestants strip down to next to nothing and go at it. No holds barred. I like wrestling."

"Yes, I remember from your story. But I would advise you not to try your tickling trick here. The wrestlers at the Carnival take their sport very seriously."

"Of course. There's a bout scheduled for a half an hour from now. I'm going to try it."

Professor Salt was now addressing the crowd. "Blasted be every herb and fruit and tree; curst be the rain that falls upon the earth and may the general curse reach man and beast. Oh, give me dagger, fire, or water!"

I looked around and met the eyes of Terhune. "Spectacle and razzle-dazzle," he said. "It doesn't mean anything."

"Murmuring streams, soft shades, and springing flowers, lutes, laurels, seas of milk, and ships of amber," the Professor continued. Then he gave a grand flourish and disappeared behind the weeping willow's low-hanging branches. The show was over.

Agib had also vanished, no doubt gone to prepare for the wrestling bout. I gathered Orn, Diarfa, and Terhune about me. "Let's have an early lunch. I have a fancy for some of that meat on a stick. And, to tell the truth, I don't know where to go from here. Let's let fate surprise us."

We were finishing our meal when Agib reappeared. He was stripped down to a skimpy loincloth and was smeared with mud. I still thought that his body was overdeveloped and excessively muscular, but I could not help admiring his powerful chest and his strongly knotted legs.

He grinned in triumph. "I won," he said. "I thought

I might. I'm strong enough to pull trees out of the ground."

Before I could answer, my attention was caught by a disturbingly familiar figure on the edge of the crowd. It was the hooded mystery man with multiple glowing eyes that I had seen while taking the wounded Talin to the Floating Head.

"Agib. Look there. Is that the man you described in your story, the one who took charge of you when the flying horse struck out your eye?"

He looked across the clearing and frowned. "Yes. I had a bad feeling about him at the time."

"I think you should know that he was also present when I rescued your brother and took him to the inn where I live. And according to your brother's story, he was on hand in Hroom just before he was sacrificed to the owls."

Agib scowled, and his mouth twisted into an ugly scar. "He needs to be captured and questioned. Now." He sprang towards the enemy, his thick leg muscles bulging as one large foot after the other hit the ground, his thick biceps flexing as if the mystery man were already within the grasp of his strong hands.

I saw the hooded figure gesticulate in the air, and a very strange thing started to happen. In mid-stride, as Agib's foot came down on the ground, it begin to stiffen and a crunching sound came up from his toes. He started to slow down and glanced at that foot as he continued to surge onward.

The entire foot was stiffening up and he seemed unable to wiggle his toes. An odd discoloration had begun at his toenails and was spreading rapidly up the toes to the rest of the foot. The foot appeared to be turning to bronze, impossible as that seemed. He stopped moving entirely and tried to flex the whole foot, but it had become extremely hard and solid. He could not move any of the muscles in his foot. It had been bronzed.

He goggled in astonishment at his intended victim, who stood about a dozen feet away with his arms crossed.

Now Agib looked down again as the same thing began to happen to his left foot. Within seconds, he was rooted to the spot and the stiffening had spread up over both ankles into his shins. He tried to lift his right leg but his foot, besides being frozen solid, was now so heavy that he could not take it off the ground. His leg muscles bulged and flexed impotently as they tried, but failed, to do their work.

As the hardness reached his knees, he broadened his huge chest to fill his lungs with air and shouted out, "No! No! It cannot be! What are you doing to me?" He was helplessly floundering, swinging his big arms back and forth, as he tried to find the strength to break free.

Inexorably, unstoppably, like the relentless movement of lava, the stiffness spread up into his upper legs, freezing the rippling muscles there into hard bronze waves and ridges. As the bronze touched his loincloth, it too turned to metal.

"No, no, make it stop," he cried, the words springing from his grimacing lips before he could even think about them. I imagined his manhood coiling into a snail of bronze, frozen and trapped within the metal loincloth.

Now that he had broken and given in to a moment of panic, Agib seemed to lose all control. I watched the hardness moving up his torso on all sides, petrifying the cobblestones of muscle on his abdomen, stiffening his back and ribs. Desperately he raised his arms and tried to reach the hooded figure with a series of violent punches, but his intended victim was out of reach, and Agib was helpless to take another step. Even as he continued to throw the pointless punches, the tips of his fingers started to harden. He tried to uncurl his fingers and found that his hands had been bronzed into eternal angry fists.

Meanwhile his impressive, highly muscled chest, expanding and contracting like a bellows as he gasped and grunted, was made bronze. He was well on his way to becoming a classical statue.

Now the bronzing effect was creeping down along

his biceps and triceps, preserving them in all their hard muscular glory as they flexed, and, having overtaken his wrists, it
was also flowing up his lower arms. He froze solid in the
midst of throwing one last, impotent punch.

With increasing speed, the bronze started up his
thick bull-like neck, and he crumbled into uncontrolled
panic. "No, not my face! I couldn't stand it–I–no!" He
whipped his head from side to side, eyes bulging in fear,
mouth open in a grimace of discomfort. "Stop it, you bastard!" he screamed, his voice suddenly high-pitched and
adolescent. "Damn you, damn you–oh, no, noooo!"

As the mask of bronze closed relentlessly over his
distorted face, he only had time for one last cry: "Oooohhh,
shi-i-i-i-t, I'm t-u-u-u-rni-i-i-ng to metal!" There was a
final crackling and stiffening, and the petrifaction was complete. The finished statue wobbled and settled into place.

I stared with open mouth and disbelieving eyes. The
hooded figure walked up to his masterpiece and strolled
around it, like a curious visitor at a museum. He gave a con-
temptuous shove that tipped the statue over; it fell backwards and rocked back and forth on the ground, the frozen
punching arm seeming to strike a blow at the sky.

The hooded figure spread his arms like a pair of
wings. He turned his hooded face in my direction, and then
he came for me.

CHAPTER 30
IT'S RAINING MEN

Sometimes the best thing to do is cut and run.

"This way!" I shouted, wheeling and bolting for the trees at the edge of the clearing. My companions pounded behind me, while Styx flew out in front as a streak of brown.

Suddenly our way was barred by a tight fist of costumed celebrants, wearing large realistic animal masks that covered their entire heads. I smashed past a cat, elbowed aside a stork, and almost knocked down a badger, and then I was into the trees.

Nearby a long shed showed me a windowless wall and an open door. I threw a glance over my shoulder and saw that the animal-headed celebrants, now being invaded by my friends, blocked me from the view of our enemy I darted through the door into semidarkness.

Straw crackled beneath my boots as I groped for the inside wall and gazed around me. There seemed to be nothing else on the floor of the shed, but when I looked up I thought I could make out strange shapes hovering in the air above my head. I waved my arms slowly but found only cobwebs.

The sunlight from the door was blotted out as several people came in behind me; muttering and the heavy smell of garlic and tobacco announced my companions. Someone closed the door quietly, and a match blazed in Terhune's hand. "Relighting my pipe," he rumbled.

The dancing match threw goblin shadows all around the enclosed space, just as the torches had done in the tunnel under the Floating Head during our escape through the Widow Toad's house. It was one of those long wooden pipe matches favored by Terhune, which gave me time to study our surroundings before it went out.

The looming shapes above us were gigantic figures of wicker, suspended from the ceiling or impaled on poles that rose from the floor. In the flickering gloom, I made out warriors, snakes, bulls, temple dogs, and dragons.

"There's to be a parade," I mused aloud.

"Aye, but how soon?" was Terhune's rejoinder. "We don't want to be discovered here if yon behooded bastard is lurking outside." He blew a musky cloud of smoke my way.

Orn ground his teeth. "Base dunghill villain. I had no cause to love this strange new boy, but to watch him changed to that..." Words failed him.

At that moment, someone came running past the shed and pounded on the door in passing, perhaps in youthful enthusiasm. Startled, I recoiled and went crashing backwards into one of the poles supporting the monstrous figures above us. Losing my balance, I fell against it and felt it bend and then snap beneath my weight.

As I tumbled onto my back in the straw, I found myself staring straight up into the leering mouth of a wicker dragon, complete with horns. Its many short legs seemed to claw the dimly lit air as the front half of its long body, no longer supported by the broken pole, bent down toward me. I could almost imagine the lifeless jaws slavering to close over my head.

And then those jaws began to spit out small dark objects that rained down upon my face, hitting hard and bouncing onto the straw. I was being peppered with small dark bits of rock, carved like men. It was raining small dark men.

"Catalan!" The triumphant cry came from Diarfa, who had rushed forward to pick up several of them and hold them to the sputtering matchflame. "Do you know what you've done?"

"Let me guess." The cascade of playing pieces dried up, and the wicker dragon completed its mocking bow to me, bouncing slightly in the air with its grinning jaws inches from my mouth. I rolled over and stood up.

I took one of the pieces from Diarfa and fingered it. "Onyx, I have no doubt. Terhune, we need more light." He promptly lit a fresh match.

Orn was pulling on his beard. "Of all the unbaked and doughy drones who have been in my life," he laughed, "you are the luckiest. You wander into this shed, you stumble against a pole, and what gets dumped into your lap?"

"It was my face, not my lap. All right, who's carrying the ivory pieces?"

Diarfa lifted the leather pouch at her side. "I took them from the raft when we left it at the Hungry Hag."

"Let's see one of them."

She fished out the tall slender Queen, with her light diadem, braids, and face of serene beauty. I found the corresponding onyx piece and cradled them side by side in one palm, noting without surprise that they matched in style, craftsmanship, and size.

"Gather them up and put them in your pouch with the others. After seeing that statue business out there, I've had enough of man-made images of man." I went to the door and put my ear against it, straining to catch any sound from outside.

Terhune came to join me, wearing his cloud of pipe smoke like a halo. "Do you reckon the boy will still be lying there? Or will they cart him away?"

"It depends on how long we have to stay here in

hiding. Best to lie low for a while and give our friend in the hood a chance to lose interest and wander off. We may be all right as long as we stay out of his way. But I would like to see the Rope Trick before we move on to the coast."

Orn's voice was almost a screech. "Are you still planning on pursuing that path of madness, after the display of dangerous magic we just witnessed?"

"We now have two people to find and rescue, Talin and his twin brother, and the only way I know to do that is to finish their part of the quest for them. So we go to the Lady Marabar's palace on her island. After the Rope Trick."

When I felt safe enough to leave the shed, the sun had passed the point of mid-afternoon. Across the lower half of the sky stretched a livid yellow band, like the trail of slime left by a slug crawling across a blue china plate. Out of it came the distant bell-like pealing of honking geese.

Two young lovers, masked as songbirds and cloaked in bright feathers, strolled past us. They were having a friendly disagreement.

"But he already has the Smile of Snow Melting," she was insisting. "Why does he need another big trick?"

"Because, my dear," he reached up under the beak of her mask to stroke her bare throat, "the Professor is a showman reduced to performing at one big carnival a year. If he can pull off the Rope Trick, he can double his income."

"I don't like it that he's going to do it right before sunset. The light won't be very good, and it'll be easier for him to trick us."

"Professor Salt has real magic, my love. He doesn't need to trick us."

They disappeared through the trees, headed in the direction of the weeping willow's clearing. I looked at Terhune. "There you have it. Perfect timing. We can watch the trick, satisfy our curiosity, get back to the Vile Aroma, hire horses, and get out of here under cover of darkness, as the sun will be down by then. Easy as cake."

"Satisfy your curiosity, not mine. I didn't need to see the great tree iced up and thawed out, and I don't need to see people climbing a rope and chopping each other up hundreds of feet above the ground. We could catch wild monkeys and get them to do the same thing."

Diarfa strode toward the clearing, throwing her voice over her shoulder. "Any more of your conversation would damage my brain. Let's go, Terhune. Where's your sense of wonder?"

"I left it back with the cannibals," he grunted.

We chewed warm spinach pastries and watched the western trees reach up to claw at the reddened sun. The crowd was even bigger than it had been for the Smile of Snow Melting. As we had suspected, there was no sign of the Agib statue.

A space had been left between the ragged edge of the crowd and the magnificently spreading willow. Professor Salt was standing there, his long arms hanging empty at the sides of his barrel-shaped body, his melancholy dogface turned to the mackerel sky. He wore a somewhat theatrical magician's robe covered with moons and stars. At his feet was a large, deep basket.

Sitting, he crossed his legs and raised his hands over the basket and intoned, "Ahora uhuru." There followed a rush of syllables so blurred and slurred that I could not catch their substance. Just as Agib had described from his dream, a rope came snaking sinuously out of the basket and swam straight up into the sky, climbing slowly but steadily until it disappeared into the gray clouds.

The Professor stood and turned calmly to his left, where assistants garbed in scarlet and orange were pushing forward a short handsome boy about fourteen years old. His loose vest hung open, revealing goosebumps forming on his bare chest. He appeared to be terrified. I had to remind myself that this must be a well-rehearsed act.

The magician spoke to the boy in a low voice and gestured to the rope, which now made a straight dark line from the basket to the lid of clouds pressing down upon the clearing. The boy stared and shook his head. Professor Salt spoke a bit more roughly and struck him about his ears.

Dipping his head in resignation, the boy leaped up, seized the rope, and began to climb. It easily held his weight, remaining taut as he inched higher and higher. Within a few minutes he was lost from sight in the clouds.

The crowd chattered and buzzed. The sun continued to sink into the trees, and the air grew cloud-gray. Finally the Professor looked up and cried, "Time to come down!" He made a show of cocking his head to listen for the boy's reply.

A thin, weak voice trickled down from the unseen climber. "I won't. I'm staying here."

The Professor swore a mild oath and reached into his spangled robe, taking out a cutlass which he brandished for the crowd's entertainment. Then, using only one hand to hold onto the rope, he slowly climbed up after his young assistant and eventually disappeared himself.

We waited and watched. A burly man nearby said to his friends, "I've heard about this trick. I know what comes next. This is the good part."

Horrible screams ripped the darkening air. Out of the clouds fell an object that hit the ground next to the basket, bounced, and settled to rest not far from the edge of the crowd. It was an arm, cut off at the shoulder and drenched in bright blood.

Little shrieks sprang up here and there, but the people mostly stared with their mouths open. There followed another arm and then a leg, both appendages cleanly severed and dripping with gore. They lay glistening and bloody like dying fish thrown on a bank by a hasty predator.

The magician's other assistants flashed into action, fighting fish falling upon disabled opponents; they snatched up the body parts and stuffed them into the basket. No sooner had they finished than a round object plummeted into their midst, bounced higher than the appendages had, and was batted into the basket. It could only have been the boy's head.

A few more body parts came down, although I did not get a good look at them because impatient members of the crowd were jostling to view the carnage more closely. It was raining pieces of boy.

Now the magician descended, holding the cutlass away from his bestarred robe to avoid staining it with the blood crawling on its blade. He reached solid ground and snapped his fingers, and instantly the rope went limp and fell coiling into the bloodstained basket. Radiating smugness and condescension, he sauntered over to the basket and reached inside, pulling out one of the arms.

In Agib's dream, following the pattern described in all accounts of this trick, the arm had been attached to a whole and complete boy, grinning and alive, who came out of the basket to accept the applause of the audience. What we saw that day before the great weeping willow was somewhat different.

The arm came easily, much too easily, out of the basket, and still ended in a dripping, freshly sliced knot of bone and gristle. There was no boy attached.

Professor Salt gave a cry of surprise and shock. He dropped the arm and leaned over the basket, plunging both hands inside. A moment later he reeled back, his mouth working soundlessly, and struck himself on the right cheek. His hand came away leaving a blotch of blood like an irregular birthmark.

"Ladies and..." he attempted hoarsely. He staggered and turned away from the basket. "Ladies and gentlemen, I regret... I regret..."

My stomach turned over. The crowd around me swayed and stomped and seethed. Shouts ranged from "Murderer!" to "Give us our money back!" I looked for my companions.

Over by one of the food stalls lurked our friend the hooded man. As I watched he was bent double, seemingly convulsed with silent laughter. I felt anger heating up inside me as I contemplated this creature. Maker of mischief. Master of motiveless malignity. A walking tumor.

I pulled my companions to me. "We go to the Vile Aroma. Now. We will hire horses and leave this place as soon as humanly possible."

Stuck on top of one of the slopes of the Madman's Head, cantilevered out over the valley like a ship run aground, the Vile Aroma was a long one-story green-painted building with a deep covered porch extending all the way around it. Its color made me think of someone gorging himself on pickles and then puking into a patch of poison ivy. Perhaps it was the name of the inn.

Having come up the hill from the Dark Carnival almost at a dead run, we erupted through the door into the dingy front parlor and headed for the corridor leading to our rooms. Terhune was grim, Diarfa grave, Orn bemused.

Terhune stopped short as we reached the door to the room he and I were sharing. He stepped aside and gestured, showing me that it was standing ajar. We had definitely left it closed that morning.

I gestured back to him and indicated that he should investigate. He drew his sword and eased the door open wider with its blade, giving him room to stick his grizzled head inside. He became very still.

"What is it?" I whispered.

He pulled back into the hall and turned to me an expression I could not read entirely, although amusement bubbled close to the surface.

"Not twins," he said. "Triplets."

CHAPTER 31
WEEPING WILLOW AT DAWN

Followed by Styx, the four of us came inside and filled the room, looking at the visitor. The candles in the light fixture had been lit, so that it was easy to see him. His long, elegant frame, in the expected dervish cloak, was sprawled in a chair by the window. While Agib had been a beefier version of Talin, this boy was delicate and fine-boned, more so than Talin, with even higher cheekbones and no visible muscles. His head was still closely shaved, revealing no fuzz to indicate that he was trying to grow his hair out. Instead of an eyepatch, he had covered both eyes with a pair of smoked spectacles.

Yet his face was Talin's.

We also looked at his companion. He was a huge sentry cat, somewhat larger than regulation size, with long fluffy hair marked with brown and gray stripes. The normal markings of a sentry cat—the darker fur on the face, feet, and tail—were absent.

Styx sat and watched him. He watched back with large chartreuse eyes set in a tiger face; I noted the pink nose, freckled snout, white chin, and glorious whiskers spreading into a bandit's mustache. A ruff of fur stood out around his neck, and his plumed tail waved behind him like a banner.

"Friends," said the boy, "for friends I hope we can be, I took the liberty of waiting in your room. I could not hope to find you among the crowds down at the Carnival, and I very much wanted to catch you while you were still here."

His voice was higher than I expected, not the vibrant baritone of Talin and certainly not the bass growl of Agib, but that of a true tenor. He shifted in his seat, and I noticed that he was holding the end of a leash attached to a leather harness encircling his cat's chest and shoulders. I had never seen a harness on a sentry cat before.

"When I asked for Catalan at the front desk, the man told me where to find this room. He even let me inside. I suppose that I have an honest face. Or maybe it was the way Oatmeal hissed at him." He grinned and scratched the cat between his ears.

"I am Catalan. Why were you asking for me?"

He opened his mouth to answer but was cut off by Terhune. "No, no, don't tell us. I'm keen to guess. Let me see. You're questing for part of an old war game. It's for a fine Lady, who sounds old enough to know better than to get mixed up in such charades. You had a dream about one of Catalan's poems and felt the urge to come here looking for the spot where he wrote it. How's that for fortune telling?"

The boy seemed stunned. "Well...Yes, everything you say is true. It's that game called chess. I'm pledged to find the board for this particular set that's being sought by certain interested parties. Although recently I've been wondering if it's worth the trouble I've been through."

He reached up to adjust the smoked spectacles, and I found myself wishing that I could see his eyes. Or what might be left of them.

"Modesty almost forbids me from asking," I said, "but which poem of mine was in your dream?"

"I saw it written on an old stone wall outside a

farmhouse, complete with title and signature. That's how I knew the name of the author. It was called 'Weeping Willow at Dawn.' I remember–"

"Damn and blast!" exploded Terhune, turning away and stomping into a corner. "It's that tree again! Are we never to escape from it? When we finally get killed at the end of this idiotic business, are they going to chop it down and build our coffins out of it?"

"Forgive my friend," I said with a smile. "He has a volatile personality, and we've had a somewhat trying day. Tell me. I don't doubt your word, but how much of the poem can you remember?"

He stroked the big cat's head while gathering his thoughts. Then he spoke.

> "The sun withholds its molten light
> Until the work is done.
> The Artist turns his wooden egg
> To meet the rising sun.
> The swarming mass of painted snakes
> Defies its binding shell;
> Medusa woman, born of ink,
> Leans out to greet her solar hell.
> Once fully drenched with liquid fire,
> The eggshell cannot hold its shape.
> The night hag melts to ropes of leaves;
> Our eyes complete the rape.
> Our daylight vision, sane and clear,
> For phantoms has no room.
> The witch egg, hatched by morning flame,
> Now crumbles to its doom.
> The Artist scatters painted shards
> With opalescent gloves,
> Then leaves his palette to a world
> Of spiderwebs and doves."

"Perfect," I declared. "Word perfect. I gather that, by

talking to people and asking questions, you figured out that I was describing that great weeping willow down in the Madman's Head."

He nodded. "That brought me here. I think that it was my fate to find you. But something tells me that the playing board is not actually here. I've been waiting for another dream to guide me to the end of my search. Any suggestions?"

My companions and I looked at each other. "Well," I said slowly, "let's just say that I have a rather interesting story to tell you. But I think that we should talk on the road. We're leaving for the coast, as soon as they can make the horses ready for us. How fast can you travel?"

He laughed. "Oh, I get around pretty well for someone who's blind. Mr. Oatboy here has turned out to be the world's finest seeing eye cat." He stood up and gave the leash a shake, and Oatmeal moved obediently toward the door.

We let him precede us into the hall and followed in single file. Terhune, who had remained silent since the recitation of my poem, took me by the arm. "Who's Medusa?"

"A woman with snakes for hair. She was one of the Gorgons."

He eyed me glumly, waiting for me to finish the joke. "What's a Gorgon, then?"

"A woman with snakes for—"

"All right, all right. Let's go."

Night's black agents were all around us, and the Vile Aroma a mere memory, when the boy spoke again. He had to raise his voice to make himself heard over the clatter of the horses' hooves as we cantered down the high road in the direction of the Scorpion Sea, the two cats loping along beside us.

"I know you said that you had a story to tell me. But I have a story too. The story of how I came to take this quest and what happened to me on my journey. I want to tell my story first. No one else has heard it."

"Fine. We have miles to go before we make camp, and a good story always helps to pass the time. I confess, though, that I'm anxious to get your reaction to my story. There are people in it you are going to want to meet."

"If we can find them again," grunted Terhune.

The boy chose to ignore his comment. "I'm not so sure about that. Wanting to meet new people, I mean. There were times during my journey when I was ready to give up on the whole human race."

"Tell us."

He ran a hand over the smooth dome of his head and adjusted his smoked spectacles again. I could barely see him in the darkness.

"My name is Bama," he began. "Although no demon barber, no great spiller of blood, I loved to hear my foster father planning to kill someone."

PART VI

THE SMILE OF A TREACHEROUS WOMAN

CHAPTER 32
WATERFALL OF BLOOD

Although no demon barber, no great spiller of blood, I loved to hear my foster father planning to kill someone.

My best childhood memories are of lying on the couch in my room, a porch open on three sides to a mild rainy day, while in the next chamber his voice, warm as wheat toast, talked of beheading or hanging.

He was the Royal Executioner, and I loved to see him in public, wearing his ornamental coat with its buttons as big as cookies, his fair wavy hair and fat cheeks making him look like the anthropomorphic winds seen blowing their mouths into Os in the corners of old maps.

And so with the wind's sudden swiftness was he plucked from me at the end of last summer, falsely accused of allowing a prisoner to escape, as if any amount of money could subvert him from his duty. The King, forbidding and hard-edged, signed his death warrant with one hand while still clutching with the other his breakfast fork, and I, not allowed to watch the execution (I could have judged the skill of his successor, I thought), was bustled so unceremoniously from the palace that the doors almost closed their jaws upon my coattails.

I was lucky to have both coat and boots, as my

adopted country was a low and rainy one, and the streets of my adopted city were streaming with water and mud. Perhaps she was weeping in sorrow and rage, to lose an inhabitant of such intelligence. I pushed on.

A chance remark overheard in the front parlor of the Cape and Cudgel led me to the back room, where a woman was hiring men to do some lifting and carrying for her.

The fire fell on a tall, razor-edged woman of indeterminate age, forbidding as my ex-King, hard as marble, her body hidden by a rain-bedaubed cloak, her eyes hidden by lenses that changed colors in the flickering light, her hair hidden by a monstrous hat like a ruined birdhouse.

"I need a man," she said, as dramatic as a badly-acted queen in a street play.

"I am a seventeen-year-old boy and have no home. What do you need lifted and carried?"

I couldn't see her eyes, but given the way her mouth grimaced I expected to see her head rotate completely around on its neck, like that of an owl. She was angry.

"Hold your tongue," she blazed.

"Your obedient servant." I stuck out my tongue and carefully grasped it between finger and thumb, waggling my eyebrows at her as if to seek approbation.

She chose to ignore my sauciness. "You will be going on a quest. One of some importance to me, and one that will bring great rewards." She looked around the room, as if trying to ferret out anyone who might be eavesdropping, and her eyes fell on the two candles burning on the mantelpiece.

"Anything to get me out of here. This city of water has kept me too long."

She snuffed out the candles and then snuffed herself from a box she took from her cloak pocket. I could actually see her assuming the role of hostess as she stood there before the fire, holding the snuffbox out to me. I shook my head. "Any wine?" I asked.

"No sparkling wine, I'm afraid," she sniffed, striding

to the sideboard. She moved like a man. "Only port."

"Ah, port. What they drink on the left side of the boat." I grinned at her and watched the color darken in her hatchet face. It appeared that I could not amuse her.

She splashed ruby liquid into a chipped teacup and thrust it into my hand. "I am the Lady Marabar. Our opponent is the Lord Tharados. He and I are engaged in a quarrel that goes back for some time, but that's past history—"

"That's all water over the stitch in time," I interrupted, taking a swig of the port and winking at her over the brim of the cup.

She scowled. "He has taken from me certain artifacts and hidden them in various places, challenging me to find them again. He has graciously agreed to provide clues to any champions I enlist to help me in the quest."

"Some people use birds to predict the future by having their entrails torn out and examined. Omen pigeons, I believe they are called."

"Not birds. Dreams. If you accept, you will take a room here at this inn and spend the night, during which the first dream will come to you with a clue to point you in the right direction. Tomorrow morning you will set off, with an assistant to help and guide you. Well? Is it yes or no?"

I drained the teacup and rolled it between my palms, while rolling her proposition between my ears. The prospect sounded entertaining, and I had very little money. "What's the artifact I'm looking for?"

"A large playing board for the old war game called chess. It is constructed of alternating inlaid squares of mvuli wood and stained sandalwood."

A silk purse appeared in her hand, a fat purse presumably filled with gold, one that seemed to wriggle in the firelight like a piglet trying to escape being turned into bacon. I took it from her and found it gratifyingly heavy.

"Bring the board to my palace on the island of Phuxor by the winter solstice, and your future will be more special than you can imagine." She indicated the door with a fingernail not quite as long and curved as a scythe, and under the gaze of her shimmering lenses I went out to look for the landlord.

At daybreak the next morning, as the rain beat against the window of my room at the Cape and Cudgel, I found myself writhing in the bed, twisting the mildewed sheet around me, while I twisted myself around the vivid dream I had just experienced.

I was standing on the bank of a foaming, busy stream that rushed past me on my right, while before me a small cloud of birds hovered above the water, what kind I could not tell, a parliament of owls, an exaltation of larks, a spring of teal, or a wisp of snipe. With a low thunder of their wings, they darted upstream, and as my eyes followed them I saw it.

From an upper terrace of rock, plunging down in an explosion of mist to feed the stream beside me, spilled a broad waterfall. And, although the images at the edges of the dream picture were a dull gray, this curtain of water was a bright crimson. It was as if someone had slit the throats of an entire lodge of otters and dumped the bleeding bodies into the stream above, to slash across my field of vision like a cascade of blood.

I threw off the knotted sheet and sat up, coming face to face with a stranger who was standing right next to the bed, holding a covered tray.

"Your breakfast, my friend."

Even though I was sitting and he was standing, our faces were on the same level. He was a little brown man in a motley suit, with eyes as hard and bright as those of a toy monkey. He had a long thin nose that twisted one way and a long thin chin that twisted the other way, giving him the look of a hairy corkscrew.

Before I could speak, he lowered the tray to my lap and stepped back. "Eat up and we can be on our way. This is an unfortunate room, rather shabbily maintained. There are balls of dust under the bed. Ghost turds, some call them. My name, by the way, is Glance."

I peered dubiously at the dried eggs under the cover. "It was the best room they could give me at short notice."

"Yes, a bird in the hand is worth a squeeze in any old port where there's an ill wind that comes in on little cat feet." He shot me a shrewd, piercing look. "So what was in the dream?"

"You don't waste time, do you? Here, put this on the table. I'm getting dressed. We can talk on the way out."

By the time I had gotten my cloak and boots on and preceded him to the stairs, I had told him about the waterfall with its aspect of blood. He nodded and struck himself in the chest, making the tiny bells sewn onto his fool's motley gently tinkle.

"I know it. Agony Falls, they call it. If we are to get there, all we need do is intercept the stream, Agony Brook that is, and follow it in the direction of the sea. It will lead us straight to the falls."

We came down to the front door and emerged into the wet street, where two robust horses were tied to a hitching post. Glance looked back at the inn.

"Whoever built this place was careful in its design, placing the door so that it faces south. In many climes, they try to have gates and as many windows as possible point in that direction because south is the home of the vermilion bird of summer, the source of fire and life."

"How nice for them. And are we headed south?"

"No, we're going north, the direction of the tortoise and the snake."

We untied the horses and mounted. "And what are they the source of?"

"Winter and death."

We rode out through the rain.

CHAPTER 33
EYEBALL KING

"If you think of the eastern end of the Scorpion Sea as a baby's hand," said Glance, "with the inlets making short stubby fingers, then your kingdom here is on one of the peninsulas between the fingers. What we are going to do is ride out and around the fingers and up to the northeast of the entire hand."

We had left the city behind and were pushing on through the soggy countryside, watching for any spot that might provide us with a dry resting place or hot food. Glance was tapping a fingernail against his front teeth and sweeping the fields and meadows with his bright eyes.

"There's one thing we don't have yet that we are going to need," he said.

"Only one? Offhand, I can think of courtesans, gold ingots, cigars, and grilled cheese sandwiches. What did you have in mind?"

"Something that might be provided by the next farmhouse we come to, if the same fellow is still living there. When I last came through these parts, he was called Eyeball King. Watch for a yellow house with two chimneys."

The house soon sprang up before us, seeming to cry, "Visit me!" and reminding me of the children's story of the girl who fell down a rabbit hole, in which a bottle cries, "Drink me!" As we rode up, out came a tall man in a long coat and wide-brimmed leather hat to ward off the ever-falling rain. His face was dominated by a pair of crawling caterpillar eyebrows and two preposterously bulging blood-shot eyes, but not quite as large as owl eggs nor quite as red as Agony Falls. He laughed insanely when he saw us.

"Cats!" he screamed. "Cats for sale! Hurry, hurry, step right up, pack up the babies and grab the old ladies and drag up your bags of loot, your filthy lucre, take advantage of this amazing offer while it lasts!" His eyes rolled in both dir-ections at once and his fingers twitched. I thought that he was going to go into a seizure on the spot.

He swept us off our horses and into a backyard drunk with overexcited vegetation of the worst variety. Tethered to a stalk that was either a huge weed or a small tree was a monstrous sentry cat: bushy, furry, enjoying a riot of stripy brown-and-grayness that gave him a ruff around his neck, a tail that could have been used to wipe the steps of a palace, and paws spreading like ivy leaves. He was magnifi-cent.

"His name is Oatmeal," our host brayed. "You will find him as warm and comforting as the hot cereal itself. Give me all your money."

Glance gave him a leather purse, which allowed me to keep the one I had gotten from the Lady Marabar. Eye-ball King, if that was the man's name, stroked the purse, held it to his nose, smelled it, licked it, opened his mouth, let roll a stream of shiny chuckles that bounced like marbles, and goggled his eyes at us. I thought that if they got any larger they were going to escape his face and eclipse the sun.

"Is he trained?" Glance asked.

The man twitched his head from side to side, as if fearful that someone would spring out of the bushes and contradict him. "Of course! I sell no other kind!"

"Then why, pray tell, is he tied up?"

"Ducks!" he screamed. "My neighbor has a duck

pond." He gestured wildly with his uncooked steak of a hand. "Oatmeal here is a good boy, but he is driven–driven, I say!–by the demonic genius of his appetite. Even though I feed him almost every day."

Oatmeal turned his face languidly toward me and Glance, and his chartreuse eyes managed to mingle amusement with contempt. He blinked sleepily.

"He attacked and ravaged the pond one day. I could not allow it to happen again. You understand. Once you get him away from here, I'm sure he'll be fine."

"Well! No time like the present to put it to the test, is there?" Glance had the tether untied from the rough stalk before he'd even finished speaking. He tossed the end onto Oatmeal's back, so that it hung down in a loop, and swung round toward the front of the house.

"Come along, boy." Without looking back, he danced toward the horses, the bells on his tunic singing as he went. The cat rose majestically and together he and I moved to follow.

Eyeball King became frantic. "Wait!" he screamed. "You haven't seen my eyeball collection!" He strode along beside me and Oatmeal, making shooing gestures to get us into the house, as if we were two of his neighbor's ducks.

Glance was already on his horse, and in a moment I was also mounted. We took up our reins.

"My collection!" screeched Eyeball King. I feared that he would throw himself down in front of the horses to block our way, or set fire to himself. Indeed, he seemed in danger of exploding at any second.

"Some other time," Glance said crisply.

"My peacock!"

At that moment, with slow flaps of its wings, a peacock flew over the house, its emerald body long and elegant, its folded tail trailing behind it in a shimmer of rainbow-tinged seafoam bedazzled with many flat eyes. Eyeball King indeed.

With a scream to rival that of its owner, it soared

over our heads and circled around to disappear into the rain. Having never seen one in flight, I stared after it. The ones you see in ornamental parks have had their wings clipped to keep them on the ground, walking decorations.

Glance shattered my revery by crying, "Away, away, my heart's on fire!" and thundering out onto the road, Oatmeal loping beside the horse. With a watery smile at the man who was now down one cat but still had his bird, I took my mount to a canter and moved to catch up.

"A handsome bird," Glance commented shortly thereafter as we continued to follow the road. "In the East, they believe that smoking a peacock feather in a pipe is protection against snakebite, that drinking the ashes of a feather will prevent vomiting, and that eating the bird's dung is a remedy for several eye diseases. The tongue, however–"

"Who was that?" I interrupted. "That was the oddest encounter."

"Yes, he's very easily excited. There at the end I thought he was going to be seized by a coronary thrombosis."

"A..." From listening to my father discuss his executions, I had heard much about the human body, but I did not know what this was.

He chuckled. "Sounds like an ivory-clawed beast lurking in wait for unsuspecting victims. No, it's an ailment of the heart."

"You must know a great deal."

"Well, in traveling one hears many things. I have heard the old belief that gifted children have the power to laugh roses. I have heard the speculation that flies drowned in wine can be brought back to life. I have heard that you should swallow a toad in the morning if you want to encounter nothing more disgusting the rest of the day."

I laughed for the first time since the loss of my father.

"Speaking of amphibians, perhaps you have heard of the Infamous Frog War of Shroom. There was a battle involving ten thousand or more frogs, biting and ripping at each other and making horrible sounds for seven days running. Inhabitants of the village of Shroom called in the authorities to investigate, but it turned out to be a frog orgy, and what they had thought were casualties were only sexually exhausted frogs."

I laughed again, and we rode on through the rain with our new cat.

At dusk we arrived at a field set about with gigantic granite boulders, found shelter beneath one with an overhanging shelf, and made a fire. Oatmeal settled himself between the fire and the rock wall and tucked his paws away.

"A cat sleeping with all four paws tucked under is supposed to mean cold weather ahead," Glance said as he opened one of the food sacks. "Cats have always been used for making predictions. They are said to smell the approach of distant rain, which is why farmers watch them closely during droughts."

"But it rains all the time here."

"Just a useful tidbit of knowledge, my friend. Besides, we are gradually passing into new country. In a matter of days we will be in the next kingdom and on our way to our goal, and who knows what we will find? Beautiful, fierce, strong warrior women who wield weapons of gold?"

He handed me something unidentifiable in the growing darkness; it felt and tasted like a sponge. I chewed thoughtfully. "This is a strange quest. I'm not sure why I took it." After a moment I asked, "How fast will we be traveling?"

"Well. We don't want to exhaust the horses or the cat. On the other hand, we don't want to have dragging footsteps." He chuckled. "There was a land on the other side of the Scorpion Sea. Their deity was known as 'the God of the Dragging Footsteps' because he was lame. One of the villages misunderstood this as 'the God of the Dragon Footsteps.' They used to find the footprints of real dragons nearby and believe that they had received a divine visitation."

He poked the fire gently, with the air of a surgeon exploring a lump, and decided not to stir it up. "We'll turn in shortly and get an early start in the morning."

By now it was totally dark, and Oatmeal's great eyes glowed in the low firelight as he watched us and, perhaps, listened.

Glance scratched him between the ears. "It was once believed that a cat's eyes shine at night because they are emitting all the light they have absorbed during the day."

"You talk a great deal, don't you?"

"Yes, it's one of the things I like best about myself."

CHAPTER 34
THE HOUSE ON AGONY BROOK

We had been following the brook for quite some time, and had begun to notice a red tinge appearing in the water along the banks, when we came upon it.

It was an ancient but stately wooden structure that sprawled all the way across the brook, its supporting pilings opening in a leer to let the water rush through. At first I took it for one of the old covered bridges, but then I noticed the windows, the second story, and the outside chimneys that ran the entire height of the building from ground to roof, and I knew it for a house.

"A good stopping place," declared Glance, "considering that we have no food left." He looked ruefully at Oatmeal. "I believe our friend is in dire need of nourishment himself. The last three times he has gone into the forest to hunt, he has returned looking decidedly unsatisfied. I almost fear that if I let him go one more time he will not come back."

"Surely he remembers that we fed him when we still had food in our sacks."

"Yes, but that was days and days ago. His recent returns have been met with nothing but helpless shrugs. And a cat bitten once by a snake dreads even rope, as the proverb says."

Slowly and thoughtfully I got out my pipe. "It could be worse. At least we have left the rainy country behind us."

"Yes, but–Heigh, Oatboy!" Glance snatched at the cat's tether as the animal suddenly sprang from our side and went bounding into the underbrush. "Come back! We need you for the danger that may lie ahead!"

Oatmeal disappeared into the maze of trees.

My companion picked up his pack and shrugged it onto one shoulder. "I'm going after him. He'd probably come back as usual, but I simply have a bad feeling about today and what it has in store for us. I aim to help make things turn out right."

"What about me?"

"See what sustenance is available at that house. I see a hitching post on this side of the brook, so there's probably a door there. Tie up the horses and wangle your way inside. I'll meet you back here as soon as I can."

He stepped daintily through the weeds and wild-flowers and was swallowed up by the silent wood, which I was sure would disgorge him again soon. What an unsuspecting fool I was.

I soon had our steeds secured and, pipe in hand, approached a tall narrow door in the side of the bridge-house. Feeling hearty dislike for having to throw myself on anyone's mercy, I decided to ask for a light for my pipe and see what developed.

Grasping the doorknocker, a hefty knot of bronze fashioned like the head of a goose, I lustily rapped an entreaty and listened to the echoes of my blows receding in the distant interior. Hunger made me ill-tempered and impatient, so when no one came I eased open the door and slipped into a large entrance hall.

A stone hearth the size of the platform atop my father's gallows led my eye to the fireplace, into which I could have walked without having to stoop or duck my head. That is, I could have walked into it but for the fire that raged there, throwing a wall of heat in my face and drying all the moisture from my eyes and lips. As I stared at it, a strange figure appeared in the flames.

I found myself gazing at the white, masklike face of a beautiful young woman with dark hair and noble features; unconsumed by the fire, it swayed subtly atop a thick scaly treetrunk of a serpent body.

And a cat bitten once by a snake dreads even rope. Why had Glance chosen to quote that proverb to me today? Her rich red lips parted.

"Help me. I am Sanoma. Deliver me."

"Of course," I answered, as if I met woman-headed serpents every day of the week. "How can I help you?"

"Help me change back to a complete woman. Various articles of my clothing are to be found in different rooms of this house. Search for them. You will know them when you see them. Bring them to me."

I sprang for the stairs in the corner of the hall, with much the same eagerness and desperation I had seen in Oatmeal's spring for the forest, and bolted up the steps two at a time. The first door I came to was open, and the daylight streaming in through the window revealed a bed piled with old tablecloths, folded napkins yellow with age, lacework intended for the backs of armchairs–and a gleaming pair of ivory elbow-length gloves.

"Ah, in your present snaky condition you'll have a bit of trouble putting these on, since you have no arms," I murmured, "but mine is not to question why." I moved forward to pick them up, and suddenly the room was full of dark flame-eyed goblins, hanging from the curtains, leaping up and down in the corners, and crouching on the bed. They had sharp-edged hammers for hands.

My limited experience with goblins has taught me that they are cowards more often than not, relying on treachery and superior numbers to surprise and bring down their intended prey. At any rate, none of these came up any higher than my waist. I drew my sword and slashed it around my head, while baying like a wolfhound at the moon.

They scattered before me and huddled trembling against the far wall, giving me ample opportunity to snatch up the gloves and dart back into the hall. I went to the next room, where I found more of the nasty creatures encircling a pair of ruby slippers in the middle of the floor. Striding in and thrusting my sword at them was enough to send them howling to all sides, as craven as a kindle of hares, and the shoes were mine.

The last chamber on the upper floor was totally empty, except for a dressmaker's dummy supporting a scarlet gown of breathtaking brilliance. When I touched one of the shoulder straps to remove it, a black goblin shot up and out from inside the dress, spurting flame from its eyes and mouth as it shrieked and swung its hammerhands at my face. I batted it aside with the flat of my sword, peeled the gown from the dummy, and hastened back to the stairs.

As I reached the bottom of the stairs, the gown and gloves draped over my arms, the slippers in one hand, I felt the thick hot air parting reluctantly before me, an unseen barrier like a curtain of invisible beads, clutching at my face and shoulders, sliding slowly over me as I pushed through to the front hall beyond.

I held out my prizes to the roaring fireplace and noticed that they were gone. At the same moment, a shimmering figure appeared on the hearth and crystallized into the woman I had seen in the flames. She was wearing the gown, slippers and one glove, and was in the final stages of pulling on the other one.

"I thank you." Her voice was musical and throaty. "I am in your debt."

"It has been my pleasure to help you escape from such a dreadful trap."

She folded her arms and gave herself a little embrace. "Escape. I never hear the word without a quicker blood."

I moved toward her. "Now tell me more about who

you are and where you come from."

Her face was still a somber mask, the skin white as mountain snow, the hair black as an ebony windowsill, as in the old nursery tale. "I am Sanoma."

"Yes, so you said. But where do you live, and how did it happen that you ended up imprisoned here?"

She came to meet me in the center of the hall, pressing the length of her body close against mine, moving her hands languidly up and down over my cloak. I could see traces of her quickening blood in her dark eyes and her crimson mouth.

"Meet me tomorrow at dawn," she murmured, her lips barely stirring. "Downstream from here, at the point where the brook goes over Agony Falls, is the inn known as the Jolly Beggars. They can put you up for the night. I will be in the courtyard precisely at dawn. That will be the time and place for me to tell you everything you need to know about me."

She peeled herself off me, much as I had peeled the gown off the dummy upstairs, and swept to the front door, pausing to look back over her shoulder, the glossy wing of her black hair covering one eye. "If you are not in the courtyard at exactly the moment the sun rises, you will forfeit all claims and opportunities to my company." Then she was gone.

I stood astounded, fingering the hilt of my sword and trying to think. In the next moment I heard an outraged neigh of protest and the pounding of hooves on the hard surface of the yard outside. Three strides took me to the door in time to see the mysterious Sanoma, mounted on my steed and pulling Glance's alongside her by its reins, vanishing around a curve in the road.

She was stealing our horses.

Knowing that I could not hope to catch her on foot, I uttered a curse and pounded my fist against the open door. The movement made me aware that something felt different about my cloak. I reached inside and groped for the secret pocket where I kept valuables.

She had also stolen the Lady Marabar's purse of gold.

CHAPTER 35
DAYLIGHT AND CHAMPAGNE

A face came out of my ceiling.

No, not the ceiling. The curtains on the canopied bed had been flung aside with a rattling of the rings on their rod. A frightening face bent down into mine, as memory swam into my brain.

I had waited all day at the bridge-house, but Glance and Oatmeal did not return. When I divined that dusk was not far off, I decided to use the daylight left to me and went along on foot, following Agony Brook as it pursued its increasingly swift rush down to the waterfall ahead.

In less than an hour, my ears filled with the hissing of the nearby but yet unseen waterfall, I saw the cupolas and gables of the Jolly Beggars and soon found myself going through its not-so-jolly front door, which was hanging from one rusted hinge. In another hour, using what little personal money was left to me, I had dined on greasy mystery meat and had retired for the night, leaving strict instructions that someone come to awake me just before–

Dawn.

The bedchamber was now filled with a milky, smoky light. It was far past dawn. I shot up onto one elbow and looked more closely at the person leaning in upon me.

He was a gaunt vulture of a man, with a bald pate, a hooked beak of a nose and a gray-white beard down to his waist. As he stood there, however, moving his hands over one another in a handwashing gesture, he also showed me kind eyes and a warm smile. He struck me as the sort who enjoys scaring people with his appearance and then surprising them with his personality.

"Awake at last, will wonders never cease. I expected you to be up long ago, yelping for breakfast. In fact, I've brought some, although it's getting closer to lunchtime. You may address me as Negawsklov."

Annoyance pricked me in a dozen places. "Why weren't my instructions followed? I asked to be woken just before dawn." I swung my feet out from under the slightly damp sheet and sat on the edge of the bed.

"My ostler tried to rouse you, but you would not wake up. It was like you were drugged, he said. Fox sleep, if you ask me."

Groggily I accepted the bowl of hot cereal he handed me. "Fox sleep?"

"An extraordinarily deep sleep generated by magic. A fox, carrying the appropriate talisman or charm around its neck, is sent to run around a house and it puts a spell on you to sleep. It's the best way I know to keep someone flat on his back in bed."

"This is most inconvenient. I had a vital appointment in the courtyard here at dawn. With a certain lady."

Negawsklov moved to the window and looked out. "Well, she's not there now. Nothing but cobblestones and a beggar boy who looks like the sad-eyed son of Moses, as my granny used to say. Daylight and champagne discover not more."

As he mentioned champagne, he picked up a bottle of that sparkling refreshment and poured a generous measure into a goblet of yellow glass. Then he drank without offering any to me.

"What do you mean, daylight and champagne discover not more?" I asked irritably.

"I mean, it's plain as day, your lady is now gone. If she was ever here to begin with. Who is she?"

"She said her name was Sanoma. That's all I know."

An ejaculation of disgust spurted from his bearded lips. "Oh, that one. She's a piece of work. A walking, talking flask of poisoned honey."

I slurped my cereal. "You know her, then."

"She comes through from time to time, putting on grand airs and preening like a peahen. Calls herself a princess but won't say what kingdom she's from. She's known in these parts for her virginity and her belligerence."

"Could she have bewitched me with this fox sleep? Is she a magician?"

"No, but she might be a famulus."

"What's that?"

"An attendant to a magician. They provide assistance as needed. The really powerful sorcerers, of course, don't need one, but sometimes they keep them anyway out of vanity."

I gave him my empty bowl and he tossed it into a corner. "How can I find her? I need to persuade her to give back some things that belong to me."

He sucked up some champagne and chuckled. "Not her. She's as bloodless as a stone. Her idea of a pleasant afternoon is having coffins sent round to try on."

I stood up. "Then I'll have to trick her."

"Putting one over on her is like trying to slip the sun past the rooster." He paused abruptly and then laughed into his drink, making it spray up into his beard. "Someone surely slipped the sun past you this morning, yes, indeed."

He gestured to my cloak where it lay draped over a moldy armchair. "If you see fit to get dressed, I'll stand you to a drink downstairs in the back room and see what else I can remember about your lost lady."

I followed him down the narrow, one-man staircase to a windowless, lamplit chamber that ran across the back of the inn. As we came through the door I was explaining to Negawsklov, "I'm also hoping to meet up with two friends, one with fur and one without."

"Might they be among these fine fellows? We're currently serving brunch to a convention of puppeteers. One helping of the daily stew and all the wine they can drink, all for one low price."

The puppeteers were sprawled around the room like a bask of crocodiles, sunning themselves in the yellow light of the lamps and yawning hugely. On the tables before them were scattered dishes of some meaty concoction and balloon glasses half full of flat champagne. One whose face was tattooed with bruises complained, "This is not my idea of a good deal. A plate of dogfood and a goldfish bowl of champagne? A man could die of putrid throat before he got a decent drink around here."

Negawsklov grasped my elbow and hurried me toward a far corner, where I found a welcome sight. "Perhaps this Fur Man is one of those you seek?" he murmured.

Sitting up in a chair intended for humans, his heavy purr shaking his body, Oatmeal was eating vanilla ice cream from an eggcup.

CHAPTER 36
TICKLING THE BRAIN OF ICARUS

"Mr. Oatboy!" I cried. I fell upon him, put my arms around his neck, and buried my face in his ruff of fur. When I pulled away, I saw that he had an uncomfortable look on his face and was trying to get his mouth back down to the scoop of melting ice cream on the table next to us. I let him go.

"Under the circumstances," said Negawsklov, "I'll leave you two alone. I'm sure you have much to... ah, discuss. I'll be in my office if you want me." He stole away.

I scanned the room but did not see Glance. "What's been happening, boy? Where's your other master?" He stuck out a very dark pink tongue and began to lick droplets of white from his muzzle.

As I studied the crowd, I noticed something interesting about the Jolly Beggars. All the workers, handing out drinks behind the scarred wooden bar or moving in and out among the tables with dishes of food, were boys my age. All of them were working barechested, in tight leather pants and boots. All of them were strikingly good-looking, all of them had spectacular bodies, and none of them had been cursed with chest hair. Obviously they had been selected by someone with impeccable taste.

My eye was caught by a very tall boy with extremely short golden hair, slightly protruding ears, long eyelashes, built-up shoulders, and nice arms. Youthful experiments had taught me that I prefer girls between the sheets, or I would have been tempted to have a brief dalliance with him, as he did have a superb mouth.

I was about to turn my attention elsewhere when I saw him place a hand on another server's shoulder and speak to him. Distance and the conversations of the puppeteers around me made it impossible to understand the entire sentence, but I distinctly heard him say, "Sanoma." They both laughed and went behind the bar.

Intrigued, I told Oatmeal to stay where he was and moved closer. I saw that the boy was now polishing glasses, while his companion was counting the coins in a large copper bowl at the end of the bar. I sat at a little triangular table within earshot and settled in for a siege of eavesdropping and spying, spinning out the next hour by ordering and consuming vast quantities of green tea that came in a ceramic pot fashioned to resemble a spiderflower blossom.

The summer sun beating down outside the walls made the room very warm, and soon all the bare muscular torsos around me were gleaming with sweat. I had just decided that one more swallow of green tea would make me vomit when fate delivered mine enemy into my hands, as they say.

My boy was reaching up with both hands to replace two clean glasses on a shelf above the bar; as he strained, his ribcage and the chiseled muscles of his stomach stood out like curves on a fine statue. His friend playfully reached over and, using a light pinching poking gesture, attacked the exposed belly and sides with his fingers.

His victim spasmed uncontrollably, yelping and gasping, "Don't!" He lunged to put the glasses back down on the bar before he dropped them, while his whole body tensed and twisted to escape the still wiggling fingers of his friend. Once he had the glasses safely down, he used both hands to grab the attacker's wrist and push his hand away. He was giggling and twitching like a madman.

"My stars, Icarus," the friend laughed, "you really are ticklish, aren't you?"

The boy grinned, obviously embarrassed. "I can't help it. It's my worst weakness. I don't know why my skin is so sensitive, but being touched when I can't do anything to stop it is my greatest fear."

The friend gave him an odd look, shrugged, and turned to the rack of wine bottles behind him, and Icarus went back to his glass polishing, and I smiled an evil smile. I would not have to use pain to get what I wanted.

Shortly I heard the friend ask Icarus to bring out two more bottles of red wine, and I saw my prey pick up a lamp and go through a green baize door next to some kind of stuffed thing with feathers that was perched on a pedestal. I looked at Oatmeal, who had overturned the empty eggcup and was wearing it on his head as a hat, and gestured for him to come to me. He tossed his big head, throwing the cup onto the table, slid down off his chair, and padded in my direction.

Together we waited until the boy behind the bar had gone to the other end to wait on a customer, and then we went through the door that had swallowed Icarus and down a short flight of steps.

His lamp sat on a shelf, lighting up jam jars and bottles of brightly colored liqueurs, painting stained glass onto the windowless walls. His tall dark shape was at the far end of the room. Oatmeal paused until Icarus turned toward us, a wine bottle in each hand, and then the cat sprang.

He hit the boy in the chest and knocked him down, so that he ended up on his back with Oatmeal on top of him, the cat's front paws pinning his arms out to the sides in the pose favored by those arranging a crucifixion. (I had seen my foster father handle a few of those, in cases where he did not plan to kill the prisoner right away.)

Desperation being the mother of invention, I went

back out to the bar and looked at the stuffed creature on the pedestal. It appeared to be a feathered serpent. It might have been a work of art, a man-made creation of feathers taken from a bird and grafted onto the leathery skin of a dead snake, or it might have been the carefully preserved remains of a real animal, a new species, a mutation. I did not care, as long as it could provide me with the weapon I needed.

I pulled out one of the longer feathers from its back and tested it against the palm of my hand, finding it stiff enough to retain its curved shape but soft enough at the tip to excite the surface of my skin. I tried to remember which areas of the human body had the most heavily concentrated nerve endings. I smiled the evil smile again and returned to the wine cellar.

Icarus was swearing quietly and grunting as he struggled to get out from under Oatmeal, but the sentry cat was large enough and heavy enough to keep him my prisoner as long as I wanted. I walked around and knelt at the boy's head, with my knees on either side of his upside-down face, gripping him along the jawline so that his head was immobilized.

"Hello, Icarus," I said with gentle menace. "I need to find the lady known as Sanoma. You need to tell me where I can find her."

He spat at me. I wiped his saliva from my chin and watched a mask of sullen defiance settle on his handsome face. I showed him the feather.

"Don't make me use this. Tell me where I can find Sanoma and I will let you go."

Quiet horror was stealing over his features as he realized what I was holding and how helpless he was. "Wh-what..." He could barely form words at this point, but I knew that I could make him talk.

I was in the catbird seat, as they say. I knew his greatest weakness, and there was nothing he could do to stop me from doing whatever I wanted to him. I am not a sadistic man, but it was a priceless moment, good beyond hope. A moment to give a lifetime for.

I touched the tip of the feather to the right corner of his mouth and moved it back and forth, aiming to duplicate that maddening sensation of having an insect crawling on your face. His body was gripped by one huge undulating shudder. He looked the way I feel when I have a piss shiver, that involuntary tremor that young men sometimes experience immediately after emptying the bladder.

"Come on, don't. Stop it." He stared up at me in forlorn hope.

I trailed the feather over his upper lip, tracing the line where his mustache would be if he had one. I could feel him trembling violently between my knees as he fought to move his head away from the annoying attack.

"Where is Sanoma?"

He did not answer, so I moved on to the next phase. The feather was just narrow enough to fit up inside his right nostril, and when I started swirling it around inside his nose I thought that his eyes would start from his face. Now he was making a sound somewhere between a laugh and a moan, and as he lost more and more control his deep masculine voice took on a higher pitch.

"Do you know what I'm doing, Icarus? I'm tickling your brain."

"You've got to stop! Someone stop him!"

Under Oatmeal's furry mass, the boy's smooth sculpted chest rose and fell convulsively as he gasped for air. "No! No! No! No!" he kept crying.

"Where is Sanoma?"

"Stop it! You're killing me!"

Indeed I was. Killing him softly with feathery kisses that he could not get away from.

I was opening a door for him, a door with feathers for hinges, a door to a place he did not want to go.

"Where is Sanoma?"

I pulled out the feather and put it down. Time to get serious. I noted with approval that Oatmeal's strong front legs were keeping the boy's arms spread out in a T-shape, leaving the most vulnerable parts of his bare torso exposed. I slid my hands into his muscular armpits and toyed with the damp blond curls there, and I had him screaming in less than ten seconds. He was flopping like a big fish on the deck of a boat.

"Rothrock!" he shouted through his agonized laughter. "The kingdom of Rothrock! Head northwest from Agony Falls! Three days by horse!"

I left him gasping and crying on the floor. I did not feel bad. I think that he secretly enjoyed it.

CHAPTER 37
BLACK GOLD

I stood at the foaming foot of Agony Falls, on a narrow wooden walkway that had not been featured in my dream. It began at the bottom of the plunging water curtain and ran for some distance along the side of the rushing red-stained stream. I watched Oatmeal's long body writhe on the planks in a rare display of feline excitement. Maybe he knew something that I did not.

"What to do, boy? I have no horse and no money. Perhaps one or the other will come floating down the waterfall if we wait long enough."

I ran my eye along the curved walkway, splashed with crimson puddles from the falls exploding behind me, and saw a young woman who was not the lady Sanoma walking toward us, wrapped in a dark blue hooded cloak. Her hair was roughly the color of rust but gleaming with inner flames, as if some dying iron trapped by the rust were applying its own heat from within.

"Nice cat." About my age, she had a little-girl voice and a pert, elfin face spattered with even more freckles than I had, but her bright green eyes were sharp and shrewd.

"Nice cloak." Showing my skills as a past master of witty conversation.

"I fished it out of a lake in a big copper vase, along with a magic purse that is always full of jewels no matter how many times you empty it. I haven't found out what the cloak does yet."

"I wish I had your luck. I have to get to the kingdom of Rothrock as fast as possible, and it appears that I will be walking there."

"Really." Her eyes grew even brighter. "I've just come from Rothrock. I've been following a princess named Sanoma, but I'm afraid that I've lost her trail."

"Really." I imitated her tone and we both laughed. "It so happens that I am following a princess named Sanoma. What a coincidence. It is proof that we are all just tiny cogs in one vast organism."

"I think it is proof that we are all just tiny cocks in one vast orgasm." She laughed again. "Why do you want to find her?"

"She took two things that belong to me. I want to see her face when I show up to ask for them back."

"The same with me. I am a fisher girl on our local lake. She had her goons take a catch of fresh fish from me and never paid me. I can always catch more, but it's the idea of taking without paying that galls me."

"Apparently she is not a nice person. I just met a man who called her a 'walking, talking flask of poisoned honey.'"

"That's an insult to poisoned honey. I'd call her an angelfood cake with a bomb baked into it."

Attracted by the talk of food, Oatmeal rose and looked at her with avid curiosity. I put one hand on his head and kept it there. "I think that she may be headed back to Rothrock. I don't suppose you would know where to find her if we could get there?"

"She has a hunting lodge outside the capital city. She doesn't hunt herself, because she doesn't like getting her hands dirty, but she has a huntsman who kills things while she watches. All of her hobbies make my blood run cold."

With one hand still on Oatmeal's head, I placed the other on the cloak where it curved over her left shoulder. "I wish that we could be in front of that hunting lodge right now."

I experienced a blinding flash of white light, a roaring wind, and the distant metallic sound of gold and silver horns in a far-flung foxhunt. The waterfall disappeared and the three of us were now standing in front of a wooden structure like a giant cuckoo clock, a hunting lodge designed by a drunkard.

I decided that I had found out what the cloak did.

"Delightful. The one making the wish doesn't even have to be wearing the cloak, just touching it." I looked at her. "If we're going to be breaking the laws of space and time together, perhaps we should introduce ourselves. My name is Bama."

"I'm Harp."

"I like your style of travel, even if you didn't know about it beforehand. Any ideas about getting in to see Miss High and Mighty, Miss Pride Goeth Before Destruction, Miss Haughty Spirit Before a Fall?"

"She doesn't let anybody in. She keeps herself barricaded behind a small army of goons, bristling and showing their teeth like a business of ferrets. That's why I had to wait until she set out on a journey and then follow her."

"Isn't that rather boring for a lady fond of causing hurt? What does she do when she isn't watching animals being slaughtered?"

"She talks to a would-be paramour named Trexler, who is old enough to be her father twice over. I think he has creeping senility, which is when you get so old that you can only move by creeping. She keeps him around because she finds him amusing in a pathetic sort of way, but she won't let his semen-squirting salamander anywhere near her bedchamber."

"His..."

"That's what the folks in the city call it. Apparently

the only part of him that's still in perfect working order."

"Well. What can we do to get her attention? Any other toys like the cloak? How about that magic purse?"

She rummaged through various inside pockets and produced a quantity of yellow and burgundy oilcloth, folded in upon itself and tied shut with a silk cord. As she opened it, she looked up with sudden excitement.

"I've got it! There's nothing like throwing jewels through a window to make an impression! Come on!"

Fumbling with the purse, she strode straight for the lodge, where I could see a great casement window standing open. When I caught up to her, she was hefting a handful of coal-like lumps and measuring the distance up to the window.

"Black gold," she explained. "Not anything like real gold, though. A hard jewel rare enough to make our double-damned villainess sit up and take notice."

In two fleeting breaths she had flung her fistful of treasure through the window. She stood there laughing. She had a merry laugh.

CHAPTER 38
DOOM IN YOUR VERY OWN BACK GARDEN

Soon the resident goons came out and strong-armed us through an arched door, sweeping us along a long hallway with a turkey carpet, past a loudly ticking grandmother clock. As they waltzed us through an art gallery, a gander at the family portraits there showed me Sanoma's nose copied faithfully down through the ages, from generation to generation, as immutable and indelible as that of an ancient ruler on an antique coin.

Out the other end of the gallery we went, into a back garden so precious that I thought I might lose my breakfast. "Enough rose trellises to furnish a royal wedding," Harp muttered, "which might happen if old Trexler gets his way."

The garden was arranged for a croquet game. I saw six wickets of white steel, hardwood mallets with leather grips, reinforced with brass strips, and a multitude of wooden balls in solid colors. There were clips, stakes, corner flags, pegs, and a rubber hammer to pound them in with. Or to pound your opponent if he annoyed you.

The garden was also bristling with doom palms, hoisting their gingerbread-flavored fruit above our heads and trying hard to look as ominous as their name sounded.

"Planted by Sanoma to strike terror in her many enemies," I muttered back to Harp. "How convenient to have doom right in your own back garden."

"Speaking of doom, here's our hostess. You were right. She did come back here."

Sanoma loomed before us, driving her goons back with an imperious gesture probably copied from one of the family portraits. She flashed me with her eyes; as fishers cast their circling nets, she spread a deadly abundance of ocular rays and caught me fast.

Behind her was a square man with a square head sitting on square shoulders. His thick white hair fell in straight bangs to touch his thick eyebrows. He wore a dagger-shaped pendant of black hematite accented with a small garnet at the tip, just at the point where a drop of blood might linger as the blade was withdrawn from a wound. How nice.

Sanoma gave me a smile not quite as large and not quite as bright as a constellation. "Ah, the persistent swain," she purred. At my side, Oatmeal echoed her with a sound more like a growl.

Gripping Harp by the elbow, I lunged forward and grabbed Sanoma by the hair, and she gave vent to a banshee cry of bloodchilling rancor.

"You shabby pathetic commoner! No one touches me without my permission!" She looked at her goons, but I forestalled her.

"I've got a surprise for you. I wish we were at the end of the Scorpion Sea."

There came again the flashes of light and metallic noise, and then we were staggering on a sandy slope as the sea boiled and foamed before us. Sanoma was half swooning into my arms, while Harp watched her with contempt. Oatmeal, unfortunately, had been left behind. I looked around.

We were hemmed in by sand dunes and tall grass and wooden posts, atop each of which perched a red-winged blackbird. A blood orange of a sun hung over the sea. There was something wrong here.

"I meant to be taken to my country, as I still know some people there who could help us, but it is a low and rainy country. It looks nothing like this."

"I know the country you mean. I think this must be the other end of the Scorpion Sea. The cloak can't be expected to know where you live."

Sanoma grew rigid in my embrace and I released her quickly. She opened her eyes, ran them briefly over Harp, pausing at the freckled face, and turned, dismissing her.

"I should have had you killed at the Jolly Beggars, but it amused me to let you think that you had lost your bargain because you overslept. Fox sleep can be so useful."

"So, you are a magician?"

"No, just a famulus, but I have learned a few tricks from my mentor. Enough to strike you down time and time again."

I moved to lay hands on her again. "You fool," she spat. "You think you can keep me here? A little dose of the fox sleep and I will have left you far behind me."

I could not help grinning. "I know. Negawsklov told me. The enchanted fox runs around the house and throws a spell on those inside. The only trouble is, I don't see any foxes here."

She gave a sneering laugh. "You don't need a fox. That's just an expression. Just as there are no real cat parts in cathead biscuits." She threw up a hand and uttered some words I could not comprehend, and immediately I felt a dark hood of drowsiness wrap around my head and drag me fainting down to the sand.

CHAPTER 39
A FRUIT TREE OUT OF A FEVER DREAM

When I awoke the blood orange sun was higher in the sky, Harp was sitting up beside me and rubbing her eyes, and the lovely Sanoma was gone. So were the cloak and the bottomless purse of black gold.

I groaned. "I suppose I am what she called me, a fool."

"It doesn't matter what they call you, unless they call you pigeon pie and eat you up."

There was a pause, while the surf crashed onto the beach below us. "I'm hungry," she said in her little-girl voice. In the absence of the cloak, I saw that she wore a comfortable two-piece traveling outfit of forest green.

I stood and looked inland over the dunes, spying at once a line of mutilated old trees. "Let's investigate. That might be the remains of an orchard, and, if so, there might be fruit."

"If ifs were skiffs, we'd all be sailors. Fruit on the trees in midsummer?"

"Maybe. You never know what the plants are like in a strange country."

She stood and walked with me, and, as we passed, the red-winged blackbirds took flight, throwing their shadows on the sand around us.

The first tree we came to was indeed heavy with pendulous fruit, but it seemed a fruit tree out of a fever dream. It was a plum tree, but instead of the familiar dark reddish-purple, it bore decidedly different plums. Those growing on the left side of the tree were yellow, a yellow I have only seen elsewhere in succulent wedges of beaver cheese; those growing on the right side of the tree were green, the pale green of inland snow.

Harp grabbed one of the yellow plums and promptly bit into it, grinning as the juice ran down her chin, while I reached more casually for a green one. Negawsklov's cereal was still congealing in my stomach. I was eyeing my plum, trying to decide whether I wanted it, when my companion gave a squawk of surprise and fear.

I looked and saw that little horns, the color of old ivory, had sprouted from her forehead; moaning around her mouthful of partially chewed fruit, she had dropped the remainder of the yellow plum and had both hands on the growths, fingering and pushing at them as if she could force them back into her head.

I was about to throw down my green plum and try to help her when I was hit with inspiration, as I sometimes am. "Here," I said, thrusting it at her. "There must be a reason for the two different colors. Bite into this one."

The look in her eyes changed from terror to hope. She spat out what was left of her first bite and took my fruit, cramming it into her mouth and chewing as fast as her jaws could move. She stared crazily at me as she swallowed.

It worked. The horns promptly began shrinking and, in a matter of seconds, had melted back into her skull, leaving her pale skin smooth and unmarked in any way. She ran her fingers over her forehead and laughed to find them gone.

"Remarkable," I muttered. "I've heard of being on the horns of a dilemma, but this presents a dilemma of horns." Before she could stop me, I snatched another yellow plum off the tree and took a big bite, and as the juice went down my throat I felt a crawling sensation above my eyebrows and the unmistakable feeling of something hard breaking through the skin there.

Harp's eyes seemed twice their normal size. "Now you've got them," she whispered. She pushed the half-eaten green plum back into my hand and forced it to my mouth. "Get rid of them, quickly. They're horrible."

I bit, I chewed, I swallowed, and I sensed the horns retracting, feeling as a crab must when he pulls in his eye stalks. Within seconds, I too touched a smooth patch of skin where the growths had been.

I smiled. "Harp," I said, "if you have pockets fill them up. Both colors. We are going back to Rothrock, and we are taking a present to Sanoma."

"It's hundreds of miles."

"We're going back to get your cloak and purse. And we're going to get my purse and my horses. Maybe even your fish. And there's a friend of mine gone missing from that general part of the country."

She narrowed her vivid green eyes. "Male or female?"

"Oh, he's just a monkeyboy."

Giving people free samples of the yellow plums, and then making them pay for the green ones to have their new horns removed, we worked our way back along the Scorpion Sea. We left behind us a trail of angry people, but every day took us that much closer to Rothrock.

We would probably still be walking now if we had not come across a magician for hire named Hyde. We found him at night, in a tent lit from within like a great paper lantern. He had very long, almost black hair that looked as if it needed restraining as it spilled down over his shoulders, and he wore evil green goatskin trousers and bracelets of leather and silver.

He looked at us somberly as we explained what we

wanted. There was an exchange of filthy lucre, he burned some incense and muttered some muddy words of magic, and instantly Harp and I were whisked to the dooryard in front of Sanoma's hunting lodge.

I had prepared a little basket of the deadly yellow plums, carefully covered with a soft cloth and innocent enough to adorn the arm of any toothless granny. We waited until we saw a goon unfamiliar to us, one who would not recognize us. Harp got his attention and sent in the basket as an anonymous gift with a suitably abject note: "I am not worthy to kiss the hem of your skirt, but I beg that you might consider this worthless token of my esteem." Blah, blah, blah.

Then Harp and I camped out in the dooryard, as inconspicuously as possible, and waited. Much sooner than I had hoped, horrendous screams came ringing from the windows of the lodge. I smiled.

CHAPTER 40
A HARVEST OF DEAD MEN

I sat looking out the window of our most recent hiding place, an inn in Rothrock called the Cast of Falcons, while Harp finished shaving my head. Sanoma's proclamation was tacked to the wall next to the window. It announced that the first man to remove her horns would have her hand in marriage; unfortunately, anyone who tried and failed would be hanged from the nearest tree.

Rather than waiting for applicants to come to her, the princess was so desperate that she and her entourage had been sweeping through the city, pausing in public squares and parks just long enough to allow failed attempts at her hideously horned brows, executing the would-be princes, and careening onward to the sound of her shouted curses.

That fall the trees of Rothrock all bore a harvest of dead men. From my seat at the window I could see one unsuccessful applicant, with facial scars and a dirty blue coat, twisting and dancing in the wind as he hung at the end of a rope tied to a witch finger tree.

Harp put down the razor and ran a warm, wet cloth over my freshly bald head. "Are you sure she's suffered enough for us to make our move now?"

"I'm getting impatient. I have my own affairs to

pursue. Let us do what we have come to do, get back what is rightfully ours, and..." I paused delicately, but she did not seem to notice.

"All right. But are you sure this masquerade is necessary?"

"The city is crawling with these missionaries of the new religion, these dervishes. And a person with a shaved head is virtually unrecognizable. I will be able to penetrate to her innermost chamber."

"It's a shame, though. People with reddish hair are superior people." She grinned and shook her auburn tresses.

"Am I no longer superior?"

"You are to me." She grasped my hand and squeezed it.

Our time in hiding had not been wasted.

The snouty sneering mouths of some unidentifiable late-season flowers were braying their incense into the crisp air. We were surrounded by the wreckage of an abandoned croquet game: the same wickets of white steel, hardwood mallets, colored balls, clips, stakes, flags, and pegs that I had seen the last time we were here.

We had decided to follow Sanoma back to her hunting lodge, where she had undoubtedly left her stolen loot. She stood now in her back garden, clothed in boredom and despair, waving a lazy hand back and forth before her frozen face, her horns leering from her head, seeming to shriek, "I am a freak." They inspired me.

"Your Highness. We have a saying in my religion. A truthful woman is a freak of nature, like a cat with horns. It is ironic, for only a truthful person can be cured of this affliction. It is only possible to cure people with clean souls."

I had the black cloak and shaved head of a dervish. On my arm was a covered basket of the magical green plums. In the corner of the garden lurked Harp, who had been brought in as my amanuensis.

"If you have any crimes on your conscience, you

must confess them and correct them before you can be cured."

She reeked with the odor of sanctity, and humility dripped from her. "I have taken things that did not belong to me," she murmured. "I will restore them to their rightful owners, if only you can help me with this affliction."

"Done," I said. "Done and doubledone." I took out a plum and brandished it before her. "Taste of this and be restored." From the corner of my eye I thought I saw Harp shaking her head, but even as I questioned my timing, wondered if I should wait until our possessions were back in our hands, Sanoma snatched the fruit and sank her very white, very sharp teeth into it.

Her horns curled in on themselves and vanished into the creamy smoothness of her forehead, and she gave her constellation of a smile. She held out her hand to one of her goons without looking at him, and he put into it a pyramid-shaped flagon containing a pinkish liquid.

"I thank you and offer you the opportunity to drink a toast to the occasion. This is the drink known as a hop-toad. Lemon juice and peach brandy over crushed ice. Cheers."

Although not much of a drinker, I took the flagon and swigged it down. Instantly I felt a rush of ominous heat coursing through me, as my senses reeled and my vision blurred.

Sanoma unleashed peal after peal of hysterical laughter. "Thrice now have you proven yourself a fool. Did you think that a shaved head would keep me from recognizing you? You have, at the same time, undone the spell you somehow placed upon me and forfeited your friend here. Seize her," she ordered her goons.

They laid their dirty hands upon Harp and spirited her through a low arched doorway into the lodge, followed by their mistress, while I stood rooted to the spot as the pernicious hoptoad drink did its work upon me, my muscles turned to pulp, my eyeballs turned to seawater, my brain

turned to mush, my tongue turned to sand. I took one staggering step, tripped over a croquet wicket, and crashed onto
my face.

CHAPTER 41
CAT WARS

Sandpaper rubbing all over my face brought me to my senses. I was no longer prone but supine, and something with the heaviness of a boulder was bearing down upon my chest. I opened one eye, nearly getting an eyeful of tongue, and found Oatmeal busy licking my face.

Seeing that I was awake, he stood up from his crouched position, walked around in a circle three times, and then fell down upon me again, this time with his banner of a tail thrust under my nose.

"That'll do, boy," came a familiar trilling voice, and I saw Glance's bright eyes looking down on me. "I've brought us some extra help, since Sanoma has taken your friend down into the catacombs beneath the lodge."

Oatmeal slithered off me and I sat up groggily. "Remind me never to drink hoptoads again," I muttered. "What kind of help–" My voice died as I noticed that between us and the back door of the lodge was a sea of fur, seeming to ripple as the creatures milled about. It was an army of sentry cats.

Glance put a hand under my elbow and helped me to my feet. "Allow me to introduce the leaders." He nodded at a sleek, slender cat with standard markings and coloration.

"Loki, named after a northern god of mischief and evil."

He indicated a large striped cat with long hair, similar to Oatmeal but lighter in coloration, more orange-gold. "Tigro-puss."

Next came a magnificent beast, solid black except for a face and bib of white. "Midnight Snowflake. You know, of course, that in the East a black cat with a white throat and chest is known as dark cloud over snow." Of course.

With blinding rapidity he jabbed his finger at other cats, some with the regular cocoa bodies and chocolate masks and some with lighter coats. "Siva. Snark. Samson. Luna. Aka. And two with a special background that bears recounting."

His voice grew drier and less whimsical.

"When Sanoma was an adolescent she came across a pregnant feral cat, Mama Doswellina, big tawny and golden-eyed, and she dragged her halfway through the city to the gates of her father's palace in the apparent hope that such activity might make her lose the kittens she was carrying in her swollen belly, as lose three of the five she did, disgorging into the world just before she died half a week later a some-what reduced but soon healthily mewing load–the identic-ally striped and tawny Macduff so called because like the legendary hero of that name he was from his mother's womb untimely ripped, no more clue to the kitten's father than longer finer fur and a bushier plume of a tail than that of Mama Dos–not to mention Alias the mutant piebald cat with lovely black fur (being rapidly forced to share this pelt with, if not relinquish it to, patches of the maternal amber) and impossibly large blue-green eyes set in a lemur face."

Having spoken that entire sentence, not quite the length of the Scorpion Sea, in a single breath, Glance waved his hand, the mass of sentry cats parted, and there they were, Macduff and Alias, lashing their tails and looking hungry for revenge over the loss of their siblings and mother.

"Let's go inside. The bird of time has but a little way to flutter, and so on, and so forth." He skipped forward, and the cats flowed along with him.

With cobwebs still enshrouding my brain, I followed them through the arched doorway, down a narrow side corridor, and down steep stone steps that seemed bent upon winding their way into the very bowels of the earth. At length we came out into a vast underground chamber, lit by a wild sulphurous luster.

The floor, although seemingly of solid material, was treacherous with slime. My forehead was bathed in a clammy vapor, and the peculiar smell of decayed fungus rose to my nostrils. I pushed forward through the cats to the brink of a circular pit that plunged even deeper into the heart of darkness.

"Lovely decorations," murmured Glance at my side. I looked around and saw that every surface of the chamber was rudely daubed with depictions of hideous and repulsive devices; the figures of fiends with skeleton forms and menacing leers, and other fearful images, overspread and disfigured the walls and floor. The outlines of these monstrosities were sufficiently distinct, but the colors seemed faded and blurred, as if from the effects of the damp atmosphere.

From beyond the pit came a dreamy indeterminate hum, and the saffron light grew brighter, revealing Sanoma and her goons standing on a dais at the end of the chamber. Behind them lurked a strange figure in a hooded cloak, and I thought that I beheld within the darkness of that hood the sparkle and blaze of multiple fiery eyes.

Between us and them, precariously balanced on a small and shallow ledge at the very verge of the pit's far side, was my dear Harp, a symphony in cream and crimson. Her hair, suddenly redder than I remembered, was bleeding down the length of her ivory neck, a blood-dimmed tide engulfing the archipelago of her freckles. Her green eyes were huge and glazed over, as if drugged.

Seeing that there was enough room to pass between the stone wall and the jaws of the pit, I started to go around it to the left, with Oatmeal trailing at my heels. "Hold!" Sanoma's voice rang through the chamber. "You know not what you do! Behold!"

She pointed up to the vaulted ceiling, where I saw a pendulum with a crescent of glittering steel, about six feet in length from horn to horn, the horns curving upward and the lower edge evidently as keen as a razor. The blade, massive and heavy, started to swing on its rod of brass, hissing as it moved through the air, rapidly descending as it swung.

"You cannot reach her without putting yourself in its path," said Glance. "And if by some chance it does not cut you in two, then it will sweep you into the pit. Find another way."

"I must go to her," was my response. Flattening myself against the dank stones of the wall, I began edging around the pit, while Oatmeal paced restlessly at the brink, giving vent to an occasional howl of despair.

Glancing back the way I had come, I noticed that a segment of the army of sentry cats had detached itself and was flowing around the other side of the pit, headed for Sanoma. She gestured and her goons came down off the dais, laughing roughly as they unsheathed their weapons.

Already the fearful scimitar was sweeping so closely above my head that, as it fanned me, I smelled the odor of the sharp steel. I felt strangely calm and caught myself smiling up at the glittering death, as a child does at some rare bauble.

Yowls of pain and rage rang out from the far side of the pit, where a wholesale slaughter was taking place. I saw one goon swing his heavy saber and slice off the heads of Siva and Snark in one blow, while another lifted the bloody limp body of Loki above his head and flung it over the stone lip into the dark abyss.

I realized that the distraction was just long enough to put me in mortal danger, as the hiss of the moving blade caught my attention in time to see it hurtling straight for my face. At the same moment, something rammed into me from the side and shoved me violently past the pit, past Harp's small ledge, to land sprawling on the slimy floor on the far side.

Even as I looked to see who had saved me, I heard an almost human scream, and I saw the sharp edge of the pendulum slicing through Oatmeal's right side as he stood where I had stood beside the pit. Upon the instant he bolted across and came to me.

There was now a bald patch on his side, showing gray-pink skin stretched tight over his ribs; it moved in and out with his labored breathing and glistened with blood. A strip of fur and skin, still attached by a thread, hung from his rump like a second tail.

When I looked back groggily at the battle of the goons and cats, I saw that the tide had turned somewhat. Midnight Snowflake had a man down on his back and was feeding on the flesh of his throat, while Tigro-puss was a stripy blur as he darted in and out among the swordsmen in a path intended to take him straight to Sanoma.

That lady tossed her head back and laughed her horrid laugh and stretched out one hand to grasp a long metal lever protruding from the wall at her side.

"I am by no means finished," she purred, and she threw the lever.

Immediately the pendulum stopped moving, but at the same time I saw another change in the chamber, one that filled me with dread. It was altering its shape—because the two side walls were moving inward.

And now I perceived many things at once: the cats shrieking, the men swearing as they fell under their claws and teeth, Tigro-puss dancing stiff-legged, tail erect, around an ax-wielding goon at the base of Sanoma's dais, the lighter Luna and the darker Aka coming up around them as the cat army slowly advanced through the chamber, Macduff and Alias springing onto the dais to land and crouch on either side of Sanoma and stare at her with avid hunger and palpable bloodlust, Glance now appearing beside Harp, clinging to her as the moving wall behind them pushed them inexorably toward the yawning gulf, until there was barely an inch of foothold on the ledge.

"Stop!" I cried to Macduff and Alias, as they wriggled in preparation for pouncing on their prey. "Only she can save Harp!" I dragged myself to my feet and limped light-headed to the dais, raising my bleary eyes to meet those of Sanoma.

"I come in peace. Surely we can make some kind of peace between us."

Without turning her head, she reached a hand out to the hooded figure behind her, and it unfolded full-sleeved arms to produce a bouquet of long-stemmed crimson roses. Sanoma stood there fingering the sharp thorns as she watched the carnage going on around us.

"Here's what I think of your *peace!*"

With the last word she slashed savagely down across my face with the roses, and the thorns tore out my left eye.

Reeling and crying out in my pain, I heard my father's voice: "When the flesh is cut, the sensation does not become pain until it reaches the brain and is registered there, but the sensation travels from the cut to the brain at the rate of ninety-eight feet per second."

I turned my good eye back to the ledge, where I saw Glance and Harp tottering on the brink, and then the moving wall surged forward and shoved them into the pit. They were gone.

Now Sanoma was leaning down to me. "Wander the smiling countryside, which you will never see again," she hissed into my ear, "and think of all that you have lost."

She slashed at my face again and the thorn-studded roses took out my other eye.

As the veil of darkness descended upon me, I heard the growls of Macduff and Alias, heard Sanoma scream in astonishment and disbelief, heard the thud of a falling body, and felt something warm and wet splash my face.

Then silence and stillness and night were my universe.

My last thought was that Oatmeal's skin and fur would grow back. My eyes would not.

PART VII

THE SMILE OF A PANTHER ABOUT TO FEAST

Chapter 42
The Piper at the Gates of Dawn

It was twilight and we were coming down through the foothills by way of a pass called Fancy Gap, about a day's journey from the coast. I had finished telling Bama the story of his brothers and could see that it had given him a lot to chew on.

"Each of us ended up a dervish, or at least in the garb of one, for a different reason. Talin was forced into it to save his life and escape from Hroom. Agib fell into the hands of other dervishes who nursed him back to health. I used it as a ruse to get close to Sanoma. But each of us, after his calamity, decided to keep the identity as a disguise in which to travel."

The horses picked their way cautiously down a flinty slope, and then Terhune grunted and spoke.

"This lad's story is interesting. One more confirmation that there's magic afoot in this business."

"We already knew that," I reminded him.

"Aye. But I'm fond of multiple confirmations. Speaking of which, I see a number of disturbing patterns in this whole rigmarole. I smell mischief."

"What kind of mischief?"

"I already told you that I had an idea about the

nature of these so-called helpers or assistants. The new lad's story only convinces me the more. They're too much alike, too identical."

"Another case of triplets?"

"No. As we have seen from the three lads, even identical triplets have their differences and their own personalities. These jaspers are another thing entirely. I think that they were golems."

Diarfa gasped. "Golems! But there haven't been golems for decades! They've been outlawed in most kingdoms."

Bama frowned. "I've heard the word, but I'm not sure what they are."

"Supernatural beings," Terhune told him. "Created from earth and herbs and certain secret ingredients. They have been called the perfect servants because they have no mind and no will of their own. And if you make a batch of multiple golems, they turn out identical. Peas in a pod, as my granny used to say."

"Well," I thought out loud, "if the Lady Marabar was providing helpers for her champions, what better way to do it than to choose trustworthy servants whom she could rely on to carry out her wishes?"

Terhune spat tobacco juice. "All right. Let's gather together our three young dervishes–assuming that we can find the first two that have gone missing–and ask them if they're happy with the way things worked out after they followed the guidance of their trustworthy, reliable, mindless, identical helpers. Eh?"

"What's our next rest stop?" Orn asked, abruptly and violently changing the subject. He did not look happy.

"There's an abandoned windmill up ahead that will give us shelter and some warmth," I said. "Terhune here could tell you about the time he was being chased by a gang of vampires and pulled the mill's arms into the shape of a giant cross. An ancient religious symbol no longer significant to anyone but the undead. The moon threw a cross-shaped shadow over them and it fried them on the spot."

"Ancient history," he muttered, but I saw a smile flicker on his lips. "Nothing quite like frying vampires."

We reached the mill, a lightning-blasted ruin, with the last of the light. Any rubble on the inside had been cleared away long ago by other travelers, and there was plenty of room for all of us on the floor. I was asleep in five minutes.

I was awakened by dim light and a hand on my shoulder. Bama was leaning over me, his delicate face still shielded by the smoked spectacles. I thought of a line in my poem about the weeping willow, the poem he had received as his second dream clue: "Medusa woman, born of ink, leans out to greet her solar hell."

His words disturbed my reverie. "I've had my third dream."

I sat up with a jerk and saw that Terhune was already on his feet, gazing imperturbably out through one of the jagged holes in the wall. The others, including the cats, were still stretched out on the floor.

"I was in front of some big building. I saw a strange statue there, with the body of a man but the head of a horse, and on the head were the horns of a goat. Its mouth was slightly open in a leering grin, so that I could see its stone teeth, and it was holding up some kind of wind instrument, not a flute. It appeared to have more than one hole for blowing."

I knew it, and so did Terhune. "The Piper," he told the morning sky.

Bama's forehead creased. "The Piper?"

I explained. "The Piper at the Gates of Dawn. The work of the great sculptor Deerga, who ultimately went mad after producing many such oddities. Some say that he was mad to begin with. He was eventually locked up for having sex in public with one of his statues. Some kind of animal, I believe."

Orn was stirring. "I never for a minute took any stock in that concocted and bully story," he mumbled. "What's for breakfast?"

We ignored him. "And here's the grand surprise. The Piper stands in front of a place with a long name, Bedside for short–"

"Tell him its whole name. I love to hear it spoken." Diarfa was awake now.

I nodded. "All right. The Bedside Manor Twilight Cocktalarium and Home for the Permanently Bewildered. It's where Deerga was put away when his madness overtook him and could no longer be winked at by the general populace."

"Why is that a grand surprise?"

"It's in Tarn, the seaport where we're headed. We will be there by late afternoon."

Tarn was in my ears and in my eyes, nose, and mouth. I reveled in its bustling traffic, its hawkers' cries, its colorful signs, its constantly moving people, its salt sea air. As I scanned the main square, I bit into a crab sandwich and felt it ejaculate its tart sauce into my mouth.

The person I was seeking suddenly appeared before me, although there had been no way to let him know I was in town. I grinned to see my favorite agent on the Scorpion Sea. Gray was a tall, skinny teenage boy with a large wide mouth. He had a gangly, hairless body that I found almost unbearably erotic because it made him look even younger than he really was. Diarfa, who had seen him at the Floating Head, said that he was scrawny and had a mouth like a frog. Tastes vary.

His appearance helped him blend in anywhere he went without arousing suspicion, because he looked too young to be dangerous. Also, because he was totally devoid of prejudice, he was willing to go to bed with anyone, male or female, which made him invaluable in ferreting out information.

Today he was wearing a full-sleeved pirate shirt of white silk, tight breeches of bronze leather, and no cloak. He always claimed that the cold could not touch him. His shaggy brown hair and black eyes made a dark hole in the gaudy crowd as he emerged from it.

"Greetings. My friends and I have no time to tarry, as we must get up to Bedside before they close the gates. Come aside."

Gray followed my horse over to a loudly gushing fountain, where the sound of the water would partially mask our words. I leaned down to mutter in his ear.

"You have heard, I am sure, of the True Word and the dervishes who are spreading it, picking up donations along the way as hunting dogs pick up beggar's-lice. Their leader is called the Snowman. Find out what you can about all this and meet me on the docks tomorrow morning."

He spoke for the first time, in the lilting tenor I remembered. "Where will you be spending the night?"

"Up at Bedside."

"The owner never lets outsiders spend the night, only the inmates."

"She owes me a favor."

Gray nodded, spun on his heel, his sleeves swishing through the air, and bolted back into the mass of people and horses from which he had appeared so inexplicably.

I returned to my party and raised my voice slightly. "Away, away. The madhouse awaits."

The Bedside Manor Twilight Cocktalarium and Home for the Permanently Bewildered, constructed of dragontongue-gray brick over a century ago, and shaped like a monstrous starfish, clung to the top of a hill overlooking Tarn, its long narrow wings dripping down the slopes in all directions. Having passed through the gates in the serpentine wall that encircled the base of the hill, we left our horses with a somber servant and toiled up the gravel path to the main courtyard.

There we saw the Piper at the Gates of Dawn, just as Bama had described it. A wiry male nude carved out of gray stone, lifting a twisted musical instrument up to lips spread in a soundless whinny, the long horse face running up to sharp curving horns. A thing out of a nightmare.

"Well," said Diarfa, eyeing it with sick fascination, "if the dreams are reliable, we're very close to the final component of the chess game."

In the wall beyond the statue, a heavy door swung open and the opening was filled by a little man whose pale yellow hair had always made me think of a sulfur-crested cockatoo.

"Kemp. Our apologies for not giving you warning of our visit. We need to see your mistress."

"Of course," he oozed, pronouncing the words as "Ob cuss." Bowing and scraping, he ushered us into an entrance hall, dusty and dim because the torches had not yet been lit.

"You may sit here in the waiting room while I apprise her of your request." He threw open a door. "There are others already here, but I am sure they will not mind sharing the room." He oozed away.

A raging fire illuminated the waiting room and its ornate furniture, throwing shadows of the two men seated on either side of the hearth as they leaned in and clinked squat heavy glasses together in a toast.

They were Talin and Agib.

Chapter 43
Slow Anger at an Ancient Crime

They gaped and sprang to their feet, coming forward as Orn trilled, "By the Lord Harry!" and Bama demanded to know what was happening. Diarfa and I merely stared, while Styx lashed his dark tail and Terhune and Oatmeal remained the calm unflappable beasts that they were.

Talin thrust his glass at Agib and came up to me, almost close enough to kiss me. His eye glistened with some strong emotion, and he gripped both my biceps in his strong young hands. I felt lightheaded.

"Well met by firelight," I managed to say faintly.

"I thought that I might not ever see you again."

"That makes two of us." I pulled myself together. "How did you come to find your way here?"

"The last thing I remember is being on the raft, the morning after we escaped from the cannibals. After that, it's as if I fell into a long deep sleep–"

"The same with me," Agib put in. "One moment I was turning into a statue at that Dark Carnival, then there was a long black period shot through with dim flashes of light. Trapped in a long dark teatime before a badly built fire, that's what I was."

"This afternoon that man Kemp found us both

asleep out in the front courtyard. We were curled up together under this eerie statue—"

"Yes, Talin, we know all about the statue. It was the clue in Bama's final dream."

"Bama?" He seemed to realize for the first time that there were other people in the room. I watched his single eye reluctantly leave mine and then widen when it fell upon the dervish behind me.

"Yes. I see that you have met Agib, and I hope that you have had a chance to trade stories. You'll both want to make the acquaintance of Bama here, since I believe that you are all related to one another."

Agib laughed coarsely and, lifting first one glass and then the other, threw the contents of each down his throat. "Related? I'll be a honeyseed rogue if we're not brothers. Tattered prodigals. Fickle changelings, farmed out to whatever second-rate royal households would take us."

"And now brought together," said Diarfa, pitching her voice a little higher than necessary in the small room, "by the most preposterous scheme I have ever heard of. What are these people playing at, to hide a child's toys and then beat each other over the head trying to get them back again?"

The door flew open and the man Kemp crept in. "My mistress will see you in the Merrythought Room." He paused slightly. "She will see you all." Without looking at us he slipped away again, and we moved to follow.

Orn eyed me shrewdly. "Merrythought is an old word for a wishbone."

"And, by extension, any place where wishes come true and destinies may be divined."

We found ourselves traveling down a shadow-speckled corridor, past iron doors with small barred windows, windows that leaked the moans and cries of the inmates.

"I is skeered of skellingtons!"

"Yay, it's the Waiter Parade!"

"Two fools die, say I!"

"I want to lick and chew!"

"Beware, beware, a witch won't share!"

"Dog waste gone!"

"Tonight I must use all my knives!"

"I smell the trees!"

"It's almost that happy, happy time!"

"Ack, ack, it's oozin' up like the Trump o' Doom!"

In the madhouse, all sentences end with an exclamation point.

The Merrythought Room was a long and comfortable parlor in the back of the Manor, furnished in the pale brown of withered leaves. At the fire, a tiny gnome of a man, either a much decayed servant or a much improved inmate, was trying to make and butter toast at the same time, holding a piece of bread impaled on a long fork which he clutched in yellow gloves, smearing both toast and himself with such vast quantities of yellow butter that I could not tell where gloves stopped and butter began.

On the mantle above him crouched dark blue pitchers, midnight blue pitchers, heroic blue pitchers, stabbing the air with their spouts like the noses of naughty puppets. They shared their space with fat black candles in the shape of owls.

In an alcove to our left, two more old men were huddled over a small cloth-covered table, playing a game of cooncan; I could see a design of cedar waxwings on the backs of the cards.

The room was dominated, however, by a magnificent painting that took up an entire wall to our right. Two attractive young women in fancy hats and long dresses, one with her right hand reddened as if by a bleeding wound, sat with bowed heads in a rowboat on a lake of lotus flowers, while here and there the irislike lily called tiger-faced peacock lifted a colorful face to the white sky. The painting was behind glass, and I could see our reflections moving as blurred images imposed over the water and the flowers.

A throaty voice came from behind us. "I'm the one on the right. My companion is the only person with whom I have shared my bed and the only person I have truly loved. That was years ago, of course."

She was just as I remembered her, tall for a woman, the shoulders of her brown gown brushed by her lush smoky topaz hair. She looked as if she had posed for the painting yesterday.

"I am Lady Tamila Cockingbird, the proprietress of this place. My first name always rhymes with vanilla, never with Pamela. I keep this room furnished in pale brown because it is the color of mourning in certain eastern countries. I am in perpetual mourning. Do sit down."

"You know me," I said.

"I do."

We settled ourselves in chairs that were decorative and singularly comfortable–a rare combination–while the others in the room continued to ignore us.

"Our business has dreams mixed up in it. We were brought here by a dream of your statue out front. The work of your mad sculptor Deerga."

"A scamp and a wretch." She took out a long thin cigar, the same pale brown as her gown and everything in the room around us, and lit it with immeasurable relish.

"But that is nothing more than a guidepost to help us on our way."

"Tell her about the contest," Talin blurted, something like agony in his voice.

"Two great figures of sorcery have engaged in a war of wits and power. My young friends here serve the Lady Marabar, who is opposed by her Lord–"

She interrupted with a puff of smoke and a wave of her hand. "The robber baron Tharados, a vile gangster. He is a volcano of hatred and evil."

"Really? Do you know him?"

"Well, no. But it's something that everyone knows in

this part of the world."

"How do they know?"

"The Lady Marabar speaks openly about their quarrel, which has gone on for years. He's never been normal since his first Lady died in childbirth."

She pulled on the cigar and let her smoke-gray eyes go out of focus.

"Marabar was already in the palace at the time, and in his bed. Some say that he took out his anger and grief on her. Blamed her because she was actually in the chamber when the first Lady died. Never forgave her. Slow anger at an ancient crime, you might say."

Terhune stirred. "How ancient?"

"Oh, almost two decades ago. They've spent some twenty years bickering and snapping and trying to best each other in duels of wizardry. Some say he'll never rest until he strips her of her power."

"He'll soon be laughing out of the other side of his mouth," Orn told her. "This lot has signed on to champion her cause and restore her favorite magic talismans to her. Everything's almost back in place."

"Father, watch your tongue." Diarfa's tone was sharp. "You're treading on cat ice."

I got up and wandered back to stand looking at their reflection in the glass of the painting, considering how much more Lady Tamila needed to hear. But then she spoke.

"I know that I owe you a favor, Catalan. I'd be happy to help the Lady Marabar. It's been no great pleasure to sit here looking out at the island of Phuxor and watching them try to chew each other into submission, like a cobra and a mongoose forced to share a courtyard."

"Which the cobra and which the mongoose?" Diarfa murmured. I watched her reflection as she rose. "I have need of a garderobe. Is there one in the passage?"

"Two doors down to the left. If you find yourself talking to a man who thinks he's a chamberpot, you've gone too far."

I saw the image of Diarfa go out the way we had come in, and then the reflection of the Merrythought Room became still again. I turned over many things in my mind.

The light clear voice of Bama came from the seated group. "My Lady, have you... had recent occasion to come across an ornate playing board? One to be used for the ancient game of chess?"

Before she could answer there was movement once more among the reflections in the glass, a figure drifting over the painted landscape as easily as a playing piece moved by an unseen hand. It came from the direction of the passage, but it was not Diarfa.

I whirled and stared at a tall gargoyle-faced man, dressed in yellow and black stripes and pointing a loaded crossbow at us. I thought of what Diarfa had said in the cabin on Hunchback Mountain: *The Bumblebee of Love flits in the garden of the world, for whose flowers destruction is in his breath.*

Tamila threw back her head and let out a gasp. "He's not one of mine."

At almost the same time the stranger said, "You must give me the little men."

"They're called chessmen, you ninnyhammer." An act of bravado from Orn.

The stranger edged slowly around the room until he stood near the cooncan players, who were rooted to their chairs by their fear. Tamila eyed him warily.

"He wears the colors of the House of Tharados. Have no doubt that he means what he says."

Suddenly he dropped the crossbow and was clawing at a short metal spike protruding from his throat, all the while gurgling as if the membranes of his lungs were inflamed with pleurisy. Bloody foam flecked his lips and he swayed drunkenly.

Diarfa came up beside me, holding a second dagger

poised in case it was needed. "Sorry there was no smothered chicken available to throw this time."

The stranger crashed down onto the cooncan players' table, making them jump up and scuttle aside. Cards fluttered in the air, a cardboard flock of disturbed waxwings. In his death throes he clutched the tablecloth and dragged it with him to the floor, uncovering the tabletop beneath.

"Let all the dukes and all the devils roar!" cried Agib. "Look!"

The top of the table was a large playing board, constructed of alternating inlaid squares of light and dark wood.

"Mvuli wood and stained sandalwood," breathed Talin. "It must be."

Terhune made a sound between a laugh and a cough. "Have you had recent occasion to come across an ornate playing board, he asks. Well, lads, I think you've finished your quests. All that remains is to deliver the goods to yon happy island."

"Which we will do tomorrow," I told him.

Orn sprang to his feet. "Oh, fine, we fling ourselves into the arms of the man who hired this knave, this poltroon, to kill us. We stick our heads into the jaws of the panther, to provide a feast for him."

"The Jaws of Darkness," muttered Agib.

Lady Tamila stood and walked to the dead man, flicking ashes down onto his upturned face. "A moment ago you were singing a different tune. 'He'll be laughing out of the other side of his mouth,' you said. 'Everything's almost back in place.' Changed your mind?"

"No, we haven't changed our minds," I told the group. "Tomorrow morning we meet Gray on the docks and hire a boat for Phuxor. Terhune, see about taking the legs off that table. We only need the board."

On the floor next to our new prize, the slain bowman seemed to be sneering at us.

CHAPTER 44
NIGHT WALTZ FROM HELL

Gray was late. The captain of the hired boat, a rogue corsair who had turned from piracy to less lucrative but safer pursuits, was anxious to set off.

"I've got plenty of trips to make this day," he told me petulantly, pacing up and down the dock and pulling at his droopy mustache. "You're wasting your time anyway. They don't like visitors on Phuxor, and you'll never be allowed to land. They've got that majordomo, what's his name, Quicksand or summat, who runs the island like a warship, strict and tightly controlled."

He herded us up the gangplank and into the glass-enclosed passenger area, where a tangled webbing of green ice on the windows made it impossible to see out. I waited until he went off to prepare for departure; then I stuck my head out the door to take a last look for Gray.

There he was, still in his shirtsleeves despite the bitter chill, striding cranelike down the dock, his eyes snapping buttons of black fire. I went out to meet him on deck, some of the others following me as the thumping of his boots on the gangplank heralded his arrival.

"I can't stay, but you're on the verge of setting off anyway," he said in a rush. He thrust a folded piece of paper at me. "This is all I could get on such short notice, but you'll find it interesting. Read it when you're alone." His eyes slid suspiciously toward the dervishes.

I tucked it in an inner pocket of my cloak and opened my mouth to answer him, but the cry of "All ashore!" sounded hoarsely from the bow of the ship and he jumped like a startled animal.

"Away, away!" he cried and was gone, moving so rapidly that the cloud of vapor from his breath was still before my face even after he had vanished down the gangplank.

Moments later, we were casting off from the dock, slicing through the slushy sea, on our way to *yon happy island.*

Phuxor was a small piece of rock with one accessible beach, one steep hill, and one ominous gray edifice on top, smoky and smudged by distance. We were allowed to land but were immediately met on the beach by the majordomo of whom the captain had spoken.

He was a squalid brown swamp of a man, cloaked in the aroma of bacon, with scum on his face and large-winged insects fluttering behind his eyes. "My name is Quagmire," he intoned.

Ah. *Quicksand or summat,* indeed.

"My mistress awaits you. This way."

The steepness of the path had Orn wheezing and blowing like a grampus, and I was feeling my own morning freshness ebbing by the time we reached the top. The high gray walls and small windows of the palace made it look like a prison looming over us. It started to snow as we approached it.

Quagmire shouldered open a heavy set of double doors and pointed us into a yawning entrance hall where a scantily clad maid was hovering. "Follow her." He seeped away.

As we proceeded down a windowless, torchlit corridor I heard Orn mutter in my ear, "The way that maid is dressed is a scandal to the jaybirds. What kind of snakepit is this?"

She conducted us into a large oblong room, featureless except for the vast fireplace taking up most of one wall. Its flames gleamed on the smooth cedar panels of the windowless walls, ceiling, and floor, reminding me of the cigar box chamber beneath the house of the Widow Toad. Down the length of the room ran a long table with nothing on it.

The maid offered to take our cloaks but I declined. I wanted all of my pockets within easy reach. She went out.

The door opened and the Lady Marabar swept in, her purple-black gown rustling as she came. I saw the strong sharp razor-edged face I remembered, the color of a dusky rose sunset. I saw the elongated withered neck like a dragon's tail, long severed yet still hard with agony. I saw the shark-gray hair tortured back from the eyes, eyes protected by opalescent lenses that changed color in the flickering firelight.

I saw the dark majesty I had seen in the picture of the boat-tailed grackle in the entrance hall of the Hungry Hag. I saw the sultry beauty I had seen in the picture of the black-crowned nightherons on the same wall. She was astonishing.

"How kind of you to come so far," she said.

"How kind of you to let us come," Diarfa said flatly.

Marabar gestured to the table and we sat, while the cats made themselves comfortable on the floor. I nodded to Diarfa, who was carrying the bags with the chess set components in them, and she gravely placed the board in the center of the table and put the pieces in their appointed places on the inlaid squares.

Marabar seemed oblivious to the prize we had brought her. She turned round to Quagmire, who had suddenly appeared at her shoulder, and ordered wine.

"My Lord is coming to join us on this most auspicious occasion. I hope you will enjoy some refreshment while we wait."

Before she finished the sentence the majordomo was shuffling back and forth among us, sloshing red wine into goblets and slamming them down. The maid followed with wooden bowls holding a savory dark brown stew. Brandishing a flagon of strange yellow wine that looked like urine, Marabar poured herself a drink. "My own special stock," she told us. She received no stew.

She held her goblet aloft in a toast. "Congratulations to us all. This assignment was very difficult from my end as well as yours. Extracting the clues and sending them in dreams. Finding and instructing reliable assistants—"

"Your golems?" Terhune's voice crashed in.

Silence.

Silence.

Silence.

Silence.

"Golems, yes. They are so much more talented than humans." She drank some of her yellow wine.

"And they do as they are told," Diarfa drawled.

Marabar ignored her. She appeared to be deep in thought, although her goblet kept moving up to her mouth.

Finally she said, "Of course I did not depend entirely on you, my young champions, or my well-trained assistants. From time to time I dropped in on you to see how things were going. Perhaps you noticed me?"

She drank more wine.

"My eyes are very special, which is why I keep them covered and protected most of the time. I have the power to give myself multiple eyes, for half an hour at a time, to look in all directions at once. At such times I wear a hooded cloak, so as not to scare the horses."

Tighter breathing and zero at the bone, as the poet says. I remembered the hooded figure with many glowing eyes, featured in the story of each dervish and seen by me at the Floating Head and at the Dark Carnival. I remembered it convulsed with silent laughter at the bloody end to Professor Salt's failed Rope Trick. Motiveless malignancy. I felt that dark burp of the bowels that meant something was very wrong here.

"And once, just for my own entertainment, I appeared to you in a different guise, to check on you at the Hungry Hag."

The air around her shimmered briefly, and in her chair was the fat old woman, complete with lumpy skin, bald head like a small boulder, bulging eyes, excessive face powder, and tomato-stained crevice of a mouth. Then the Lady Marabar was back, smiling at me.

"I believe that the real Widow is a neighbor of yours back in Andor. Don't look surprised. There is very little I don't know."

The door opened and in came a large fleshy man. His shock of hair was gray but his bushy mustache was red, presumably dyed to its former color. He stopped when he saw our gathering and stood just inside the door, twiddling tobacco-stained fingers on the lapels of his crimson dressing gown.

"We have guests, how nice." Then he noticed the chessboard. "What is this?"

Marabar waved her goblet. "My dear Lord Tharados. This is the enchanted chess set I received from the Grateful Dead, over which you and I quarreled. Surely you remember?"

He frowned. "I–"

"With all due respect, my Lord, I am not finished."

He spread his hands, and his frown turned to a smile. "Then please go on. I always find entertainment in your infinite variety." He came over and sat at the table. "Take all the time you want."

"I thank you." She drank more wine. "I realize that all of you here have made sacrifices in bringing me what I asked for. I have seen some of these sacrifices myself."

She looked in the direction of Bama, who had grown uneasy, fiddling with his now empty bowl.

"You may have been wondering about the where-abouts of your beloved Harp. Of course I was in the underground chamber beneath the hunting lodge of Sanoma. I'm afraid I have to tell you that, at the behest of the Snowman, she was kidnapped, brought here, killed, chopped up, cooked into a savory stew, and served up to you. You have just eaten her."

Bama turned slowly and vomited onto the chessboard.

"No!" cried Talin.

"Oh, no need to worry about the chess pieces," she purred. "They have no special powers and never did. They were a mere subterfuge to help me in achieving my true purpose."

She drank more wine.

"I have led you all on a merry dance. Well, not so merry at times. A night waltz from Hell, some might call it. Or perhaps a strathspey, similar to but slower than a reel."

I found that my mouth was hanging open, and a rapid glance around the table showed me that my companions were equally shocked.

"Did you actually believe that your quests were real? Did you actually believe that what I told you was true? Did you actually believe, if this so-called treasure was so easily retrievable, that I would need you?"

At the end of each of these sentences she had snapped a scythelike fingernail against her goblet. Now she slapped the table and flared up, "You are nothing and I am everything!"

I jumped as if I had been stabbed and heard a crackling of paper inside my cloak. I reached in and pulled out the message Gray had given me just before we sailed for Phuxor. I unfolded it and the words leaped up at me.

The Snowman is a woman.

CHAPTER 45
PUNISHED AND BURNISHED AND BURNED

The Lady Marabar placed her hands flat on the table and rose slowly, uncoiling like a poisonous reptile.

"Time for us to take off our masks."

She drank more wine.

"There was no quest. I fabricated the entire thing. I planted the components of the chess game and knew where they were at all times. By my power to induce dreams, I have led you to them as the lamb is led to the slaughter."

Diarfa stirred in her chair. "But not by yourself. You had help from your golems."

"Oh, yes. Three little men who looked like monkeys and talked like encyclopedias. With the names Prance, Trance, and Glance. Did it really take you so long to suspect them?"

"Where did you get them?" Orn asked in genuine fascination.

"It doesn't matter. The magic of the mud. Unfortunately, they cannot be here because I killed them to ensure their silence. That which tasted air and drank the sun is dead. And dead puppets tell no tales."

She turned her face to the vomit-flecked chessboard. "Games. I could have been playing demon patience, that most excellent card game, but I preferred to play with you. You are all pawns. Prawns. Spineless creatures. Invertebrates. Helpless twitching creatures to be pushed around the game-board of this treacherous lurid life."

She turned her face to Lord Tharados, who sat silent. "Look at these fine specimens of young manhood." By now she was spitting out her words as poisonous pellets.

"Each of them, by his own idiocy and folly, has maimed himself." She chuckled, and the sound was iron-dark and ice-cold.

"Each of them, by his own idiocy and folly, has killed an object of his affection." Now she was openly laughing, and what I heard was the same sound of tearing leather I had heard when she masqueraded as the Widow Toad.

"Each of them, by his own idiocy and folly, has ensnared himself in a false religion that I created for my own amusement. Drugging people with religion and then taking their money is such a rich source of entertainment."

Diarfa could no longer contain herself. "What about this True Word? What's going to happen to all the innocent people who have been duped by it?"

"The next logical step is to start rounding up those who refuse to embrace it and burning them as heretics. The difference between a heretic and a loaf of bread is that a loaf of bread doesn't scream when you put it in the oven. My favorite joke."

"How can you speak so lightly about such a thing?"

She shrugged. "It gives me something to do. It's been a great deal of work, but the labor we delight in physics pain."

"You monstrous creature," Diarfa said with gritted teeth.

"'Be well aware,' quoth then that Lady mild, 'lest sudden mischief ye too rash provoke.'" She drank more wine. "As the poet says."

Diarfa dared to give a small laugh. "Mild is not the

word for you."

Marabar flared up. "I repeat my warning. Do not provoke me. I have eyes of horn and a heart of steel. I shut up the sea with doors and rape the treasures of the snow. I put my hand on the sun's face and make it night in the earth; I bite a piece out of the moon and hurry the seasons. If old age is to be a shipwreck, then I shall leave as much wreckage behind as I possibly can."

She surveyed the three dervishes. "Do not pretend to be guiltless in your destruction. Whether we fall by ambition, blood, or lust, like diamonds we are cut with our own dust."

She turned her face to Talin. "I sent the genius who killed Zayo, but it was your drunken braggadocio that triggered his attack."

She turned her face to Agib. "I made you fall on your catamite and stab him to death in the Devil's Oven, but it was you who chose to indulge in the deadly combination of the bottle and illicit sex."

She turned her face to Bama. "I sent you Sanoma, my walking, talking flask of poisoned honey. But you accepted the deadly hoptoad that sent your inamorata underground. You have all been victims of wine and magic."

I looked at Talin, who had one eye. *That owltorn, that gongtormented sky*

I looked at Agib, who had one eye. *A huge sun-yellow portal... like a hook in my mouth, tugging and tearing me to it*

I looked at Bama, who had no eyes. *Wander the smiling countryside, which you will never see again, and think of all that you have lost*

I could remain silent no longer. "This is sheer flummery! If you did all that you claim, you are mad."

"Ah, yes. The celebrated poet. You, too, have been used. Your poetry has been perverted in my service. Bait for my dream traps. Your soul has been sullied."

"What! Why?"

"You I dragged into the business because you once had the effrontery to laugh at me in public."

I remembered the story I had told Talin back at the Floating Head: celebrants acknowledging her arrival in their native custom, turning their backs to her, bowing away from her in a slowly spreading wave, and my ignorant laughter.

"No one, man, woman, child, or animal, does that and remains unharmed."

My senses reeled. What animal had laughed at her in public?

"I do not suffer fools gladly, and anyone who crosses me is doomed. When I was a young girl and just beginning to learn the ways of sorcery, someone gave me two ducklings as a birthday present. Looking back on it, I find that they were vulgarly charming and disgustingly sweet. At the time, however, I doted on them."

She drank more wine.

"A boy of my acquaintance came to visit, picked them up by their necks, and proceeded in total oblivion to tighten his grip unconsciously and strangle them to death as he talked to me. I turned the three of them, the idiot boy and the two dead baby ducks hanging limply from his hands, into a statue on the spot.

"That was the first time I reached out and punished someone who was annoying me, and I can still remember the initial surge of black joy. There is nothing like it. It beggars description. It is the perfect drug.

"Later I put them on a horse and placed the whole revolting ensemble on top of a mountain." She turned her face toward Agib. "I believe that you had the pleasure of viewing that particular piece of artwork on Bent Mountain. Before you threw it into the sea."

She drank more wine. "Since then that trick has been one of my favorite forms of revenge. You could fill a country town with the people who have offended me and been turned into statues. The landscape is littered with such masterworks. What do you suppose was the origin of the frenzied contessas in the back garden of the Hungry Hag? Alas, that story would make us tarry too late, and I have other fish to fry."

"Then why," I asked calmly, "after turning Agib into a statue at the Dark Carnival, did you turn him back into a boy?"

"Because I wanted him to be awake, alert, and sentient for the climactic revelation of this delightful reunion party."

"Reunion?" piped Orn. "We don't know you."

"But I assure you that none of you is here purely by accident, even though some are here only as hangers-on." She appeared to contemplate Terhune. "I am reminded of a story. There was a spoiled young gentleman, heir to the throne of his kingdom, who liked to summon courtiers to him in the palace garden. There he would force each lackey in turn to read aloud the inscription on the collar of his spaniel: 'I am the Prince's dog at Kew; pray tell me, sir, whose dog are you?'"

Terhune bristled but held his tongue. I could not be so controlled. "Terhune is no man's dog! He is a valued friend and companion!"

"Indeed. How touching."

Now she turned on Tharados the blithe, demure smile of a nine-year-old at a birthday party.

"And as for you, my dear Lord, my sweet Lord, my precious lamb. Light of my life, fear of my loins. My sin, my sun, my soil, my soul." She drank more wine.

"You must be wondering who these callow striplings are, and why I have used my valuable time to bring them down. Be still and I will tell you."

She paused, seemingly lost in thought. "You were my senses' idol when we met. You took up with me when your first Lady was with child and refused to let you into her bed. Of course, harlots and their hunted have pleasures of their own to give, the vulgar herd can never understand. And all cats are grey in the dark."

Suddenly her demeanor changed, and now her voice was caking the walls with blood. I could see it and smell it and feel it clotting on my skin.

"You led me to believe that I would inherit her place. In fact, you used me, you manipulated me, you lied to me, you disrepected me, and for that you had to be punished. You would have tossed me aside if your first Lady had not died in childbirth.

"I remember being present, beside the midwife, kneeling by the sills of those exquisite flexible doors when they gave up their gory dead burden, the burden that killed her. I remember how you were wracked with grief, bursting forth into the autumn night, smashing pumpkins, screaming at the trees. Ignoring me."

She grew somewhat calmer. "You may have wondered about that death. There are, as a matter of interest, certain marvelous and useful drugs... But I digress.

"And then I was with your child, and you shunned my bedchamber, having found the next mistress in line. And when I lost the child I found that I had lost you. I have never understood your obsessive pursuit of a son.

"Oh, you kept me as your Lady, but you never touched me again. You insulted me, and for that you had to be punished with a pain as great as molten metal, as raging fire. Punished and burnished and burned."

She drank more wine. "Actually, when I saw you with the pathetic trollop that was to follow me, I came to a decision while I was still with child. I made certain plans. I'm afraid when I sent word to you that I had lost your child, I was not being entirely truthful. I'm also afraid I forgot to mention that I gave birth to triplets."

The room was so quiet that the fire seemed impossibly loud. I felt like an idiot for not seeing the truth. Those cheekbones.

"I'm also afraid I forgot to mention that I had them separated that night, spirited away to three distant kingdoms, and raised in royal foster households until the right time came to make use of them."

He stared. "You lied!" he cried hoarsely. "Why?"

"It's my hobby."

A low moaning was coming from the side of the table where the dervishes sat, but I could not tell who it was. The sonorous words of the Lady Tamila Cockingbird sang in my ears, sang in my brain, sang in my bloodstream. Blood music. *He is a volcano of hatred and evil.*

I looked around the table. There was a volcano in the room, but it was not male in nature.

"With my scheme, knotted and gnarled and whorled as it was, I have caused them to shatter themselves. They will never live as normal men, they will never be happy, and I have been the architect of their destruction. What I have done, I have done for one reason, for the exquisite pleasure of standing here today and telling you what I have done and watching your face."

Tharados had turned the same color as the vomit drying on the chessboard. "The thing I have greatly feared has come upon me."

A movement in the corner of my eye made me glance at Styx. He was rocking back and forth on his front paws, his gaze fixed on Marabar. I looked from beast to woman back to beast, but by this point it was almost impossible to distinguish between them.

The face beneath the fur, the skull beneath the skin. Each had the horrible grin of a panther about to spring, about to feast, about to gobble up everything in front of it, about to consume the entire world. And the rest of us could only sit and watch them do it.

Marabar showed her teeth as her grin grew even more terrible. "And now, to state the obvious—"

And now

And now

And now

And now

And now her face becomes marble and now her hair

comes undone and now the pictures in her hair come alive and now we waltz with witches and now we tango with turncoats and now we pavane with perverts and now we dance with death and now we drink requital on a reef and now we scream for her and now we writhe because she withholds her grace and now time holds us green and dying and now we sing in our chains like the sea and now her voice becomes the Trump of Doom and now it rolls and tolls and now it sings and rings and now it bells and tells and now it bays and brays and now it says, "They are our sons!"

Tharados gripped the edge of the table, breathing deeply as he regained his color. With great deliberation, keeping his eyes fixed on the tabletop, he began to make complex hand gestures while muttering to himself. In half a minute, he was finished. He looked at her.

"The danger of boasting about your crimes, my Lady—and at this point I assure you that I use the term purely as an honorific—is that you run the risk of their being overturned. Your will has been undone. All losses are restored and sorrows end."

She turned her head slightly to one side. "What have you done?"

The door opened and Harp came in and crossed and put her hand in Bama's and said in her little-girl voice, "The reports of my death, dear friend, have been greatly exaggerated."

The door opened again and Droo came in and crossed and put his hand in Agib's and said, his face ablaze with adoration, "Yes, yes, I said yes then, I will say yes again, yes."

The door opened again and Zayo came in and crossed and put her hand in Talin's and said serenely, "I burn. I burn."

The door opened again and the three golems came in, their heads and shoulders powdered with snow, and lined up against the wall, as identical as the vomit-flecked onyx pawns on the chessboard, their eyes all aglitter with the same species of mad hilarity...

And lastly, in prancing parade, came the ebon Ransom and the patchwork pussum known variously as Smogley or Smudgepot. Oatmeal rose and went to meet them, and they danced and shouted out their glee.

Once upon a time, in the front room at the Floating Head, I had observed a family trying to finish a quiet dinner. The plates for the main course were not quite empty, but a bungling waiter had served the cake early and it sat in all its succulent glory. The mother was making sure that it stayed out of the reach of a very young girl, who was being held by her father as she lunged across the table, shrieking, "Cake!" In her aspect was the blank-eyed terror of someone who has always had everything she wanted and suddenly faces the possibility that such may not always be true. "Caaaaake!" she wailed, keened.

Although her eyes were concealed by her protective lenses, the Lady Marabar now showed the same blank terror, as she saw her horrific sweetmeat being taken from her. She was quivering all over, and flecks of spittle appeared on her pulsating jellyfish of a mouth.

"You cannot do this!" she cried. "My murders have made my masterpiece! You cannot do this, you cannot do this, you cannot do this!"

I could. "Sticker," I hissed.

With a growl as thick as a dreamless night of dread, Styx sprang and struck her in the chest. As she went flying over backwards, I saw his jaws close on her screaming face. They disappeared behind the table. There came the hideous wet slick slurping sound of a large carnivore feeding.

Talin stared, horror scrawled across his countenance. "Aren't you going to stop it?" he said, whispered.

"Stop what?" I asked blandly.

Warrior poet evolving into poet warrior.

CHAPTER 46
IF I COULD TURN BACK TIME

I was waiting in a small chamber with a large fire-place and the odor of pine and roses. I had divested myself of my cloak and sword-belt, because a sword can sometimes get in the way.

Terhune was elsewhere, handling the details of our return to the Floating Head. I reflected that I would be wanting larger quarters at the Head.

Well, Talin had asked to meet with me alone. What else could that mean? I remembered our reunion at Bedside Manor, how he had come up to me, almost close enough to kiss me, his eye glistening with some strong emotion, and gripped both my biceps in his strong young hands, making me lightheaded. What else could it mean?

He came through the doorway, his patch gone, his restored eye completing his face, now no longer that of an eagle but that of a healthy earthbound mammal.

Behold, he comes, bounding over the hills, my beloved is like a young stag—

Tell me whom you love and I will tell you who you are.

Suddenly he stopped, two strides away from me, his face very solemn. His eyes looked huge, frightened in the firelight, and the smile lines around his mouth were invisible.

"Thank you," he said, whispered.

Thank you? Thank you?

I held out my hand to him as one does to his beloved. He held out his hand to me as one does to a comrade.

A century of silence. His hand unmoving. His eyes unwavering.

"I asked to meet with you so that I could clear the air of any misunderstanding. I could tell from the way you kept looking at me... I admire you but I am not like you."

I could not speak.

"Well. I must go. Diarfa and Zayo are waiting for me."

Of course. Diarfa and Zayo. An embarrassment of riches.

I turned to the window and saw nothing. Felt him close behind me, his warm breath on my hairline.

"I'm sorry." He was gone.

Lord Tharados, I said, cried in my mind. Where are you? Where is your magic? You can restore lost eyes. You can raise the dead. Make him love me. Make him want me.

More silence.

I felt like such a fool. If I could turn back time to when I had never seen his face...

Outside the green snowflakes were slowly turning into rain. Icing melting on a cake.

At least he had not been smiling. There are some smiles more terrible than frowns.

The fire snickered at me.

I put my sword on and went to look for Styx.

ACKNOWLEDGMENTS

Many thanks to my editor Rose Mambert,
whose keen eye, good sense and impeccable taste
have made this book better than it was
when I showed it to her.

ABOUT THE AUTHOR

Lyle Blake Smythers is an actor, writer and librarian in the Washington, D.C., area. Since 1976 he has performed in over 100 stage productions, including three appearances at the National Theatre. He has published fiction, poetry, satire and literary criticism in *Manscape, FirstHand, Playguy, The William and Mary Review, Insights, School Library Journal* and *Children's Literature Review*. He is a former children's librarian and is currently providing cataloging support for an ongoing project at the Library of Congress.

Feasting with Panthers is his first novel.

www.ingramcontent.com/pod-product-compliance
Lightning Source LLC
Chambersburg PA
CBHW051236260626
47162CB00002B/451